Sand and Water

Anabelle Hazard

© 2010 by Anabelle Hazard

Cover illustrated by Maria Pennefather

Published by
Bezalel Books
Waterford, MI
www.BezalelBooks.com

Printed in the United States of America

All rights reserved. No part of this publication may be reproduced, stored in a retrieval system, or transmitted in any form or by any means-for example, electronic, photocopy, recording-without the prior written permission of the author. The only exception is brief quotations in printed reviews.

ISBN 978-0-9823388-4-1
Library of Congress Control Number 2009936651

Prologue

"Mom, why do you come here everyday?" Alana asked, tugging on her mother's sleeve.

It wasn't that six year old Alana minded coming to Mass everyday with her mother because she did enjoy playing with the other home schooled kids outdoors when Mass was over. She enjoyed playing with them far more than Mass, in fact. It was just that she was curious why her mother came to the statue of Our Lady of Fatima on the right side corner of the church every time they exited the church. Why couldn't her mother pray for instance to St. Therese of Liseux on the left side or St. Anthony of Padua by the front and what on earth was she persistently asking the Mother of God for?

Maria O' Keefe looked down at her adoptive daughter and whispered, "I come here to pray one Hail Mary everyday for the man you are someday going to marry."

"Who am I going to marry?" Alana asked, a mystified look on her beautiful face.

"Well it's your choice, really. You can either marry Jesus or a man."

"But I don't want to marry Jesus. He already has so many brides... St. Catherine, St. Clare, St. Teresa... I want to be the only wife."

"In that case, maybe you can pray for a man who loves you just like Jesus loves you," Maria suggested.

"How does Jesus love me?"

"Remember what Fr. Brian talked about that Jesus loves you so much that he died on the cross for you--" Maria began.

Alana interrupted her. "But mom, I don't want to marry a dead man," she said with a profuse shake of her head.

Maria did not know how to explain this concept to a six year old as Alana was her first and only child but she was going to attempt it, heaven help her. "Lanie, the kind of

Anabelle Hazard

love Jesus has is called *agape* love. It's a love that dies to self, uh... that doesn't think about oneself but the good of the other person all the time. Its like when your dad gets up early on the weekends to make breakfast for you and me even if he got home late and was so tired from the night before."

Alana, precocious as she was, understood that, but she had a point to make, too. "But I don't need anyone to do that for me. I already have you and dad."

"Honey, your dad and I are each other's partners and we aren't going to be around forever so you may need your own partner to love you and take care of you when we are gone."

"Can Laura be my partner?" Alana asked in wide eyed innocence. Laura was another homeschooled six year old, Alana's best friend and favorite playmate.

Maria stifled a laugh. "No sweetie, God ordained men and women to be married. There are a lot of things men can do for women that other women can't and vice versa."

"Hmm," Alana said thoughtfully, as they headed out of the Church doors. She wasn't entirely sold on the idea of partnership or marriage yet. *What could possibly be better than living at home with mom and dad?* Aloud, she asked, "What will my partner do for me?"

Maria tried to make her explanation as relatable to Alana as she could. "Let's see... he would play "house" with you all the time, you can be the "mommy", he can be the "daddy" and you would have a baby or lots of babies...he would make sure your playhouse is all fixed up when the roof gets broke and...if there was just one slice of pineapple upside down cake left for desert on the dinner table, he wouldn't eat it, he would give it to you."

Alana's eyes grew wide at the thought of having a playmate all the time, of getting her broken toys fixed instantly and especially of not having to share her favorite cake. She might even be able to boss him around. "He must be *very* special, mom. I think I will pray a whole rosary instead of just one Hail Mary everyday for him."

"Sure you can do that too. Maybe it will help you stop complaining every time we pray the family rosary after dinner," Maria said pointedly.

Alana gave it some thought. Sometimes, the rosary did seem too time-consuming and tedious. "Well, maybe just three Hail Mary's everyday, ok?"

"Ok," Maria agreed. "Three Hail Mary's from you and one from me, everyday, before the Immaculate Heart of Mary who is also known as Our Lady of Fatima." And because she was a home schooling mom, she couldn't resist throwing in a quick lesson. "So now, three Hail Mary's plus one Hail Mary, what does that equal to?"

Alana gave her a melodramatic sigh. "It means, we're going to be in here after Mass for a very looooong time."

Chapter 1

Twelve years later...

"Well??? Is it true that they have Julio Iglesias impersonators stationed all over Spain like they have Elvis impersonators walking the streets of Vegas?"

Coke sputtered all over Lukas Swenson's computer screen as he snorted out his drink, laughing at the absurd question. Barely five seconds ago, he had just logged into an internet chat room online using the nickname *LSAbba* when a message popped up on his screen from someone who called himself or herself *HawaiianLanie*. Most likely a "herself," he concluded.

Lukas had to answer this unusual question with an equally ridiculous answer. He typed: "Seeing how Julio is still alive, wouldn't that be awkward if two or three Julios were in the same room together?"

Alana, also known in cyberspace as *HawaiianLanie*, laughed at the image. "No," she disagreed. "That would be heavenly."

Lukas argued back: "Hawaii is heavenly. Julio Iglesias is past his prime. That's why his sons are taking over show business."

Alana replied: "Shame on you! You are Spanish, you ought to be proud of your fellow countryman! They should deport you for saying that sort of thing."

Now Lukas was amused *and* intrigued. *How does she know I'm Spanish?* he asked himself silently. But he went on with the light hearted banter, "Oh please do tell the Ministry for Immigration what I'm up to. I will gladly get deported to Hawaii and I will play *Abba* songs on the entire flight."

"Don't you know it's suddenly become illegal in Hawaii to play disco music? It upsets the tropical beat, the say."

Anabelle Hazard

Lukas chuckled. "Oh really? I hope the natives haven't banned my favorite past time. You know how I love putting on a grass skirt and reciting poetry written by Pedro Calderon dela Barca."

Alana was a big fan of the famous philosophical Spanish poet and playwright turned Franciscan priest, Pedro Calderon dela Barca. Since she discovered his works, Alana was constantly begging Laura to translate all of his works for her, much to her friend's exasperation.

Alana answered: "This native will carry you to the Kilauea Volcano and make you a human sacrifice if you come to the airport without a souvenir from Mr. Calderon."

"I'm afraid security at the museum is tight, my friend. You'll have to settle for a forged autograph on a reprint of his poetry books."

Alana laughed again then glanced at another pop-up window on her laptop. Someone with the nick name *LSAbba2*, known in cyberspace lingo as 'nic', was inviting her to chat. "Hold on. There's another *LSAbba* that's inviting me to chat. It appears you have an impostor on cyberspace."

Lukas replied. "Tell 'em to bug off. You are entertaining the original *LSAbba*. First come, first serve."

Alana told *LSAbba2* to go away but *LSAbba2* was insistent.

"Lanie," her computer pop-up screen from *LSAbba2* read, "it's me Laura... someone else took my nic so I have to use *LSAbba2* for tonight."

"What?!?!" Alana shrieked in alarm. *So who in the heck had she been chatting with the last few minutes? Why did he or she have Laura's initials and Laura's sense of humor? How was it possible that he or she even shared Laura's love for Abba and distaste for Julio Iglesias? And pray tell her, how did he or she know about Pedro Calderon dela Barca? This was so eerie, no, creepy.*

Alana told Laura to hold on and resumed chatting with *LSAbba*.

"So who are you?!?" she demanded to *LSAbba*.

Lukas replied, "The question is who are *you* and why did you initiate a chat with me?"

Alana almost shrank in her seat. She *did* initiate the chat with a complete stranger. Feeling like she was about two inches tall, she answered, "Oh I am so sorry. My name is Lanie as you can tell from my 'creative' nic. There's been a misunderstanding. I thought you were someone I knew. My friend is in Spain on a month long vacation so we usually chat around this time. She uses your nic or rather, you're using her nic."

Lukas was relieved. He had to admit that he thought it strange that *HawaiianLanie* knew he was Spanish. "Oh I see. That explains your supernatural knack for correctly guessing my nationality. Well, that was an interesting conversation we just had, Lanie."

Alana was about to close the chat window with *LSAbba* but hesitated. She had to admit she enjoyed the conversation, too. In a split second, she decided to prolong the chat instead of saying goodbye. "So what are you doing online answering strange requests to chat?"

"I'm working on a biolab, waiting for an experiment to finish. I needed some human company. Since the microspecies and boiling liquids can't exactly converse and it's an ungodly hour in Spain to call someone just to chat, I just hung around somewhere in space… and where are you?"

"I'm in Hawaii, trying to stay cool indoors on the hottest time of the day," Alana answered.

"Now it's my turn to say "Shame on you!" You should be out on the beach, *HawaiianLanie*."

"Oh I was there this morning and will be there later in the afternoon. Don't you worry, I get my daily dose of "beachiness". I'm just on a break. Do you really like Pedro Calderon dela Barca's poetry and plays? I've never met anyone here who shares my *gusto* for ole Pedro or any plays for that matter. Most of the teenagers I meet are pop culture aficionados —which I'm hopelessly not."

"Yes, I'm a closet fan so don't tell the intellectual scientists I work with or I'll never live it down. My mother had all of *mi amigo* Pete's writings and translated most of it in English for my American father."

Alana gasped. "I have to bribe my Spanish speaking best friend to translate all of his works. The last one she did cost me my precious baby sitting time. She says the next one will cost me my first born child."

"LOL," Lukas typed, using the chat abbreviation for laugh out loud. "I have a proposal for you then: I'll send you a translated work of your choice if you keep me company tonight."

Alana didn't think that was such a bad bargain. "Deal. I have two conditions though: no personal info—names, addresses, emails, birthdays, schools, offices, and certainly not, social security numbers. And all topics have to be GP—General Patronage."

"Sounds fair. Can we exchange credit card numbers? You didn't mention they were on the restricted list." Lukas teased.

"Haha. Now, let me go tell the impostor to get lost."

"Wait, won't you hurt her feelings?"

"Are you kidding? She'll be grateful never to have to translate another piece of literature for me again. In fact, if she knew where you lived, she'd be over there in two seconds, promising to be *your* best friend forever if you take me off her hands."

Lukas chuckled again. He checked on his experiment while *Hawaiian Lanie* said goodbye to her friend.

"Where were we?" Alana asked Lukas when she had finished explaining things to Laura.

"Let's start over and introduce ourselves. a/s/l please?" A.S.L was the abbreviation for age, sex, and location.

"18/female/Hawaii, USA. Your turn."

"20/male/Barcelona, Spain. Would you by any chance be interested in discussing the World Cup with me?"

"Absolutely. Here are my thoughts: men in knee high socks belong in the eighties and Go Croatia!" It was the first time in history that a soccer team from Croatia made it to the World Cup finals.

"Croatia!?" Lukas almost choked on his coke. *I really should stop drinking beverages around this woman,* he thought to himself. He continued typing: "I'm rooting for any Latin team. I thought you were Spanish at heart considering your taste in culture."

Sand and Water

"Since Our Lady Queen of Peace has been appearing in Medjugorje, Croatia for the last 20 years, I'm assuming she is rooting for Croatia. So I am, too-- even though I may be a Spanish senorita by heart." Alana was referring to the ongoing apparitions of the Blessed Virgin Mary to six children, now adults, in Croatia.

"That's treason, *mi amiga*! And who is the Queen of Peace?"

"She's *only* the Mother of God," Alana rolled her eyes as she typed.

"Well let's chat all the way till the world cup finals and see just how powerful the Mother of God is."

"You're on."

Alana wound up leaving the chat room three hours later. It was past two o'clock in the morning when Lukas finally logged off.

On July 12, 1998, France won their first world cup title. Alana explained to Lukas that the Mother of God had also appeared in Lourdes, France to a fourteen-year-old girl named Bernadette Soubiroux and it was evident that Our Lady also had her protective mantle around the French.

Chapter 2

Alana looked outside her open window, feeling the cool evening breeze blow her hair away from her face. She never tired of the view from her strategically placed second story room. Alana's desk sat on the corner of her room. On the side of one of the windows was the Pacific Ocean, and on the other was the hilly terrain of the Oahu Island. Her father, Joseph "Joe" O'Keefe, a brilliant architect, had designed their home so that every window on the second floor enjoyed a picturesque landscape. Even at night, like tonight, when the ocean and the hills failed to show their blue, green and brown hues, Honolulu was still gorgeous. The sight of the bright city lights and illuminated buildings against the shadows of nature was spectacular.

Alana tore her eyes away from God and man's combined masterpiece to glance at her blue and white computer screen.

"Stay," Lukas pleaded.

Alana thought about his request for a minute. She did not want to go, but she had signed up to read the first readings for Mass the next day and could not afford the chain reaction of effect of sleeping late and being late for church.

"I have to go," she typed into the MIRC chat exchange.

"Please stay. I want to give you something," came the reply.

"You've got two minutes." Her arm did not need twisting. Alana had grown fond of her chat pal of six months, and both of them were notorious for losing track of time whenever they chatted. Two minutes had often extended to twenty and once, it had gone up to two hours.

Their friendship began on that fateful night of mistaken identity right around the time when the (mIRC) Internet Relay Chatroom had just been launched. Lukas often marveled at the wonder of the mIRC which allowed for complete strangers who had a computer from any part of the world to download a program, log-in and meet each other in a chat room in cyberspace and become fast friends.

The following weekend, chats were resumed between *LSAbba* and *HawaiianLanie,* covering topics from weather (they both liked humidity) to chewing gums (they both detested it) to waterskiing (she liked it, he didn't) and snowfall (he liked it, she didn't). The weekend after that, on appointment, *LSAbba* and *HawaiianLanie* were chatting exclusively in their own chat room.

Over the last six months, *LSAbba* would change his nick names, every now and then, surprising Alana with his zany humor, which she appreciated more and more each time they chatted. Today on a cooler January night, he was Mr. Julio Iglesias, taking a direct jab at Alana's curious taste in old fashioned music.

The chats sometimes delved into deeper topics like their families, their struggles in studying, their ambitions in life and other angst-ridden issues that young adults commonly encounter. The chats were always very innocent; after all, Alana was not your typical 18 year old American high school girl. Alana was a cradle Catholic, adopted, and raised by two conservative parents in Hawaii who had ingrained in her an obedience to the Catholic Church, a moral responsibility for her actions, a passion for literature and an unusual love for the Julio Iglesias songs her parents played over and over.

"Here, I'm sending you a movie clip that I made. Tell me if you like it." Lukas typed.

"If it's more than two minutes, Mr. Iglesias, you'll have to wait for my commentary next week because I need my sleep or else I'll be reading the wrong verses for Mass tomorrow."

"Reading schmeading! The people in the pews fall asleep anyway and won't notice a thing. You could be reading National Geographic and they won't care, oh wait maybe that will wake them up."

For the first time since they met, Alana felt uncomfortable and slightly offended. "Ok that's not funny. I take my faith very seriously so you can't joke about it. The only time its funny is when you become Catholic too and we can both share a laugh about the people in the pews."

"Sorry Lanie. I just made the clip all of last week and was exited for you to see it. Even though I don't believe in God, I still respect that you do. Peace?"

Alana was surprised at Lukas' apologetic approach. She had often dealt with kids her age calling her a 'stick in the mud' for her strong beliefs but Lukas' unexpected reaction was a welcome reprieve. "Peace," she typed. "But I do have to go. See you next week with my commentary, I promise."

"Don't go away mad or I might be tempted to pray to a God I don't believe in for you to keep chatting with me. Oops religion humor, it slipped!"

Alana laughed aloud and typed in her reply accordingly. "LOL. Now THAT was funny. I just might say I'm mad so that you can start praying and become a convert."

LSAbba smiled at his computer screen approvingly. "Good night then. See you next week."

Suppressing a yawn, Alana viewed the 5 minute clip. A blonde, blue-eyed and fairly attractive teenager with glasses, presumably *LSAbba's* face, came into view. Alana was taken aback as they had both previously agreed to keep everything in their lives private. Since Alana had been cautioned by her parents not to divulge anything personal online or to post any pictures of herself, she had been extremely careful to adhere to this rule. The only thing that Alana had unwittingly revealed during her excitement was that she had been accepted into the English literature program at St. Ignatius of Loyola University in Boston, Massachusetts.

"I know what you're thinking," came the slightly accented voice. "We agreed not to ask about personal stuff, but I want to tell you some things about me because, well, because, I need to and you'll find out why in a few minutes. My name is Lukas Swenson. I was born in Barcelona, Spain on January 17, 1978 to a Spanish mother and an American father. How they met is a story fit for the movies but this is my movie, I mean, my five minutes of fame, so let's continue."

The camera panned to a sprawling beige and brown Mission style house with a red roof. "This is our two story home in 17 Avenida Carlotta, Barcelona, Spain. Here, I grew up with my father, 2 brothers and a cat that all three of us have occasionally tortured. This is our cat Zoro, whom my grandmother says she found on her white family heirloom bedspread quilt one day, bloody, because one of us, I won't say who, cut off his ear."

"I studied briefly at an American private high school. I am now a college sophomore at the University of Barcelona, majoring in biochemistry. I live with my brother in an apartment across from the university." The video showed a brief scene of the University of Barcelona's main building and a tiny apartment complex. The clip ended and resumed filming Lukas' face.

"Since I was a child and lost my grandmother to cancer, I had always hoped to one day find the cure to cancer and uhh, also, I always hoped to find a girl who could make me laugh like you do and like my grandma used to. You will probably cringe that I've compared you to my grandma, whom I call *abuela*, but I hope you take that as a compliment. *Abuela* was the most loving, warm, kindhearted person in my life. My father says she was a good Catholic woman who tried to get him back into the faith he was raised in, but my father was firm that we would not be deluded like he once was. You remind me of her, full of wisdom, unlike any other girls or women I have ever met."

"Lanie, I don't know what your last name is, where in Hawaii you live, or what church or school you go to, but I do know that my feelings are real even though they are *unreal* in some kind of sense. I guess you could say I am cyber-in love with who you are—your spiritual thoughts and outlook on life, your positive attitude about everything, your goals of writing unusual sentimental pieces for boring, objective newspapers, most of all, your humor. And, and I guess I should describe you right around here but ... you know what, I don't even care about what you look like. Wait, I'll be honest, I am imagining and crossing my fingers that you are not taller than me or more round than me and if you have kind of an olive skin tone and dark hair and eyes, as I assume from the Hawaiian cartoon movie *Lilo and Stitch*, then really, that would be just a bonus."

"Ok, I am babbling. This is supposed to be a love letter, but I will let this song tell you how I feel. I wrote it years ago and have just finished it. I wrote it in Spanish but I've translated it and it doesn't sound as quite as good. Anyway, here goes:

> *Where are you? Who are you?*
> *I've never seen you, but I know you exist.*
> *Deep into the night, I think of you and long for you*
> *I wonder if you are thinking of me, too.*
>
> *Where are you? Who are you?*
> *I have to believe that someday destiny meant for us to meet.*
> *What do I say when we finally cross paths?*
> *What will you say when I chase after you with words you think aren't sweet?*
>
> *You are here, you are real.*
> *I've found you and my heart at last begins to heal.*
> *But still I don't know where you are, who you are*
> *And yet my soul knows you are my home.*
>
> *I am here, I am yours.*
> *I will follow wherever you go.*
> *I will love you as long as I live*
> *I know now that love is true and true love is you.*

The movie clip ended with a goodbye salute from Lukas.

Alana buried her face in her hands. Sleep would evade her now for sure.

Alana lay wide awake that night, her confused thoughts spinning around her head like an amusement park ride. She liked *LSAbba*... or rather Lukas, enjoyed talking to him immensely and looked forward to the weekends when they could chat. She had to admit she had feelings for him that she never felt for any boy her age.

"*But,*" she argued with herself, "*Lukas is the wrong person at the completely wrong time, not to mention the wrong place!*"

"*But then again,*" she debated, "*he is sincere, charming, funny and deeply profound when the topic called for it. And the fact that he is cute makes him that much more appealing.*"

"*On the other hand, the one thing he has against him is that he does not share my Catholic faith, which is essential to me and my family. And an internet relationship? C'mon! I am 18, on the brink of my new college life, where is this going to lead to other than a broken heart?*"

"*But I want to let myself fall head over heels because there is no danger of ever losing my purity in this set-up, is there? Besides, it's not like I'm going to marry the guy. Did I just say married? Wait, am I head over heels already? Oh Lord help me, I am! How could I have let this happen?!?*"

Alana had always been very careful to guard her heart. When she turned 12 years old, Alana had had made a temporary vow of chastity to God, in the presence of her father and mother, which she swore she would keep until her wedding day. Until now, Alana had not even gotten close to entertaining any thoughts of marriage. No boy had ever stirred such powerful emotions in her. She secretly thought that too many young men were immature. But Lukas was different—sensitive, kind and he could be silly and serious about life all in one breath and she, no doubt, had fallen in love with him.

Alana sighed and turned to the statue of the Immaculate Heart of Mary, the patroness of her purity, standing on her bedside. When Alana had made her vow, she consecrated herself to the Immaculate Heart of Mary. Since then, Alana had always counted on her devotion to the Blessed Mother to protect her heart. Tonight, she felt somehow guilty that she had failed her patroness and her divine Son, Jesus.

"Dear Lord," Alana prayed. "Forgive me for being careless. I had no intention of letting things get out of hand. Please bless me, tell me what to do to set things right again. If you can do it before next week Lord before we chat, I would sure appreciate that. Please bless Lukas' heart, please do not let me break it. If you have set him apart for someone else, change his feelings for me, again before next week. Amen."

Alana grabbed her rosary from her night stand and began the Apostle's Creed. Midway through the third decade of the rosary, Alana fell asleep.

Chapter 3

Thankfully, Sunday after Mass found Alana at her friend Caroline Morgan's birthday party. It was a typical birthday party at a local beach on a warm tropical day in January. Adults could be found grilling on the barbecue while the kids, even the teenagers, were playing games with each other. Most of the adults and their children at the party were part of the home schooling group of St. John Bosco's Academy, which consisted of about forty families from the combined city and county of Honolulu.

Despite her attempts at joining in the competitive volleyball game, Alana's thoughts kept returning to Lukas. Alana's best friend, Laura Carmen Sanchez, immediately noticed her preoccupation. As soon as the game was over, Laura pulled Alana aside.

"Ok spill the beans," Laura said, nudging her on the rib. Laura was a bubbly, frank and self-effacing girl of Latin American ancestry. Everyone liked Laura because she pretty much liked everyone. Next to her in public, Lanie appeared composed and recollected. But when they were together in the privacy of their own circle, Lanie could let her guard down and be just as gregarious as her best friend.

"Huh?" Alana stared at her.

"Since when did St. Mark start writing letters to the Galatians? Something's obviously on your mind for you to change the bible like that this morning."

Alana gasped. "Did everyone notice?"

"Of course they did. You rarely make mistakes in public speaking or writing. But Jimmy Lawrence's painful singing of the psalms got more attention than you, so you're safe."

Alana heaved a sigh of relief. "Remind me to thank Jimmy later."

"You can thank him for saving your butt on the volleyball game several times, too. I don't know if you noticed but the ball did whack you on your spaced out head twice and grazed your inattentive nose once."

Alana looked mortified before she realized that Laura had a tendency for the dramatics. "Oh Laura, I have to show you something, but we need the code of super-secrets here because if your parents find out so will mine and I'm not sure I'm ready to tell them yet."

Laura gave her super-secret signal by zipping her mouth and throwing the imaginary key away. They had thought of that when they were both nine years old.

Alana dragged Laura into her parent's car, pulled out her laptop and turned it on. Then Alana opened the windows player program and showed Laura the movie clip from Lukas. "I received this from *LSAbba* last night," she explained. "I mean, the other *LSAbba*."

After watching the five minute clip, Laura took a deep breath. "Wow," was all she said. "Wow," she repeated herself and then her vivacious, chatty self took over. "First of all, Lanie, he is gorgeous! I knew I should have stayed in that chat room the first time you met. Girl, I could have snagged him up for myself. Second of all, how dare you not tell me it was so serious between you two?"

"It is not!" Alana replied hotly, feeling her cheeks grow warm. "I mean, I didn't think so anyway."

"Wait, what did you tell him?!"

"I couldn't reply. I told him I'd look at it and get back to him next week. That is, if I show up at all."

"How could you not after a guy opens his heart up to you like that? That's rude. You at least owe him a reply—good or bad. How do you feel about him, anyway?"

"I don't know. I like him I guess. My heart races every time I think of him but it's so unreal! I've always thought that internet relationships are soooo not for me. The plan was to meet some guy in college, get married after graduation and start popping out kids. You know that."

"Yeah, life doesn't go according to plans, does it?," Laura said sympathetically.

"No, I guess not. What would you do?"

"I'd tell him I like ya' so let's keep chatting till one of us gets tired of it."

Alana frowned. "That's not very mature. That's exactly how other girls would react."

Laura looked hurt. "Are you calling me immature?"

"No, I'm sorry Laura. You know how tactless I can be. I meant that's exactly what I would do if I let my feelings rule too so actually, I'm immature."

Laura rolled her eyes heavenward. "Then ask someone who is mature. Your mom or dad, Fr. Brian or Sr. Emma."

"You know that is good advice. Thanks."

"Anytime. Are you up for another round of volleyball?"

"And risk getting a concussion? No thanks. I think I'm going to head off to see Jack now."

"Catcha later."

With a wave, Alana headed down to the water to find her five year old brother, Jack. She found him in the water, playing with the waves. He had brought his body board along and was splashing around with the other kids his age and their dads. Alana decided to sit on the sand, under her umbrella and watch her brother silently. Although he sometimes got on her nerves when he teased her, she loved him dearly.

"Jack," she yelled out. "Have you reapplied sun block lately?"

Jack dismissed her question with a wave. Sometimes, he thought to himself, his sister tended to think she was his mother but he adored her in spite of the occasional overbearing stuff.

Alana looked far out into the horizon to where the sea seemed to end. Living in the island of Oahu sometimes made her think the world was so small but when she glanced at the ocean, she knew that the state of Hawaii was part of such a large country and a much larger world.

In the vast ocean out there, she mused, *there is the country of Spain and in that country somewhere is Lukas.* She guessed that he was probably sound asleep considering Spain was eleven hours ahead of Hawaii.

Alana wondered about Spain, an important figure in the history of Christianity, having spread its influence all over Latin America and even the Far East, into the Philippine islands. She wondered about Spain's rich culture and heritage and customs that to her seemed exciting and exotic. She thought it paradoxical that most people were impressed with exotic Hawaii and here she was, fascinated about Europe. Not that she would ever want to live anywhere else other than Hawaii but she did want to venture out to Europe someday.

Alana listened to the roaring waves as she sifted the powdery sand between her fingers. She was grateful that this sandy part of the earth was her home. The state of Hawaii was indeed a beautiful archipelago made up of eight major islands formed by volcanoes erupting from the sea. Hawaii was most famous for its year round tropical weather, stretch of exquisite beaches, lush green foliage, volcanic wonders, and exotic culture, making it a widely popular tourist destination. Alana always counted it a blessing that she was not a tourist but a native.

The Hawaiian capital of Honolulu, where Alana and her family lived, was inhabited by mostly Asian-Americans-- of Japanese, Polynesian and Filipino origin. Alana had grown up in Honolulu all her life. Her mother Maria, of mixed Filipino and Spanish blood was born there. Her father, Joseph "Joe" O' Keefe had moved to Honolulu as soon as he left his parent's typical Irish home in the Midwest. Alana called Honolulu home, loved Honolulu and had planned to return there after a four-year college stint in the mainland.

~ ~

The next morning, a determined Alana made an appointment to see one of her favorite people in the world, Sr. Emma Hauoli. Sr. Emma was a cheerful, fairly young nun who had established a rapport with most of the students at the nearby St. Anne's Catholic High School. Sr. Emma's reputation for being kind and easygoing easily earned the student body's trust and confidence even when it came to topics like premarital sex, contraception and abortion. Sr. Emma's sweetness however did not negate her uncompromising obedience to the Catholic Church's teachings. She had single handedly saved thousands of teenagers' souls from committing the mortal sin of abortion and was the main force behind the school's "true love waits" campaign for sexual purity. Sr. Emma also worked closely with the home schooled teenagers in the suburbs of Honolulu. Sr. Emma was the very person Alana wanted to talk to.

Alana knocked softly on Sr. Emma's mahogany office door. Sr. Emma's head covered in brown habit came into view. "Come in, come in, Alana," she said warmly.

Alana sat on the comfortable couch across from Sr. Emma and felt unsure for a minute. But Sr. Emma's affectionate squeeze of her arm immediately assuaged her discomfort. "How are you, my dear?"

"Well, quite frankly, I'm a little confused today, Sr. Emma."

Sr. Emma nodded. "That would explain why your nails have been bitten down to quarter of an inch."

Alana laughed. Sr. Emma knew her all too well. She was comfortable enough now to tell Sr. Emma about her predicament. Alana narrated her tale to Sr. Emma's understanding ears.

Sr. Emma thought for a moment before she said, "Lanie, when you are in a bind like this, I want you to always remember to seek God's will first. Do you want us to pray silently for a minute?"

Alana nodded.

"Do you still remember the retreat we had on St. Ignatius of Loyola about discernment?"

Alana nodded again. "He said to look for God's leading in the outside circumstances of your life as well as the inner workings of the Holy Spirit."

"You're absolutely right. Is there any strong emotion in your heart that jumps out at you today?"

"I guess I could call it a... a tenderness. A tenderness at Lukas?"

"Wait, don't explain the feeling. Just sit with it for a while and let it lead you to God."

Alana closed her eyes and allowed herself to soak in the feeling of tenderness. She felt protected and protective at the same time, like she felt when she first held her baby brother, Jack. When Alana began to relax, she also felt a strong peace wash over her. Alana somehow knew that in this time, God was with her, that this was strangely something from God and that God would take care of it in due time. She liked the feeling so much, she sat there at least a good five minutes.

Sr. Emma closed her eyes as well, praying for the Holy Spirit to speak to Alana. When Alana opened her eyes, Sr. Emma sensed that the Holy Spirit had stirred in Alana's soul. Since Sr. Emma did not want to press her until she was ready to talk, she waited for Alana to say something.

"Boy Sister, I could fall asleep here in your psychologist's couch. That felt really good -- I feel like everything will be ok. I don't know what to do about Lukas just yet but I have a feeling that all will be well."

Sr. Emma smiled compassionately. "That's all you need to know right now, my dear. God will speak to you in specifics if you keep listening to Him. The right thing to do will come to you at exactly the right time. It can come while you are in the shower, while you pray before the Tabernacle, while you read the Bible or the words of a book, while you walk to class or talk to someone in your family or even in a conversation with a complete stranger."

"How will I know if it is God speaking, Sr. Emma?"

"Your heart will know that God has visited your soul. Some people say it's like being hit by a ton of bricks but I'd say it's like being hit softly and peacefully by a feathered pillow. God's prodding is usually gentle, in a still small voice although sometimes, when we play deaf, He can use loudspeakers, too. And if the message isn't quite clear, that's when you come to your spiritual director. A good director will guide you into recognizing God's will, His voice. What's important is that you do as God asks."

Alana nodded. She knew she had a lot of listening to do for the rest of the week so she resolved to keep her heart and ears very open.

"Sr. Emma this really wasn't on my agenda today, but may I ask you something?"

"You sure can."

"How did you know when you were called to become a nun?"

Sr. Emma chuckled. "I was 8 years old when I went to church with my mother. My mother had on a black lace veil over her head. Beside her sat a nun with a plain black veil. I wanted to wear a veil the next time I went to church so I asked my mother to get me one like the nun's, not lace like hers, but plain black like the nun's. Mama answered that only brides of Christ wore that kind of a veil and that was that. From then on, I wanted to become a nun and no one could convince me otherwise."

"Well if discerning a vocation is as easy as that, Sister, I think my preference for lace may indicate I'm leaning toward the marital vocation," Lanie quipped.

"Its takes more than that, of course. Naturally, I had to go through years of discernment, years of listening to God's voice but that was the very first time I believe I heard Him."

"Kind of like I think I first heard God today."

"Yes, Lanie, kind of like that. Keep practicing. You will learn to listen for it when you get used to Him speaking."

As Alana got up to leave, she had one more question. "What are veils for anyway, Sr. Emma?"

"Hmm, my mind is searching for the theological explanation but it escapes me at the moment. I believe it is a symbol of obedience to your husband, whether it is Christ or a man chosen by Christ, but don't quote me on that."

"In that case," Alana couldn't resist saying. "I probably won't be wearing any veil since I find it hard to believe men and women are not equal."

Sr. Emma opened her mouth to correct Alana's misconception but Alana had already left. "Oh Lord," she prayed, "Lanie has a good head on her shoulders but do tame her spirit of rebelliousness."

~ ~

Sand and Water

Try as she might, Alana still did not hear God throughout the rest of the week. Even though Alana fasted on bread and water on Wednesday and Friday and prayed more than the daily rosary with her family, she still had no idea what to say or do. By Friday night, Alana finally gathered up the courage to talk to the one person she considered the wisest, her father. Though most politically correct people would call him her adoptive father, Alana and her family dispensed with those titles. To them, she was simply daughter and he was father.

Alana found her father reading a book written by some saint in the study while her mother put her Jack to bed.

"Dad," she whispered.

Joe O'Keefe peered from his reading glasses. He found his daughter nervously biting her nails by the doorway of the O'Keefe study/prayer room. "Come in, Lanie. Something on your mind, today?"

"Yeah. Got time to talk?"

"I always do," Joe replied. Joe had sensed Alana's preoccupation over the week but he knew her well enough to know that she would approach him or his wife Maria when she was ready. Usually, she talked to her mother but tonight, she obviously needed her father's opinion.

Alana cleared her throat. "There's this guy —on the other side of the world," she began. The rest of her story came out, including the sound advice Sr. Emma gave her.

As Alana talked, Joe listened attentively. There were so many breaks and pauses in her monologue that made Joe want to interrupt and break out in lectures but he stopped himself and forced himself to listen, to listen as God would, without interruptions or lectures. He waited, as he always did, when anyone invited his advice before giving it.

"What do you think? What should I do?" Alana asked, troubled.

Joe O'Keefe was an architect. He was a successful partner for a downtown firm in Honolulu. Joe approached life and its challenges the way an architect would-- by looking at the big picture. "Well, if Sr. Emma asked you to look deep in your heart, I guess I'm going to ask you to look outside of you, at your circumstances, to see where God is leading you. Is God guiding you into marriage now or is He guiding you into further education?"

Alana almost snickered at her dad's silly question. "I think my scholarship to St. Ignatius of Loyola University was or is a huge pointer to go in that direction, to pursue my English degree and its not like Lukas proposed marriage or anything so I don't see how marriage is even an option, dad."

Joe hid a smile. Alana was wise. To his memory, she always came to the most responsible conclusion. "So if marriage is not an option, then what would be the point of getting into a relationship —even if it is just chatting or writing to each other for however long--"

"None, I suppose. There is no point in pursuing things, is there?" Deep inside her, Alana knew what the right thing to do was but having someone with authority in her life spell it out like that was like a shot right between the eyes. "But why do I like him so much and why does he like me?"

"What man would not like you?" Joe asked his daughter affectionately.

"Oh dad," she rolled her eyes, "You think everyone loves me as you do."

"Not quite but I think the man who marries you *should* love you as I do. Now, I am glad we are having this conversation Lanie because I've been wanting to tell you something before you go off to college in the fall. Lanie, you have a beautiful soul – always caring about other's people's feelings and needs before your own, wanting to serve your brother and parents, your friends, the Church and your community. You've always been very respectful to your mother and me and taken care of Jack wonderfully. But I don't think you realize how beautiful you are outside. I guess your mother and I tried not to encourage you to be obsessed over your looks, but I'm sure you are by now aware that men and boys will always find you attractive. Thank God you don't look at all like me or you'll never get a marriage proposal!"

Looking at Alana, most people assumed that her tanned skin, dark mahogany hair, slender 5'7 frame and green eyes were inherited from her adoptive mother's Hawaiian-Filipino ancestry while the only thing she could trace to her Irish father was the extraordinary eye color. The O'Keefe family often laughed at this misconception and mostly never bothered to correct the speculation. They wanted people to think they were just your average American Catholic family.

Alana snorted and teased her father. "It's too bad I've got your temper and stubborn nature though."

"Ahh yes, I'm afraid you will struggle with that and so will your future husband, God bless him! My point Lanie is that when good-looking and suave men try to come and woo you, as they definitely will when you won't live with me anymore, you need to remember that the one qualification he needs to have is..."

"A solid Catholic faith," Alana finished.

"More than that, my dear. The man you marry has to be handpicked by God to be a good faithful husband who will raise you and your family into holiness and who will love and serve you and your family in time and in eternity."

"Gee dad, how will I ever find that man? You make him sound like he's a dead saint who's probably already in heaven."

Joe laughed at his daughter's joke. "Oh, he'll be working out his sainthood just like you are with your temper and stubborn and feisty nature and all. But trust me when I say that God will tell you when he's the one you were born to marry. But now Lanie, before God tells you it's the one, you have no business playing with fire. If you play with fire, you will break hearts and your heart will get broken, too."

Joe and Alana sat in companionable silence for a few minutes.

"Dad, I think I have the answer to my question... I think the reason I like Lukas so much is because he has not seen me at all and he says he likes me for my, my soul, I guess. It's like how you and mom love me even when I wake up with bad breath, have a runny nose, don't brush my hair, wear my ratty old pjs and make Jack cry. You know that kind of love that's there even when you or I don't have a smile on. What do you and mom call that—agape love?"

"Yes, agape love—unconditional, self-sacrificing, volitional, active love. Lanie, if it's true that Lukas finds your beauty on the inside attractive, I like the guy, too. But honey just remember that if he breaks your heart, will you be willing to give your groom a broken heart? And more importantly, if you break his heart, you will be responsible for him giving his future wife just pieces of it."

"Hmmm... so I guess I have to end things without breaking his heart or mine?" Alana sighed. "I'm afraid it's too late for that though."

"It's never too late, Lanie. God is beyond time. Pray for guidance. He will supply you with grace since you are His precious child. I trust you will do the right thing."

"Thanks, dad. I love you."

~ ~

The answer to her prayers came to Alana at 3:00 Saturday afternoon, while she was watering the plants in her mother's garden. Alana finished up her chores and went straight to her computer. She would not chat with Lukas for another 5 hours but she was ready with her commentary to his video.

Chapter 4

Lukas nervously logged into the MIRC chat room Friday night. For the first time since they met, he used his real name. Alana was already there, waiting a little impatiently.

"Hello, you're early," he began.

"You're late," she chided jokingly. "But I forgive you."

His reply was totally unexpected. "What is "forgive"? Silly Spanish boy cannot find that in his dictionary."

"Oh, it means to write off a debt owed. We Christians say that when we sin, we offend or hurt God but when we say we are sorry, God forgives us. We are restored in a right relationship with God because Jesus already died for our sins. Is that more than enough explanation than you needed?"

"My *abuela* used to say that all the time. Forgiveness and the cross or something like that. I never really understood it. So... you forgive me because my movie offended you or hurt you?" Lukas took a puff of smoke from his cigarette in his anxiety.

Alana blew her bangs off her face and tried to think of how she could explain this one. "Well, since we're on the subject of your movie, we might as well discuss that. No, Lukas, you did not hurt me. On the contrary, you've touched me."

Lukas heaved a sigh of relief. "And your promised commentary?"

"I'm a writer so I wrote it down. I can send it to you in word format and give you time to read it. Take as long as you like. If you don't want to speak to me again, I'll understand but if you want to talk, I'm going to be right here all night. OK?"

Lukas hurriedly closed the chat page and eagerly read Lanie's letter.

Dear Lukas,

   Thank you for the video, for being honest about your feelings, for the sweet song that you wrote for me, and for the wonderful things you've said about me. I will admit that over the last six months, I have felt something for you too. I like your humor, your sensitivity, your intelligence and your compassion for the sick and the suffering. I hope you don't think this is shallow, but your movie star looks have only served as icing on the cake, if you know what I mean. I guess what I'm saying is that you are deeply admired on this side of the world. I would say I am "cyber-in-love" but I don't know if that is accurate since I've never been truly in love before. If it means my heart races every time I think of you or that I get tingles in my toes when we chat or that my stomach does flip flops when I play your song over and over then maybe I have fallen in love.

   But being in love is not the same as true love. Early on, my parents have taught me that true love waits, true love is patient and willing to suffer and die to self. If I really loved you, I would not hold your feelings for me to entrap you. I would set you free to do as God wants you to live your life. And on further reflection, I find that I do love you, Lukas, as a sister loves her brother in Christ. Because I do, I cannot continue chatting with you anymore. Lukas, you have to live your life outside this computer, go to college, help find the cure for cancer, save the world, fall in love, go skiing in the Alps with a woman like you always dreamed of, and start a family when the right time comes. And if you "love" me as you say you do, I ask that you let me go too. I need to live my life outside this chat room too, finish college, write, and follow my dream. This is my dream: I'll write for the paper on the side and teach literature to kids. Many days, my husband and I will hold hands, take long walks on the beach, pray together, serve the Church together and raise our own family of 6... or more!

My dear Lukas, I do not want a temporary romance, even if it is only virtual, because I want to preserve my heart for this special man God has promised me. I want a lifetime of true love for me and if you are not looking in the same direction, working for the same goal, then we both need to end this while our hearts are still intact.

I guess the gist of what I am saying is this: Lukas, I do return your feelings, you are not alone. I like you very much but I have to say goodbye. I am crying as I write this because there is so much about you that I still want to discover and so much I want to talk to you about and because there is a hope in me that you will someday be the man I could walk on the beach with. And thinking about it, I am almost tempted to take this all back, to just live in the moment and not think about the future but that wouldn't be the right thing to do. And that's not what I know God wants me to do for right now. I will have to trust that the future is in His loving, capable hands.

So thanks for everything and I pray the God bless you when we part ways. I'll be in the chat room for one last chat tonight, if you still want to. I want to make sure you're ok and even though this sounds selfish, I also want to live in the moment to enjoy in the bliss of being in love, if only for just this once.

Yours,
Lanie

Lukas stared at the letter and read it again slowly. He did not know if he felt ecstatic because Lanie liked him too or if he felt devastated because after tonight he probably would never see or hear from her again. He didn't know what to think or say really. A part of him wanted to shut down the computer, leave her heart broken as his and forget everything that's happened in the last six months. But another part wanted to savor what they had for tonight and to leave in good terms with sweet memories of his first romance. But the bigger part wanted to make sure Lanie was ok, too. He wanted—no, he needed to make her laugh, to make her remember that she was loved so innocently, to leave her with his heart on his sleeve and give it to her completely without expecting anything in return. If this was her idea of love—to selflessly give of himself, despite the cost, the vulnerability, the pain-- then that's what he would give her.

Lukas returned to the chat room, his heart breaking severely and yet bursting with the irresistible delight of first love. He began.

Debonair Lukas enters the room dramatically, looks around for the prettiest lady, walks over to her with a white rose, takes her hand and leads her to the dance floor. He speaks: They're playing our song, Lanie. Would you care to dance with me?

In the privacy of her room in Hawaii, Alana laughed out loud, relieved, her heart enamored with this dashing, charming man who always made her laugh. "Certainly, but I can't hear the song from over here. What exactly is our song?"

"My dear, let me send you a clip and we can both listen to it and imagine ourselves dancing and twirling all over this room, but make sure you don't step on my toes."

Alana received the file he sent over mIRC. She opened her media player and heard the upbeat rhythm of the Abba song "Dancing Queen."

"Disco?!?" Alana typed. "On a romantic night like this, you pick disco music?"

"Hey, Abba is a lot better than Julio Iglesias and besides, I don't know how to tango, so show me what you got, lady."

Lanie pouts. "I think I like your song better."

Lukas blushes. "I'm glad you like it. Care for a slow dance, I'm getting tired of the bright disco lights."

"I thought you'd never ask."

"Mmm your hair smells heavenly. Jasmine and honeysuckle."

"Actually, its vanilla and Playdoh – my brother and I played before bedtime. Then she added teasingly, "Besides, how can you smell my hair when I'm the one who's resting my chin on your head?"

"You can't possibly be taller than 6 feet or…are you?"

"6'2 and 500 lbs., that's me but don't worry, I have dark hair and olive skin tone…not to mention crossed green eyes."

Lukas decided to do some teasing of his own. "Then we're a perfect match because that wasn't me you saw on the video, that was my best friend Erik. I'm actually 8 feet tall, 1,450 lbs., blue eyes, brown hair no teeth."

"Gorgeous. Now, I don't feel too bad that this is our last night together."

Lukas could not help but be dazzled by her quick wit. *This woman truly is amazing*, he thought. Not for the first time, he found himself wishing they met differently and would continue to meet after tonight.

"Even if you had orange hair, striped skin and 50 something moles and warts on your nose, I'd still miss you," Lukas said truthfully.

"Even if I'm going to miss you, I'll never regret knowing you. Do you have any regrets, Lukas?"

"That I didn't know my mother. When she died, *abuela* used to come over all the time to tell me about her. Now that *abuela*'s gone too, I forgot what mama was like. My father doesn't want to talk about her at all. *Abuela* says that my father lost everything when he lost my mother — especially his faith in God. So my regret is not being able to have been loved by her and I do wonder about the kind of life my brothers and I would have had if she had lived."

"I wish you knew Our Blessed Mother, Mary. She is the perfection of God's creation and Jesus gave her to you and me as our mother at the foot of the cross. I run to her all the time and she always understands and helps. It's like having the most powerful, most loving mother in heaven."

"*Abuela* had Mary's statue and pictures in every room so I have met her, but find it very hard to relate to her."

"Do you believe in life after death?"

"I'm a scientist so it's hard to prove the existence of anything beyond what I can see. But I want to believe in it because my mother is dead and if it is true then that means one day I will know her."

"Then if you want to believe your mother's soul is alive, it can't be such a stretch to believe she is somewhere watching over you, praying for you, still loving you, right? And if you believe that, then couldn't you believe that Mary, your Blessed Mother, whether you like it or not, is watching over you and loving you?"

"That's what I love about you, Lanie. You can stimulate my thoughts and you wreak havoc on my emotions — you have me laughing one minute and crying the next."

"Shucks, so you're not after my orange hair?"

"Anymore than you are after my 10 million euro bank account. What would you do if you had that much money, anyway?"

"That's easy. I'd give it to non-profit organizations in third world countries. My mother's parents were born in the Philippines, a country that's as beautiful as Hawaii but enslaved in government corruption and steeped in poverty and yet this country has the happiest, most faithful Catholics you'll ever meet. So that's where my money would go ··to reward a suffering people who love God despite their suffering."

Lukas decided to play devil's advocate. "But if you believed in eternal life, wouldn't they be rewarded richly then after their lives are over? If you gave them money now, you'd risk robbing them of their eternal reward."

Alana was surprised that Lukas did know something about Christianity. It must have been his grandmother's influence.

She answered, "I never saw it from that point of view, I guess. What would you do with the money, then? Give it to the religious communities in rich countries who are starving in the faith?"

"I'd go to Hawaii, hire a private investigator to track you down and offer you the rest of the money in exchange for eloping with me. Would you accept, I wonder?"

"Oh I suppose so, for the sake of third world countries. But only if you promise me that I wouldn't have to write "obey" in my vows. We'd be equal partners."

"You can write whatever you want. I'm not bound by traditional vows or ceremonies."

Alana squirmed in her seat. This latest difference of opinion was just what she needed to affirm that she was doing the right thing. She felt like a self-righteous religious snob, judging him for his lack of religious belief. But it wasn't that that bothered her as much as the thought that if she and Lukas did get married, they would fight about such a major issue of raising their kids in the Catholic faith and where would that leave their children? Laugher was not exactly the best foundation for a marriage. Still, he was cute and she liked flirting so she tried to ignore the thought and went on to more light hearted banter.

"You wouldn't mind if I wore a flamboyant ski suit to our wedding and we said our vows "to have and to hold until irreconcilable differences" before some internet certified criminal?"

Lukas thought about that a good deal. The truth was that he did mind. He wanted a bride in a white gown and veil, vows that lasted forever and said before some minister or priest. "No bride of mine is getting married in anything but a while dress and veil. The vows would be "until death do us part" but you can walk down the aisle to a Julio Iglesias music of your choice."

On and on it went. They talked about everything and nothing, switched from serious and silly until it was time to say their goodbyes.

"It's twelve o'clock your time, Cinderella."

"I know. Should I run and leave my glass slipper with you or should we try for a more original ending?"

"I wish I had your picture. I'd kiss you...on the cheek, so you won't slap me. I'm a gentleman after all."

Lanie blows Lukas a kiss. "Just so you know, that was my first kiss—cyber or otherwise."

"Then I'll send it right back so you can save it for the man you are going to marry. Here now, this is how we'll say goodbye: "Give me five, girl!"

Alana laughed and cried. "Here's five, my silly Lukas. Now slap me some skin."

"Until we meet again, sweet Lanie."

Lukas stared at the monitor long after Alana logged off. *Come back,* he begged. *Please come back.*

Chapter 5

When it became obvious Lanie was not going to return, Lukas turned off his laptop and paced his room. He suddenly couldn't sit still after four hours in front of the computer. His heart was so heavy, having found a girl so unusual, fallen in love with her, only to lose her as quickly as he found her. Lukas grabbed another cigarette from his pack. Two cigarettes later, he tried to close in eyes and a tear rolled down his cheek. He buried his face on his sleeve, willing his tears to stop flowing. But even if he could stop the tears, he realized he could not stop the pain of a broken heart.

He tried talking himself out of it. There would be other girls, of course. But his mind argued back, *Not like her*. He had already seen plenty of them, some who threw themselves willingly at his feet whenever he and his rock band played at the school functions and none of them had any substance at all. They were frivolous girls everywhere, obsessed with looks, money, clothes, with everything but anything that mattered. He never had a decent conversation with a girl as he did with Lanie and most of all, they could never make him laugh.

"*This is insane!*" his mind cried out. To be heartbroken over a girl he had never seen, a girl he only imagined to be as beautiful on the outside as she was inside was completely irrational.

Lukas longed to talk to someone but, as always, there was no one to listen to him. His dad, Frank, was always called away at the hospital for one of his patients was always having a baby. Besides, they didn't have that kind of a relationship to be talking about girls. His oldest brother, Tomas, was gone on some party or date, no doubt busy with his own social life. Lukas would talk to his youngest brother, Stephen, who always listened, but being autistic would not be able to give him any sound advice.

Anabelle Hazard

Lukas wished his grandmother was still alive. She was the only one who said anything worth listening to.

Lukas glanced at a picture of his mother, Monica and his grandmother, Elena, on his bookshelf. It was a rare photo of Lukas and Tomas in the arms of their mother and grandmother. Nestled behind the frame was a thick, hardbound book that Elena owned and had given him while she was dying. Lukas pulled it out from the top shelf and sat down on his desk chair. The bible, it read. It was well worn, used by his grandmother daily. Lukas often saw her reading it in front of the fireplace or on her rocking chair by the porch during the summers. When he asked her about it as a young boy, Elena would read it to him and tell him stories: about brave David slaying Goliath, Moses parting the red sea, Noah building an ark, Jesus multiplying bread and fish, Jesus walking on water, Jesus dying on the cross and rising from the dead. Even though Elena had insisted they were true stories, Lukas now thought of them as fairy tales. When he was younger, he had believed in Jesus because he faintly remembered going to church with his family. But that abruptly stopped when tragedy struck their home.

As Lukas grew up, his father repeatedly told them that believing in God was nonsense, and Lukas accepted what his father reasoned was the truth: God did not exist except in the mind of unfortunate, gullible people like his grandmother. Although the many pictures of Jesus and Mary in his grandmother's house sometimes made him wonder what if they were true, his father had fully convinced him that there was no scientific evidence to support that. His father's winning argument was that if Jesus and Mary were real, his own mother would not have died giving birth to Stephen. By now, Lukas knew beyond shadow of a doubt that there was no God. His own life belied any presence of a loving creator. Perhaps, he reasoned, his grandmother's life was prettier and she had reason to believe that God loved her.

Nevertheless, Lukas needed to speak with his grandmother today. He thought that reading her favorite book might help him feel connected to her in some way. Lukas opened a page randomly. The words from Tobit chapter 6 verse 12 read: "You before all other men have the right to marry her."

He had no idea the bible had love stories of predestination in them. Lukas straightened his back and read some more. "...it is your right, before all other men, to marry his daughter..." The words jumped out from the book, catching his undivided attention. Lukas felt the hairs on the back of his neck stand on end. It was almost as if his grandmother knew what he was thinking and was answering right back.

"*Could it be?*" He thought, "*Lanie was meant to be mine from the beginning of time?*" Lukas read on and he decided to read the story from beginning to end.

Lukas vaguely remembered his grandmother narrating to him the story of a young boy going in search of treasure who met an angel. The angel led him to the house where there lived a young woman that he fell in love with. He slayed the demon who had haunted the girl, married her and brought her home. After reading the book of Tobit in the next hour and a half, Lukas' memories became clearer to him.

That day, his father, Frank and mother Monica, along with Monica's mother Elena, took seven-year-old Tomas and six-year-old Lukas to a friend's wedding at a Catholic Church. Monica was then pregnant with Stephen. As they made their way out of the Church, Monica took Lukas' hand and patted it.

"Did you like that wedding, Lukas?" she asked.

"Yes, I liked playing with the fire and the candles at the back of the church. You should have seen it, mama!" he bragged proudly. "I almost caught that lady's dress on fire until Tom stopped me."

Monica hid a smile. "Thank God Tom is always looking out for you. But did you see what was going on at the altar during the wedding, Lukas?"

"What is wedding?" Lukas asked, bewildered.

"Its when a man and woman love each other and they declare their love for each other and promise God to love each other forever. Like Kirsten and Nicolas did today and your dad and I did along time ago, and like you probably will someday," Elena explained.

"Mother, he could be a priest you know. I offered my sons to God's service, if you remember," Monica said to her mother in a slightly reproving tone.

"Oh, you'll want grandchildren too if you have two as wonderful as I have," Elena argued.

"Yes, well, God's will be done, mama, God's will—whatever it is," remarked Frank.

"Tonight Lukas," Elena spoke, "I will tell you the story of young Tobias, whose reading we heard today. He was a boy who ran into an angel and the angel led him to marry a wonderful girl..."

"What about Tomas, here, Mama? Can't he listen to your story, too?" asked Frank.

"Ahh, he will hear the story of St. Peter. Tomas will be my little priest," Elena answered, rumpling Tomas' head affectionately.

"Tsk, tsk Mother, you are just saying that because Lukas gets himself intro trouble all the time," Monica rebuked her.

"Oh no, I am saying that because Lukas is determined, passionate and sensitive. Although he is restless at times and impulsive, he will make a fine husband and father and if his children want to burn the house down someday, he will understand."

Everyone laughed at that.

Just like that, Lukas remembered how happy his family was up until the time his father stopped taking them to Church. Occasionally, Elena would take them to Sunday Masses until Frank altogether banned it. Frank remained kind to his sons and mother-in-law despite his new found atheism and tried his best to be a good single father but he was just too busy earning a living and trying to maintain their mansion. Often it was Elena, a housekeeper and a nanny who took turns in raising the three boys. Elena did try so very hard to become mother and father to the boys but she almost always felt that she fell short of what they deserved.

Lukas sighed and a desperate plea escaped his lips. "*Abuela*," he called out to his grandma. "Help me out here. What do I do about Lanie?"

Abruptly, Lukas got up from his desk chair to pace the floor again. As he did so, he accidentally knocked over the bible he had been reading. The bible fell face up on him. When Lukas bent over to reach it, he noticed that his grandmother had underlined in red ink the following words from Psalm chapter 37, verse 4:

"Find your delight in the LORD who will give you your heart's desire."

Again, the hair on Lukas' neck stood momentarily. He brushed it off automatically. "*This is ridiculous. Abuela is dead, she cannot communicate with me at all!*"

And then an unsolicited thought popped in: *But was she dead, really? What if Lanie was right that there was life after death and mama and abuela were more than bodies but souls floating... somewhere, somewhere close?*

Lukas shivered then he shrugged off his fears. If this was his grandmother and mother, he certainly didn't need to be afraid of them. And if this was his grandmother's answer to his question, he wanted to give it a lot of thought.

The language on the bible was plain so there was no need to unravel any mystery to the instructions: *Find your delight in the Lord, who will give you your heart's desires and he had a right to marry her—Lanie, that is.* Lukas believed in destiny when it came to romance, thanks to the entertaining movies of Hollywood but he wasn't quite sure what to believe in when it came to God. There was no God, right? How could there be a God who would cruelly take his mother away from him? And yet, and yet, his mother and grandmother both believed that this God would send His own son, Jesus to suffer and die a horrible death on the cross for the salvation of mankind. They both lived and died believing that unfathomable mystery. Could this God have a reason for allowing suffering that Lukas did not know of? Could there be a purpose behind his mother's death that Lukas could not understand?

Then it hit him clearly: his grandmother lost her own daughter too and she still believed that God loved her, still trusted that God's reasons although unknown to her, were trustworthy. Why did she not give up her faith even when her heart broke? Was it possible there was more to this faith story than Lukas knew, than Frank himself knew?

Lukas wanted answers. It wasn't that he wanted proof that God exists or doesn't exist but he wanted to find out more. About what, he didn't exactly know. He just wanted to know. Period.

As he turned off his desk lamp, Lukas made a firm resolve to seek answers. He couldn't very well ask his father and so he decided to seek answers in the Church his mother and grandmother attended. Yes, today was Sunday and he was going to Church. Nervous but more than determined, Lukas grabbed his keys.

"Ok God", Lukas prayed, or rather challenged. "If you are real, I am ready to find you."

Chapter 6

It was past one o'clock in the afternoon when Lukas left the apartment. Since the University of Barcelona was at least three hours away from his grandmother's home town of Zaragoza, he had a long drive ahead of him. But there was only one church he knew of and that's where he was off to. Lukas put his biker's black leather jacket and helmet on, and mounted his black and silver 1997 Ducati 750 Monster motorcycle, an extravagant graduation present from his father. Lukas navigated his way through streets of Barcelona to Zaragoza to find the old parish of Santa Monica.

On the northeast of Spain lies the city of Zaragoza within in the province of Zaragoza, positioned between Madrid and Barcelona. Surrounded by mountains and situated on the river Ebro, Zaragoza is blessed with a Mediterranean continental desert climate. Since the city was founded by the Romans, architectural remains of the Forum, Thermal Baths, the River Port or the Great Theatre reflect the one-upon-a time grandeur of the Roman Empire. Amidst the Roman architecture of the Zaragosa terrain stands the famous pilgrimage destination, the Pilar Basilica.

The legend of Basilica-Cathedral of Our Lady of the Pillar (in Spanish Catedral-Basílica de Nuestra Señora del Pilar) traces its roots to St. James the greater, the apostle first to be martyred for his faith. In the first known apparition of Mary, she appeared to St. James, gave him a small wooden statue of herself and a column of jasper and instructed him to build a church in her honor. It is believed that the popular destination site has been visited by many of the kings of Spain, other foreign rulers and Spanish saints like St. John of the Cross, St. Teresa of Avila and St. Ignatius of Loyola. All of them, alongside common folk, have paid their devotion before this statue of Mary.

One of the many pilgrims who frequented the Basilica was Lukas' own grandmother, Elena. When Lukas passed the Basilica of Our Lady of the Pillar on his way to Santa Monica's, he remembered that his *abuela* had taken him and his brothers there on several occasions. He recalled that the Basilica was impressive in size and majestic in appearance. He considered visiting the Basilica today but decided against it as he was in search of a more quiet, less touristy place for answers.

After four hours of driving, Lukas arrived at the old parish of Santa Monica's. Walking past the statute of the church patroness, he noticed for the first time that his mother shared her name and curiosity for the saint took over him.

Lukas sat at the farthest end of the left side pew. He did not remember what to do inside the church. Since he did not want anyone to detect that he was a stranger in this place and call undue attention to himself, he tried to keep up with the parishioners' lead: stand, sit, stand, sit, kneel, sit... *Oh for crying out loud*, he thought to himself. *Why can't they just sit still for the entire service?!?*

By the time Mass was over, he realized that his attempt to blend in was of no use. The handful of regular parishioners had figured out he was a new comer and greeted him with a warm welcome. *Obviously*, he thought drily, *what gave me away was because I stood up last or knelt down last. Consistently.*

After the friendly parishioners had made their small talk and returned to themselves, Lukas tried to slip past Fr. Juan Mendoza who was talking to an elderly parishioner hobbling on a cane. But the ancient Fr. Juan was quicker than Lukas was. Fr. Juan deftly maneuvered himself out of the elderly parishioner's grasp and reached out to shake Lukas' hand. Fr. Juan was no doubt excited that a young man, a possible priest, had graced his parish.

"Hello, my young friend. Did you see the bulletin over there? There is a youth group that meets every Saturday night to watch some games and hang out. If you care to join us, we meet at Kaviar's at 6."

"Uh, thanks. I'm not sure if I'm up for some company. The thing is, the thing is...," His voice trailed off as he raked his blonde hair self-consciously, "I was looking for a one-on-one conversation with a... a counselor or a priest," Lukas began.

"In that case, you can call me at the parish office. I am always available for a chat and," he added, sensing that if he didn't snap up the opportunity, he would never see this young man again, "if you want it sooner, I am available now. This is the last Mass for the day."

Lukas did not want to impose on Fr. Juan's dinner plans, but he was afraid that if he was given time, he would lose his resolve. "Um, I guess I have nothing going on the rest of the evening."

"Then let me take off my vestments and I'll meet you in the back, by the grotto. There are some lawn chairs there."

Lukas walked slowly past the church to the grotto of what he knew was Our Lady. She was bathed in light. Her arms were extended, beside her hips, palms facing downwards, as if greeting him. Lukas looked at the statue intently. What was that prayer his grandmother mumbled with her beads? "Hail Mary, who are in heaven..." *Hmm, that really didn't sound right.* He tried again. "Holy Mary, Mother of God, who are in heaven..."

"What brings you here, son?" Fr. Juan asked, startling him.

"My name is Lukas. My grandmother, Elena Monteverde, used to take me here a long, long time ago."

Fr. Juan scratched his beard and then gave him a huge, warm smile. "Ahh, Elena's grandson. What a good woman she was but I have to admit," he whispered, "that I would avoid her at all costs outside the church because she would feel the need for an impromptu confession whenever she ran into me—which was usually at the farmer's market. My goodness, your grandma was practically a saint and I tried to tell her so but she wanted to confess for every single thing, God bless her. Now tell me which grandson are you? Are you the handsome one she said would break hearts someday when you enter the seminary or are you the other handsome one that she had me pray would never become a famous rock star?"

Lukas laughed heartily. "I'm afraid I'm the singer of the family."

"I'd offer you to join our church choir, if you want to put your talent to good use. Otherwise, you can be our oldest altar boy." Then Fr. Juan winked.

Lukas found himself laughing again. If there was one thing he appreciated, it was good humor. Humor made Lukas relaxed and comfortable around Fr. Juan. He suddenly felt free to blurt out his reason for being there. "Fr. Juan, I won't beat around the bush. I'm really here to find out if God exists, or if He does care about me at all or you know, why my grandmother and mother believe He does… because I don't believe or I'm not so sure anymore…"

Fr. Juan wagged a finger at him. "You're grandmother had pure, solid faith, Lukas. She knew her grandsons and son-in-law would come back some day. Come and sit, I will tell you the greatest love story every told…"

Thus began Lukas' love story with God.

Lukas eventually enrolled in Catechism classes that spring and began his journey back to the Catholic Church. Over a period of two years, Lukas learned that God, infinite wisdom, perfection and mystery created a finite creature like him out of love. God was not only his creator but His heavenly Father. God intended for Lukas to love all of created things with the end goal of uniting with God in eternal life.

Love, Lukas found out, is not the sappy *eros* lustful falling in love kind of love but love is *agape* love, giving up of selfish wants, desires and needs for the good of the other. Lukas was sorry to learn that whenever he failed to love, he sinned and that his sins offended and hurt God very much. Completely remorseful, Lukas wept unashamedly over his sins – mainly, the failure to love a Father who created him out of love.

When Lukas came to the lesson about God sending His only begotten Son Jesus Christ to die on the cross for his sins, Lukas gratefully embraced God's mercy and forgiveness for the salvation of his soul. Lukas came to believe that Jesus' suffering and death on the cross paid the price for his sins. When Jesus resurrected on the third day,

Jesus opened up the doors of heaven to all who believed in the Son, including Lukas' mother, grandmother and someday Lukas, himself. Lukas finally learned the value of suffering, completely understanding that Jesus' passion opened the floodgates of heaven for mankind. In this light, Lukas realized that his own suffering, his mother's and his grandmother's had merit because it could be united to Jesus' suffering and could be used to help save souls in this unbelieving world. Ultimately, Lukas discovered that true agape love is often painful because it means letting oneself humbly and obediently "die" just as Jesus died on the cross for our sins.

As if Jesus passion, death and resurrection weren't enough, Jesus sent the gift of the Holy Spirit to his disciples and to guide the Catholic Church. To Lukas, the ultimate treasury of the Catholic Church, not found any other religions, lay in the seven Sacraments as instituted by Jesus himself.

In receiving the Sacrament of Baptism as a baby, Lukas learned that he was freed from sin and reborn. Through this Sacrament, he was incorporated into the Church as a member of the Body of Christ. Lukas understood and believed that it was Jesus himself who illustrated by his own baptism, that baptism is necessary for salvation to those whom the Gospel has been proclaimed.

Lukas was taught that in The Sacrament of Confirmation, those who have been baptized with the Holy Spirit are enriched with the special strength of the Holy Spirit. Hence, he knew that Confirmation increased in him the gift of the Holy Spirit to spread and give witness to the Catholic faith.

The Sacrament of the Holy Eucharist, as explained to Lukas by his Catechism class instructor, is the "source and summit of the Christian life...for in the blessed Eucharist is contained the whole spiritual good of the Church, namely Christ himself."[1] This lesson took a while to descend on Lukas. He initially struggled in believing that Jesus himself became the humble species of host and that

---

[1] Catechism of the Catholic Church 1324

the host was the true Body of Christ. However, the more Lukas attended the Mass, even without receiving communion, the more he listened to the words of the priest during consecration. At one point, he was entreated by the words of the gospel of John 6:51 "Whoever eats of my flesh and drinks of my blood has eternal life." As Lukas echoed the words over and over in his head, grace poured on him and he became convinced that Jesus was being very literal in saying that the consecrated bread was truly the Body of Christ.

In studying the Sacrament of Penance, Lukas learned that Jesus Christ forgave sins while he was on earth and He willed that His Church continued this sacrament by the power of the Holy Spirit. During Jesus' public ministry, He gave his apostles authority and power to forgive sins and reconcile sinners with the church. The apostles passed on their power and authority to the priests of the Church. In a nutshell, the Sacrament of Penance obtains mercy for offenses committed against God when the penitent confesses his sins to a priest and the priest grants absolution, pardon and peace.

The Sacrament of Penance and Reconciliation was personally Lukas' favorite one. He had an easier time accepting this Sacrament than the Holy Eucharist because Lukas longed to confess many sins that haunted him and he was eager to believe that he was thoroughly forgiven. During his first confession, as Lukas was absolved of all his sins in the name of Christ, he readily understood that he was restored to a state of grace, free from mortal sin, and could partake of the Sacrament of the Eucharist worthily.

Although he had been to many weddings, Lukas learned first hand from his Catechism class that the Sacrament of Holy Matrimony establishes a covenant of lifetime partnership between a man and a woman for the good of the spouses and with the end of procreation and education of their offspring. This covenant consists of consent given mutually by the spouses and is sealed by God himself. Hence, "from their covenant, arises an institution, confirmed by the divine law."[2] This marriage bond has been established by God himself in such a way that a marriage can never be dissolved. In this sacrament, the love of the spouses joins them in unity and they are no longer two but one flesh. Lukas further learned that the Sacrament of Matrimony signifies the union of Christ and the Church and being so, it establishes a family which becomes the domestic church.

According to the Catechism class instructor, the Sacrament of Holy Orders, is the sacrament through which the apostles confer their power and authority to those with a vocation or call to the priesthood. Though he had never seen this sacrament, Lukas read that it is conferred by the laying on of hands followed by a solemn consecration prayer which asks God to grant the recipient graces of the Holy Spirit that is required for his priestly ministry. Thus, "Through the ordained ministry, especially that of bishops and priests, the presence of Christ as head of the Church is made visible in the midst of community of believers."[3]

The Sacrament of Healing/Anointing of the Sick is that given to those who are sick to strengthen them during their illness and suffering. In this sacrament, the sick are anointed with sacred oil just as Jesus touched the sick during his public life. It was not necessary for Lukas to receive this sacrament as he was not seriously ill, nevertheless he appreciated its full value and desired to receive it if he should ever need it.

Although Lukas learned to believe and appreciate the richness of Catholic teachings and tradition, he had to admit there were some things he did not easily understand and could not possibly know given his limited knowledge. Lukas however, trusted that God was infinitely wiser and more loving than anyone he ever knew and that was enough for his faith.

The day finally came when Lukas was scheduled to receive his First Communion at the San Marcus parish in Barcelona. By this time, Lukas was beginning his fourth

---

[2] Catechism of the Catholic Church 1639
[3] Catechism of the Catholic Church 1549

and final year at the university. As an adult, his father could no longer stop him from practicing his faith. When the moment came for Lukas to receive Jesus' body and blood, he knelt down in pure reverence for His Lord and Savior and opted to welcome the host in his tongue. Lukas returned to his seat and was overcome with joy that he had at last found union with the God who loved him most.

Lukas marveled at the realization that to his once unbelieving scientist's mind, he had been given the grace to accept the most mind-boggling mystery: that Jesus is God's supreme proof of his existence and the cross is God's greatest evidence of His love. He knew that such a grace was so undeserved by a sinner like himself.

When Lukas received the final blessing after Mass, he was ever so thankful that he finally received Jesus body and blood. Even the absence of his father from church did not dampen his spirits that day. His two brothers and Stephen's caregiver Magda, had made it to Mass, as did his spiritual director, Fr. Juan Mendoza. When Mass was over, Lukas' three guests met him outside the Church steps.

"Well, my boy, now all three of you are here," said Fr. Juan. "Your grandmother and mother must be looking down at this special occasion with such joy."

"Which would be more complete if Tomas would decide to become a Catholic as well." Lukas elbowed his brother.

Tomas smiled and bluntly replied. "Man, I don't know if this Church thing is for me—I mean, look what it's done for you. You gave up your band, smoking, drinking and yikes, girls. While I respect your newfound faith and am happy for you, I'm also happy for me because that means I get more girls to myself."

For a moment Lukas was horrified that he had joked like that in front of Fr. Juan but Fr. Juan was unfazed. He said, "I'm sure there was a time when Lukas thought of nothing but girls, but look at him now. I'm quite confident that the girls here can't think of anyone but him. I mean, he's even completely changed the way he looks." Fr. Juan added teasingly, "Did you get rid of your glasses, get a clean cut and return to your natural dark hair color because you realized you are a temple of the Holy Spirit, son?"

Lukas blushed. "No, I ditched the glasses because I had to keep looking in a microscope all the time and the hair kept falling into the test tubes. It was rather a hindrance to my future career. As for my hair color, I found that dark haired scientists get less dumb jokes and more respect than blonde ones."

"And how did your skinny arms fill out with muscles? Carrying your 500 ton microscope?" Tomas joked.

"Biking across Europe with my arms, of course," Lukas joked back.

Stephen looked around bewildered and struggled to speak with his speech impediment, "There aren't any young girls here though so I don't think any of you will have your share of admirers today."

The three men looked at young Stephen and chuckled. Since he was borderline autistic and said whatever came to his mind, Stephen's honesty was often refreshing.

Tomas patted his youngest brother on his back. "Too true Stephen. You won't find any girls at church, which is why this definitely is not where you'll be finding me on Sundays."

Lukas turned to Fr. Juan. "I don't get it Fr. Juan. If this is Jesus' body and blood, why don't more people come to Mass every day, instead of just one day out of the week?"

"Ahhh, Lukas, that is a decision one has to make for himself. I'm sure you could find a Church close to the university that you can go to daily."

"I'll do just that and I won't be sad at all that there will be no girls at Mass." he said, glaring at Tomas meaningfully.

The truth was that Lukas had not thought of any girl since Lanie. He had a date here and there but none of them engaged him in lively conversation and could not hold his attention long enough. Funny as it sounded, he preferred the company of laboratory chemicals and species than the women he had met. He had since gotten over Lanie, of course. God does that for you, he realized. When one brings his broken heart to God, He heals it and pieces it back together.

In prayer that night, as with every night, Lukas still prayed for the woman God had destined for him to marry. Even if it wasn't Lanie, he was confident that she would be as perfect as Sarah was for Tobias. It was just a matter of time before they met.

Chapter 7

Later that same year, an exhausted Lukas came home to the apartment that he shared with his brother Tomas in Barcelona, Spain.

The city of Barcelona, once the site of the 1992 Summer Olympics, is located to the east of the Iberian Peninsula.

The artistic architecture of Barcelona has earned it the name "city of modern art". It is a well-publicized fact that world-famous painters and artists like Picasso and Miro have worked in Barcelona at one time during their lives. Hence, their most important works are featured in some of the city's museums and art galleries, buildings that Tomas often frequented.

Apart from Barcelona's rich connection to art, a quaint feature of the city that delights the tourists is its aerial cable car system which runs across the Barcelona port. To the locals, like Lukas, the most fascinating find in Barcelona are the sandy beaches, which are a walking distance from the city's center, the Plaza de Cataluna. Since Barcelona faces the Mediterranean Sea, it boasts of a Mediterranean climate with warm, dry summers and mild, humid winters that make it possible to enjoy the beach all year long.

Barcelona, other than being Lukas' hometown, is home to the University of Barcelon. The University, founded in 1450, is an all-encompassing public university that offers at least one hundred departments and two universities. The University ranks among the top 200 universities of the world and enjoys a student population of at least 63,700. Additionally, the University of Barcelona has a world-renowned research and teaching facilities and holds one of the finest biochemistry programs in Spain.

It was early in the summer when Lukas finished his last exam for his final year. He looked forward to the rest of summer where he would probably spend his time alternating between working and swimming in the ocean.

Lukas tossed the keys to his motorcycle on the dining table just as Tomas walked out of his room to head out the door.

"Hey Lukas, there's a big party tonight at Ricardo's place. I heard lots of girls will be there, buddy. Care to come?" Tomas asked.

Lukas winced. He loved his older brother, they always had a good relationship but in the past two years they didn't exactly share the same interests anymore. In fact, it seemed as though Lukas was the more responsible older brother of the two as Tomas languished in college, taking his time before he graduated, partied on the weekends, sometimes coming home drunk, sometimes staying out with a girl while Lukas worked late at the laboratory. As a result, Lukas and Tomas were now both on their senior year, scheduled to graduate together.

Lukas vocally reproved of his brother's lifestyle and vice versa but that did not stop either of them from trying to get the other to do stuff together. Lukas would drag Tomas to Mass on Sundays and sometimes Lukas would half-heartedly attend a party with his brother although he would leave early. They both knew they were different as night and day but they worked at trying to maintain the bond they shared as children.

Lukas did not answer the question directly. He was still undecided about what to do that night. "Oh yeah, what's the big occasion? Someone flunked his finals this time and wants to drown his frustration in deafening rock music or did someone actually get an A and wanted to show off to the girls his winning paper on beer making?"

Tomas laughed. "Actually, Carl and Diego are leaving to go on some student exchange program to an American University, St. Ignatius of Loyola University or something like that so this is a going away party. Supposedly, some of the other American summer exchange students will be there – three or four girls will be coming to see the Spanish college life. So you just might get lucky tonight, little brother if you gargle some mouthwash and don't let on to the girls that you really are a dweeb underneath your deceptively normal-looking clothes."

The mention of that familiar university piqued Lukas' interest. He found himself agreeing to go to the party. "Alright then, but let me go and leave my lab coat and microscope behind," he said drily.

The party was as appalling as every other college party Lukas had been to. Smoke everywhere, loud music, immodestly dressed women with thick make-up, drunk men ogling the women, and coeds sniffing drugs behind closed doors. Lukas cringed. It was a safe bet that as soon as they came in, some girls would make a beeline for Tomas. Ordinarily, when Tomas was not interested, he would encourage Lukas to talk about his latest project in the biochem lab and that pretty much would end any flirtatious conversation with the ladies. But when Tomas was interested, he would take over the conversation, charm the girl outright and she would very likely be charmed. Lukas found himself wishing that tonight's girls wouldn't be interesting not for his brother's moral sake but so that he and Tomas could at least spend a few hours hanging out, poking good natured fun at each other.

Sure enough, Tomas had barely crossed the entrance into the room when three almost identical blonde girls spotted the Swenson boys and headed straight for them. One of them leaned over flirtatiously and drawled an overused line in halting Spanish, "Hola, soy Kelly. You Spanish boys sure know how to make an entrance."

The accent was unmistakably American and Lukas immediately knew these were the visiting co-eds.

"Hello," Tomas said in perfect English. "Would you senoritas care for a sangria or a tequila?"

Fifteen minutes later, Lukas and Tomas both had to admit that the girls were interesting. While Tomas' interest solely focused on their looks, Lukas truly was intrigued by the college they attended. What is St. Ignatius of Loyola University like? How many students are there? Do they have a good biochemistry program? What is Boston like? Is St. Ignatius a party college or do they have other extracurricular activities for an anti-social dweeb like himself?

"Look," the bored American girl named Ashley pointed out, "I don't mean to be rude, but like, if you are so interested in the school, look it up online. They have tons of international students over there, ok?"

An unscathed Lukas literally almost ran out of the party. After bidding Tomas a hasty goodbye and warning him to come home sober, he headed straight for his computer.

Lukas spent hours on the computer that night. He found all sorts of information on the world wide web: St. Ignatius of Loyola University was built and founded by the Jesuits in the early 1880's. The Jesuits, or the Society of Jesus, is a Catholic order of priests dedicated to providing academic excellence and more importantly, educating its graduates to become men and women for others. St. Ignatius of Loyola University was accordingly named after the founder of the Jesuit Order.

Lukas further learned that there was an excellent biochemistry program in the reputable Chemistry department and they also offered doctorates and master's degrees for graduate students. There was a campus ministry for Catholic students and spiritual directors in the Jesuits. There were religious extracurricular activities for athletes, musicians, artists, writers, and every kind of hobby. There were theology and philosophy classes for those who wanted to minor in them and study them as electives. Lukas also found that the city of Boston was a safe college town with hundreds of living places in and around campus. Lukas researched on how to apply for a post graduate studies program to St. Ignatius of Loyola University. To his relief, he noted that he had two weeks till the deadline for the incoming school year.

By the time Lukas heard the front door unlock and Tomas came staggering in, he learned all that he needed to apply for St. Ignatius of Loyola University. That is, everything except the one thing that would have mattered to him: whether there was a dark haired, olive skinned, green eyed Hawaiian student named Lanie studying in the English department and whether she remembered him at all.

Sand and Water

~~

Lukas could not concentrate on the Sunday homily the following day. It wasn't that he was sleepy from a night spent in front of his computer. It was recurring thoughts of Lanie after almost three years of trying to forget her, that distracted him. It dumbfounded him, really.

Lanie. Why should thoughts of her come unexpectedly? He rubbed his forehead in confusion. He sincerely believed that the reason she walked into his life was to lead him back to the Catholic faith. He had since rationalized that the reason he had fallen in love with her was actually because he subconsciously wanted what she had—an unshakable faith which caused her unrivaled optimism and deep spirituality. Thus, he convinced himself that when he had found God, he had no desire for a concept of Lanie because he had been given what she had: faith. So, why oh why was he reminded of something that seemed so juvenile now? And why, oh why did his heart start racing when he thought of applying for post graduate studies at St. Ignatius of Loyola University? This was almost as insane as falling in love over the internet with a girl he had never seen!

Once Mass was over, Lukas walked over to the statue of the Sacred Heart of Jesus at the back of the Church. The image of the Sacred Heart was Lukas' personal favorite. In It, he found Jesus bottomless love and mercy. Lukas' affinity for the image of Jesus' heart enflamed by love shaped his entire outlook in life: that Jesus' sacrificial love would help him overcome anything that he had to do in the name of love. Lukas prayed:

"Lord Jesus, I don't know why I am getting such ridiculous ideas. The last time I did something impulsive, I got my heart broken. I don't want to be misled anymore. Help me stay on the right path or know if I should start on another one. Please bless me and guide me that I may only do what God wills. And please hurry up, Lord. The deadline is in two weeks and I have to get started on the paperwork right away."

The ride home was quiet. Lukas never thought he would say this but thank God Tomas did not come to church today. He needed to think and pray and listen alone.

Lukas' thoughts focused on the gospel reading for the day where St. Joseph had a dream of an angel to take Jesus and Mary to Egypt. Lukas prayed for a clear sign on whether to stay or go. "Make it simple," he pleaded to Jesus.

Immediately, the red light turned green.

Oblivious, Lukas did not step on his gas as he continued to pray for an angel to show him the way. The angry motorist passed him, honked his horn and yelled, "Green means go, buddy. Move it!"

Lukas continued to cruise along leisurely in his motorcycle. He passed by the American Consulate General's Office, praying to the Holy Spirit for guidance. If he had looked closely at the glass door, he would have read the notice that said, "Applications for student visas accepted here." But he did not.

Lukas parked his motorcycle at the apartment's parking lot. On and on he prayed, pleading to St. Joseph for directions. The car beside him had two bumper stickers: one of St. Joseph and another of St. Ignatius. He thought nothing of it.

Lukas realized he forgot to pick up yesterday's mail so he backtracked to the mailbox and grabbed a stack. Preoccupied with his thoughts, he barely noticed the flyer until it landed on his shoe. It was distributed by the Student Exchange Services. The headline screamed: STUDY ABROAD! Lukas threw the flyer on the nearest trash.

He let himself into the apartment. Just then, Tomas opened the door of his room, grabbed milk from the refrigerator and said, "Boy, this is the only time I'm jealous of you little brother. If I was in your shoes with more studies ahead of me, I'd study abroad like Carl and Diego are doing. That girl last night, Kelly, said it has been the best week of her life."

Something inside Lukas just clicked and a peace covered him like a warm blanket on a cold night. He could hardly believe it. Jesus had answered his prayers in a hurry like he requested and he had used the last person he thought it would come from: his atheist brother.

Now, Lukas knew he was America bound.

Chapter 8

St. Ignatius of Loyola University, or SILU as the students like to abbreviate it, sits on a slightly elevated hill in Boston Massachusetts, along the row of Ivy League schools. While not as famous as its scholastic neighbors, it was considered as just as prestigious to be accepted into the Jesuit run institution. SILU boasted a history for educating the crème de la crème of Catholic families. Due to the wealth and privilege of its students, the majority of SILU's student body is collectively snobbish and arrogant, with only a handful of humble, cause-oriented coeds genuinely committed to making the world a better place after their graduation.

The quaint brick style buildings of the University form a small town of approximately 5,000 undergrad students and 3,000 graduate students. The different departments are separated by stretches of well manicured lawns, and impressive oak and Sequoia trees. The departments are connected by walkways lined with a colorful panoply of petunias, sweet peas and hyacinths. Every few feet or so, benches dotted the sides of the walkways.

The beauty of the sprawling university however is usually lost on Freshmen on the first day of school. Most of them have trouble distinguishing one brick building from another and wind up roaming the crowded halls of the campus, searching for their next class. Today, one particular freshman was staring at Alana instead of paying attention to what she was saying and that was annoying her immeasurably.

Alana impatiently rolled her eyes at the gawking Freshman. She tossed her long, painstakingly straightened dark hair and repeated herself, "Patridge Hall is that way. Two buildings from here. This is Parkins Building."

Her sorority sister, Faye Cashman, was equally irritated and snapped, "Oh just look at your map and quit

Anabelle Hazard

making up excuses to talk to her." She dragged Alana upstairs with her and huffed, "Sometimes, your supermodel looks are such an asset to us. It can get us into just about any club but seriously, times like these, it's such a hassle to get rid of unwanted admirers."

"Hurry up, you two," Courtney Holloway nudged them from behind. "Now, Alana remember that we have to get there early so that you can sweet talk Professor Casey into switching us to the 9AM class. That's the only way we'll ever get to be on the play and make it to rehearsals in the winter evenings."

Alana was now annoyed at her sorority sisters. Sometimes, they made her feel so used—like the only reason they had asked her to join their sorority and were nice to her was to get the boys' attention or some other ulterior motive such as auditioning for a play to get close to Jeff Ackerman. Jeff Ackerman was an up and coming Hollywood actor/director who was a former alumna of SILU and who would be directing this year's annual Christmas play.

"What about our weekend parties?" Alana asked her friends. "Aren't you in charge of this year's socials, Faye?"

Faye snorted. "Oh, campus parties are getting too old. We're juniors now and the only boys we haven't met are the freshmen, the transferees, and the graduate students. Clubbing is way more fun and Jeff Ackerman is cuter *and older.*"

"Did you hear that he broke up with his actress girlfriend Sydney Fairchild?" squealed Courtney. "Wow, if he takes one of us to the Oscars, Hollywood here we come!"

"It's a long way off to the tabloids and paparazzi life, Courtney, so don't count your Oscars before they hatch," Alana said wryly.

Faye narrowed her eyes at Courtney. "Especially not when I *am* going to be Jeff Ackerman's date for the Christmas Charity Ball. He just doesn't know it yet." The Christmas Charity Ball was always held on the day after the final night of the Christmas Play. It was usually the biggest university event as it was well attended by students, faculty and distinguished alumni.

Alana rolled her eyes again. "Focus girls, focus. First we need to switch our schedules, then we can talk about the play and then Jeff Ackerman and then the ball and then Hollywood. By the way Faye, I heard Jeff and Sydney are back on again."

"They'll be off the minute he sets his eyes on me," Faye sniffed.

Alana was not particularly interested in Jeff Ackerman or in theatre. But she was somewhat interested in pursuing a career as a news reporter. Faye and Courtney had convinced her that meeting Jeff Ackerman would open doors for her in journalism. She was already a writer, they'd insisted, now all she needed was the right connections to get into broadcast and print media. Hence, Alana agreed to audition for the upcoming play as long as she wasn't required to sing. Besides, it wasn't so bad that the proceeds of the annual Christmas program benefited charity. She would be able to write that in her resume as an honorable gesture of volunteering for a cause.

Alana, Faye and Courtney entered an empty lecture room and waited for Professor Conrad Casey, their World History teacher to arrive. As soon as he came in, Alana turned on her feminine charm full blast and successfully switched the girls' schedules to the already overbooked 9 AM class.

Over the next few weeks, Alana found herself actually liking Professor Casey's class. He was a feminist disguised in a man's body. Professor Casey advocated for women's rights every chance he could harp on it and Alana found herself agreeing with everything he said on that point.

"Why shouldn't women be presidents, lawyers, doctors, soldiers, politicians, theologians and even priests?" Professor Casey lectured constantly.

Alana would nod, thinking arrogantly along the same lines. *Hmmph! No one is going to stop this woman from taking on the world, least of all a man.*

~ ~

The fall audition results soon revealed that all those years of playing Mary in the St. Anne parish plays had paid off: Alana was cast in the role of Mary. Faye and Courtney, both talented dancers and performance arts majors, formed part of the ensemble.

Alana became excited at this new turn of events. If she was honest with herself, she would admit that she was beginning to get bored with the sorority parties herself. The play would be a much needed diversion from the poor grades she was getting in her media classes.

Maybe, she thought to herself, her parents would stop nagging her about her sudden shift in majors if they saw that she was doing well in theatre.

It bothered Alana that her parents were getting on her case all the time. In their eyes, Alana had come into St. Ignatius of Loyola University, a bright naïve freshman who was determined to major in English literature and minor in journalism but somehow the sorority rush lured Alana away from her goals. It was, after all, Alana's senior sisters who had advised her that it was a much more lucrative choice to get into TV. Thus, despite her parent's adamant objections, Alana abruptly changed her major. Since that impulsive shift into broadcast journalism, Joe and Maria constantly blamed Alana's friends for their bad influence while she resented her parents for being so closed-minded. As a result of the tension in the O' Keefe household, Alana worked around the campus for the summer so she would spend as little time as possible at their home.

More parent-child tension was also caused by Alana's non-attendance in Church. Alana's involvement with the Church naturally slowed down when she started staying up late for the Saturday night parties. First, she would skip a week or two Sunday Masses until eventually, she stopped attending Mass altogether. Alana's logic went something like this: Since she dabbled with smoke and alcohol during the parties, she reasoned that she could not receive communion in a state of grace and since she could not receive communion in a state of grace, what was the point of going to Church anyway? Truth be told, Alana did not like the bitter taste of alcohol or the smell of nicotine on her fingers but she wanted to look sophisticated for the parties and there was nothing at all to do with her hands except to hold a drink and a cigarette.

Alana tried to convince herself that her parents' disapproval of her lifestyle did not matter to her. She was an adult who had a right to take control of her life and besides, they were not her real parents, anyway. An insidious thought began to nag her: What if she was raised by her biological parents, would they have been more supportive and understanding of her choices?

From the outside, Alana was having the time of her life. She was young, beautiful, popular, surrounded by friends, was always invited to parties and never wanted for any dates at all. However, deep inside her, when the party was over and she climbed to her bed, she felt the ache of emptiness. She knew the emptiness would disappear in another party, on another date and so she lived for the wild weekends.

Alana also knew but she did not want to admit that the two years of college life brought her soul on a downward spiral. From an atypical teenager, she had morphed into the "normal" college girl—seduced by pop culture, angst ridden, fixated on image, centered on self, combating her parents, partied out, and sadly, faithless.

~ ~

Jeff Ackerman surveyed the cast and crew of the annual Christmas play. There was a mixture of excited students crowded around the front of the auditorium, waiting for the director to address them on the first day of rehearsals. They ranged from business majors to pre-meds to the artists. All of them were staring at him, but the one person who caught his eye was the tall, dark haired, beautiful student who was going to play the part of Mary.

Alana O'Keefe wasn't that great of an actress, he thought, although granted she could do a decent job of playing Mary. But she had her looks going for her, and in today's show business that was apparently all that was needed. Recalling her audition, he recognized in her the xfactor that he saw in his on-and-off-girlfriend, Sydney, and mentally patted himself on the back for handpicking her. His keen director's mind assessed that Alana could just be the next big thing that could catapult his fame and secure his place among the A-list directors of Tinsel town. Either that, or she could become his latest dalliance while Sydney was licking her wounds at his refusal to commit to an engagement.

Jeff spoke commandingly into the microphone, "Alright everyone, congratulations on being the cast and crew of SILU's 47th Annual Christmas play. I thank you all for your contribution of time, talent and treasure to this year's presentation. As you all know, this tradition goes way back. In fact, it wasn't too long ago that I sat in this auditorium as an audience, utterly wowed by the genius of the then director Allen Smith whose artistic rendition of the Nativity was unlike any other I've ever seen. This year, it's our turn to show off. We'll top 26 years of Nativity versions, and while we're doing it, we will make some children in Latin America very happy. "

Everyone cheered and Alana found her spirits buoyed.

From where she sat next to Alana, Faye felt the charge of excitement too. "Its not even Christmas and I feel the Christmas spirit," she remarked.

"I want Jeff Ackerman for Christmas," whispered Courtney "or that hot guy in the navy jacket, row 5. Do you think he's a freshman? I've never seen him before. And oohlala, check out row 8, looks like a foreign exchange student..."

"Hush, pay attention. Jeff's trying to tell us the schedule," chided Alana, although she briefly checked out the good-looking crew members. To Courtney, she said pointedly. "Slow down. One hot guy at a time, please."

"Geez, you're not actually the Queen of Heaven and you're acting like the queen bee around here," Courtney said jokingly.

Faye and Alana giggled. Alana replied in a voice filled with self-importance. "That's right, I'm queen bee, you are my subjects. You be quiet and you," she nodded in

Courtney's direction, "leave Jeff Ackerman alone. I'm staking my claim."

Faye put her hands on her hips. "Your highness, I staked my claim long before you laid eyes on him so with all due respect, back off. And it is rather unethical for the *Virgin* Mary be involved with the director."

Alana glared at Faye. Faye and Courtney were the only two people who knew that she was a virgin. Alana had sworn them to secrecy. The rest of the sorority sisters would have laughed in her face if they knew that she wasn't as liberated as they were. This liberal college was so different from the conservative Catholic homeschooling family and friends Alana had grown up with. She was actually embarrassed now to admit that she was once a proud member of the "true love waits" program in her parish.

Alana looked Faye in the eye, cocking her eyebrow. "Maybe I *will* lose my prized possession to someone as gorgeous as that," she said, not entirely sure if she meant it. Jeff Ackerman really was gorgeous, she acknowledged, maybe it was time she broke her own self-made vow. At that thought, she wondered why she strangely felt herself still bound by a silly vow she had made eight years ago.

"Ooooh," said Faye with mischief in her eye. "Then I will gladly step aside, my lady. Where's option #2, Courtney?"

"Huh? I'm already scoping out #6. Keep up, girl!" she exclaimed.

As the two girls assessed the male population in the auditorium, Alana listened to Jeff describe the entire program and became impressed by his artistic vision. Looks aside, he really was an impressive man. She couldn't help but notice that his authority came with age. Jeff must have graduated 6 or 7 years ago. She perceived that the maturity was the one thing the college students did not have going for them. Alana had gone on plenty enough dates to conclude that the college men, at least the ones she met at the parties, were not emotionally or intellectually stimulating. All they wanted was a good time: beer and sex. The one advantage to it, she thought to herself, was that this made it harder to fall in love with them and thus, easier to keep her virginity. Or was it really an advantage? Being the last living virgin in the campus did not exactly that rack up her popularity points.

Alana's thoughts strayed further. Why was she holding on to her virginity anyway when she hardly went to church? Who was she saving it for and what was the matter with her thinking about giving it up for a man who probably didn't know her name?

She sighed. She was so confused these days. It used to be so much fun talking about boys and parties, what to wear and who was dating who in Hollywood. Lately, though, she felt so disconnected --like she was playing a role, building up a persona that was not really who she was. She wished something would happen to change this rut—anything, for crying out loud. Maybe Jeff was exactly what she needed.

Jeff was wrapping up his little speech: "As you noticed, we've assembled such a large number of people today. It's impossible to work with a circus this size so we're dividing you guys into the following groups: Choir, Orchestra, Singers/Soloists, Dancers, Cast, Lights, Sounds, Costume/Make-up. After this, we're breaking up into our own groups and you'll meet with your team heads. Your team heads will give you your individual schedules. All of us won't actually meet together until the last week of rehearsals. By then, we should all know our parts and it will all come together, nicely, I hope. So good luck everyone."

"Did you hear that?" whined a dismayed Courtney. "That means we won't actually get to work with all our 15 prospects, Faye."

"Duh. It's just like working in the movies, Courtney," Faye said in a condescending tone. "There's the little production people and there's stars like you and me."

"Stars in the ensemble?" Alana asked in mock arrogance. She started off half-joking but was liking her new role so much, she had to rub it in. "Does that make me a superstar?"

Faye, a spoiled socialite and daughter of a famous and wealthy real estate developer, had had enough of Alana's attitude, even though some of it was made in part-

Sand and Water

jest. Faye selected her next words in a calculating manner; picking a notoriously sore topic that she believed would seal Alana's lips permanently. "You would be if you dyed your hair blonde or at least got some highlights from my hairstylist," she remarked with disdain.

Alana took her time thinking of a biting reprisal. While most women resented comments on their weight, Alana's pet peeve was any derogatory comment on her hair, especially when it came from her sorority sisters, and her sorority sisters knew it would needle her. It appeared to Alana that the official Alpha Lambda hair color was blonde, in all possible shades. Her naturally rebellious streak fought against this almost farcical peer-pressure driven trend. While she wanted to blend in with the latest styles in designer fashion and be included in the hippest socials, she also wanted to stand out and be counted as special. The struggle to keep her natural hair color almost took the last ounce of her resistance to pop culture mania.

With slow deliberate movements, Alana ran her fingers through her thick dark hair, held them up and let them loose on her shoulders. Imperturbably, but with a sugary smile, she retaliated to Faye, "Women should only need their brains and talent to succeed anywhere. At least I thought that's all *I* needed to land the lead role."

Faye, a true brunette, caught on to the hidden implication behind her words. She gave Alana a cold look but kept silent, sulkily.

"Look, look!" Courtney continued. "Number 3 is headed for choir, 12 is in sounds and 7 is... make-up? Yikes! How San Francisco!"

Alana laughed at her friend and teased her. "You should have known by the way he dressed. That cashmere sweater makes your angora one look like toilet paper."

Courtney made a face, hiding her hurt feelings. "Well, you have nothing to be upset about. You're working with number 1. I wonder if it's too late to learn how to sing or play the drums."

Alana was instantly sorry that she had insulted Courtney with put-down humor and quieted Faye with spiteful insinuations. She put her arms around her friends

68

and said, "Never too late, my little drummer girl. Come on, let's take you to a Karaoke bar, where you can practice your pa-rum-pa-pum-pum and then Faye can sing all the solos she wants while I'll be the shoo-be-do-wap back up girl. It's on me, ladies."

Despite themselves, Faye and Courtney giggled. Unknown to Alana, the reason why Faye and Courtney valued her friendship was not just because Alana was funny or popular but because Alana wasn't nearly as mean as the other Alpha Lambda's. They appreciated that Alana was always genuinely contrite when she put her foot in her mouth and tried to make amends when she hurt anyone's feelings. Every once in a while, underneath Alana's glamorous polished guise, Faye and Courtney caught a glimpse of something inside Alana that resembled the soft kindness she had carried with her when she was an unaffected homeschooled Freshman from Hawaii.

~ ~

"That's it for tonight," Jeff said, rubbing his tired eyes. "Great job, guys."

Although she was exhausted, Alana was disappointed that rehearsals were wrapping up. Rehearsing for this Christmas play was the most fun she had in a long time. She didn't realize that pretending to be Mary brought back so many memories of Christmases with her family and friends and the community she once belonged to. On top of that, she was meeting people outside her sorority circle and she genuinely enjoyed socializing with diverse personalities. Mostly though, Alana was saddened at the thought that she would not be seeing Jeff anymore once the play was over. After working closely but professionally with him for the last two months, she had begun to develop an impossible crush on Jeff. Alana often found herself performing to impress the broad shouldered, sandy haired, brown eyed director.

"Alana?" Jeff's familiar voice queried from behind her.

"Yes?" She whirled around. *Too eager*, she chided herself.

"I need your opinion on something. It's been a while since I was in this school so I don't know what's still cool in this college or not. Now, I'm thinking of having this band play some Christmas carols for the grand finale on the program. Have you heard of The Gingerbread Men?"

Alana's jaw dropped. "Are you serious? They've only got like the best selling album in the universe."

"I take it they're still cool?"

"No, they're *hot*. Hot is the new cool and bad is the new good. Didn't they teach you that in director's academy or something?"

Jeff laughed. "I must have been too partied out to get the memo, just like the good old college days."

Alana tipped her head to one side. "Frat boy?"

"Yup, party animal all four years," was the answer.

"Well if you turned out successful, there's hope for all of us party animals," she said earnestly.

Jeff was surprisingly charmed. "There's one more thing I need your opinion on."

"What's that?"

"Would it be a good idea, er bad idea for a director to take his leading lady out to a front row Gingerbread Men concert next week?"

Alana gasped. "Yes, I mean, no it would be a good idea. I mean, that would be awesome. She would love to." And then, to cover up her embarrassment at her incoherent response she added, "The correct lingo to use is, 'That would be bad!'"

Jeff chuckled. "I'll have to read the memo if I'm going to start hanging out with you."

Alana smiled and said smoothly, "I wanted to get one thing straight: my reaction was solely because the Gingerbread Men are hot. It had nothing to do with your temperature." *Good grief,* she thought. *How lame!*

Jeff smiled broadly, impressed by Alana's wit. "Then I wonder what you'll do when I tell you I know them personally and can arrange for you to meet them backstage."

"Ok, I feel like jumping up and down and hugging you but I won't do that. I'm going to practice self-restraint so that the Gingerbread Men bodyguards won't throw me out when I actually meet them. Wait, did I just say that aloud?" *Put a lid on it, Lanie,* she said to herself furiously.

Jeff was laughing uncontrollably, now. "In the name of self-restraint then, I won't say 'woohoo'. Now let me put on my poker face and say: you've got yourself a date, Alana."

With a nod, Alana bit her lip but allowed a smile to peek through. She did not say anything else until she was out of earshot with Faye and Courtney. Then she let out a shriek.

Jeff got into his sleek black convertible Camaro that evening, completely won over by Alana. He had always thought she was attractive and as he studied her over the past month, he grew fascinated by her. Now the fascination may have jumped to the level of captivation. *It looks like there's more to this than I had originally planned,* he thought with a shake of his head.

Chapter 9

  Lukas slowed down his mountain bike as he appraised the scenery before him. Red, orange and yellow oak and maple tree leaves formed a shade over the pack of bikers as they glided peacefully along the quiet streets.
  "*Wow*," he thought to himself. "*America is such a beautiful country.*" He was immensely grateful that he joined the St. Ignatius cyclists association. This was such an ingenious way to see the countryside. He had no idea that the fall landscape in Massachusetts was breathtaking. It was almost as satisfying as being in the water.
  Lukas had always considered himself a water fan and by that he meant that he liked the ocean more than the sandy beaches, the lakes more than the mountains, the rivers more than the forests, even swimming pools more than parks. While he was studying in Barcelona, Lukas couldn't count the number of times he would head to the Mediterranean waters to cool off in the middle of the day. While most people lounged and strolled on the beaches, Lukas spent most of his time swimming, snorkeling, or floating in the saltwater. The longest he had ever spent on the beach was the time Lanie had mentioned she liked going out for a stroll in her bare feet, to feel the cool sand on her toes. Back then, Lukas had sat on the beach for two hours, gazing at the breadth of the ocean, thinking about how the water connected him to Hawaii, to Lanie. That was the only time he liked sitting on the hot sand. Other than that, his restless nature generally found more pleasure moving about in the water.
  Lukas switched his bike to low gear, sped up and climbed uphill. Once he reached the summit, he could see the stretch of pristine blue water below. *Ahh,* he mused, *there's that water.* With half a smile, Lukas marveled at the varying blue shades and then looked up to where the arms of the trees formed a reddish golden arch. This sight was something else. Lukas thanked God that he had the

opportunity to see one of His finest creations on water and on land.

"Are you starting to miss the rumble of your motorcycle, Luke?" asked his buddy Sean Speigel, who was biking alongside him. Sean was a junior at SILU, majoring in philosophy, most likely headed for the seminary as soon as he graduated. Though he was three years younger than Lukas, Sean had a quiet maturity about him that made Lukas instantly like him.

"No way. The only thing I miss about Europe are the old Churches," Lukas replied.

"Since you're obviously not missing any ladies, maybe you've got a vocation to the priesthood," Sean suggested.

"Well, I'm missing a lady but I don't know who she is and where to find her," Lukas confessed.

"Is there a story behind this?" Patrick Donahue asked with a gleam in his eye. Patrick was Irish, a junior foreign student transferee, majoring in business and marketing.

Lukas debated with himself quickly whether to tell his two buddies about Lanie. He had never spoken about her except to Fr. Juan and he really needed to talk about it every once in a while. He gauged that Sean was safe, he would keep a secret, could possibly give him sound advice. But Patrick? Although kind, his humorous roommate could be reckless. But what was the use of keeping something like that a secret anyway? Didn't he need all the help he could get tracking her down, especially since he didn't have much luck himself in the last two months he had been at SILU?

Exhaling, Lukas released his unusual story out in the open. "The long and short of it is, and don't laugh now, I met a girl through the internet when I was a sophomore in college and she was a senior in high school. I knew only three things about her: She's from Hawaii, her nickname is Lanie and she was going to major in English lit at St. Ignatius of Loyola University. We lost touch and she resurfaced in my mind three years later. I've decided to come here with nothing but those clues and a... hope of some sort...but I haven't found her yet."

Sean prodded, "Where have you looked?"

"In places I thought I'd find her. I've asked around the English department subtly so I wouldn't seem like a desperate stalker. No luck. I thought she would be at daily Mass, in campus ministry or some Catholic orgs around campus but there's no sign of her. I'm beginning to think she decided not to come here at all or worse, that it was some online predator masquerading as an 18 year old," Lukas joked.

Patrick interrupted. "This sounds like a job for flyers, lad."

"Flyers?" Sean and Lukas stared at him, perplexed.

"Get out her pic, make copies and we'll pass it 'round. Surely, one of these cyclists will recognize her face."

"Why don't we post her picture on a milk carton under the headline "Have you seen me?" and put Lukas' contact number in there? I'm sure she'll jump right into Lukas' arms," Sean said sarcastically.

"As brilliant as your plan is Patrick, I don't have a picture of her. Besides, I hear they put people in jail for this sort of thing—I believe it's called stalking or copyright infringement or something that'll definitely lock me up for good," Lukas said, laughing.

Patrick's eyes grew big. "You mean you don't have a recent picture of her or you've never seen a picture of her?"

"I've never seen a picture of her," Lukas admitted.

"Hooooh boy," hooted Patrick. "Your story keeps getting more and more outrageous. You can't be in love with someone you've never seen. That's like getting married without having sex first."

"Who said post-marital sex is outrageous? The bible certainly didn't," Sean challenged.

Patrick answered, "Well, our theology of marriage class teacher Fr. Adrian Danburry, gave that lecture the other day. He said God isn't a god who cares about the date of marriage. All that God asks is that one be in a committed relationship in order to have sex."

Sean's eyebrow dipped into a frown. He lectured Patrick with his trademark directness, "Buddy, I hate to tell you that liberal professor of yours is inaccurate. God does care about the date of marriage. Marriage is not just a piece of paper or a social contract, it is a sacrament. When a marriage is celebrated before Jesus Christ, man and wife say their vows before Jesus Christ and before the Holy Trinity. From that moment on, those vows are binding in heaven and on earth. Hence, on the date of a Church marriage, a couple enters into a covenanted relationship with God through Jesus Christ and by virtue of that covenant they are entrusted with the sacred and awesome responsibility of procreating life."

"Whoa don't judge me, Sean. You're not even a priest yet," said Patrick defensively.

"I'm not judging you. I'm informing you what the Catholic Church teaches. It's black and white, right and wrong. If you feel guilty, that's your conscience judging yourself," Sean shot back.

"Look," Lukas said gently. "If you want to understand Church teaching better, you may want to get a copy of the Theology of the Body as written by the Pope. I know it totally changed my mind about sex before marriage."

"So, you were what? Sleeping around until you decided to become celibate?" Patrick asked incredulously.

"I guess you could put it that way. Think of it as though you were riding motorcycles all your life until you saw the light and discovered bicycles. To some people it seems like downgrading but to those who see the truth, God allows us to upgrade."

"Now that's profound. But it still doesn't explain why God would expect us to save sex for marriage."

Lukas sighed and searched inside his memory for the one thing that remained with him from his reading of the Theology of the Body. "Patrick, marriage between man and woman has been likened to Jesus and his bride the Church. The love that Jesus had for us was completely illustrated when He died for us on the cross. In the Last Supper, recall that Jesus says "This is my body, which is given up for you."

"Sex within marriage or nuptial love is the love of total self-donation. Just as Christ gave us His body, spouses are called to give their bodies to the other as a total gift. God intended for man and woman to be gifts to each other, to love each other and to express that love through their bodies in nuptial love."

"Once I realized that, I knew that I wanted to give myself to my wife completely or at least, as completely as I can. I've made mistakes by giving my body away in the past but Jesus has forgiven me and made me understand that my nuptial love is still a gift to her. So I am saving myself for my marriage to her."

"But what if I want to give the gift of experience to my wife?" Patrick asked.

"Then you wouldn't be using sex as it was intended for and as demonstrated by Jesus. It would be like using a bike for sailing in the ocean."

"Wow, I get that. You'd make a better priest than ole Sean here, Fr. Luke," Patrick joked in an attempt to lighten up the mood.

"Sure thing. My first homily will be about the immorality of online dating," Lukas added.

Sean laughed. "Maybe we should do the Church a favor and not help you look for Lanie."

"Maybe I should stop looking for her until I discern a vocation to the priesthood," said Lukas seriously.

"Amen to that," Sean agreed.

"Say, what do the cyclists do when fall is over? Do we keep biking through the winter?" Patrick asked Sean.

"Some of them camp out in cabins by the lake, others hibernate. I like to join the Christmas program St. Ignatius holds every year, so rehearsals keep me busy throughout the winter."

"What's that Christmas program about?" Lukas asked.

"Every year, the university produces a program and incorporates the Nativity Play. I usually join the orchestra since I play the piano. If either of you are interested in the choir or orchestra, auditions are next week. It's open to undergrads and grad students."

Lukas felt a shot of excitement course through his body. "I haven't played the guitar publicly in years, but joining the choir sounds like a great idea."

"My only question is: will there be any good looking girls there?" Patrick asked Sean deviously.

"Oh there's lots. The entire school, all the colleges and departments get involved. Your sorry soul will have a heyday," he said with a grin.

~ ~

Three months later, Lukas and Patrick reported for the last week of rehearsals together. Rehearsals were held at the imposing Gonzaga International Center where the Christmas Program would be playing. The Gonzaga International Center was the state of the art sports and entertainment facility of SILU built in 1991 and named after the Jesuit saint Aloysius Gonzaga. The modern grey, silver and white minimalist-designed building boasted a maximum total seating capacity of about 10,000. It was by far the largest and most contemporary looking facility in the campus that freshman almost always used it as a landmark for finding their way around.

Lukas and Patrick searched around the vast auditorium and spotted Sean sitting with some members of the orchestra while waiting for rehearsals to begin. They sauntered over to Sean.

"What a madhouse this place is tonight," Patrick observed, eyeing the endless stream of students coming into the auditorium.

"You should see it when the audience is here. It's like Rockefeller Center on New Year's Eve."

"I hope you don't lose your nerve singing up there Luke. I sure am glad I'm just a lowly stage hand. Wouldn't want to have an untimely attack of stage fright in front of those ladies," Patrick commented. He gestured in the direction of some of the dancers who were doing some last minute practicing.

"Patrick, here's my idea: if you see me barfing, just run to the fuse box, turn the stage lights off and we'll pull the old switcheroo, ok?" Lukas joked.

Patrick laughed and formed a circle with his forefinger and thumb while holding the rest of his three fingers in the air. "*No problemo, mi amigo.* I've got your back. I know the whole repertoire." Then Patrick turned to Sean and added, "Sean, while the lights are off, you provide the diversion. You just keep playing that piano until someone turns the lights on again."

Lukas laughed and suggested, "Or you can grab the closest mike and belt out the "hokey pokey song" so we don't cause a stampede."

"Wonderful, I know that piece on the piano by heart so I can sing and play it at the same time," Sean chimed in, chuckling. "But what's the plan in case *I* get stage fright and pass out?"

"No worries," Patrick said smoothly. "I will have to get on the stage with my tutu and do cartwheels or tap dance."

"Nice plan," laughed Sean. "What happens when our stage hand Patrick trips over a wire and the set falls on top of him?"

"That's easy. I'll just start a food fight," Lukas said, guffawing.

The three guys were now laughing hysterically, bending over and hooting.

"Boy, we're such a barrel of laughs today, aren't we? I think they pay people to do this sort of thing on stage," Lukas said.

The three guys were still laughing when a pretty blonde dancer wandered off to where they were lounging around.

"What's so funny?" she asked the men flirtatiously.

"Oh nothing," Patrick said, "We were just going to suggest to the director to add a new comedy act to the program."

"Really?" she said eagerly. "My sorority sister is dating Jeff. I could bring up the idea to him."

"No," said Lukas hastily. "Its nothing really spectacular. Slapstick comedies probably won't go with the whole program anyway. So, uh, are you cast or crew?"

"Cast. We get to twirl and jump in such pretty but heavy costumes," she complained, wrinkling her nose in distaste.

"Patrick twinkle toes here's a dancer. I believe he knows how to tap dance," Sean muffled a grin.

"I do not!" Patrick said in embarrassment. Then he gave Sean a glare, "He meant I used to do the *break* dance back in the good ole eighties."

"I'm Courtney. Maybe you can save me a dance at the Charity Ball this weekend, Patrick?"

"I'll look forward to it, Courtney," Patrick said.

"Jeez man, where's your pride? Play a little hard to get," Lukas said, good naturedly.

"That is not in my vocabulary," Patrick said, looking at Courtney meaningfully.

"Nor mine," she countered.

Just then, another pretty blonde dancer came up to join them. "Courtney, who are your new friends?"

"Oh," Courtney said, "This is Faye, my sorority sister and this is Patrick and…"

Patrick jumped in, "Sean and Luke."

"Nice to meet you," Faye smiled brightly at Lukas, tucking her curly blonde hair daintily behind her right ear.

"What sorority is that?" Sean asked curiously.

"Oh, the Alpha Lambdas of course. Have you ever been to our parties?" Faye answered with an air of superiority. She gave Lukas a sideway glance that made him extremely uncomfortable. "I mean obviously not since I would have noticed *you*."

"Can't say I have," Sean answered. "And these two blokes are foreign students so they've been preoccupied with touring the country on weekends," Sean added, his eyes darkening.

"Oh, that explains it. Where are you from?"

"Faye! Courtney! There you are," exclaimed another female voice.

Lukas turned to look at the speaker and found himself staring at the most striking face he had ever seen. She had a smooth oval face, pouty lips, and a straight dainty nose, but her most attractive feature was by far her thickly lashed sea green eyes. As pretty as these two blondes were, they paled in comparison to this 5'7 tall, dark haired, olive skinned beauty who had come up to them. Even Sean was visibly affected by her features and Patrick no doubt was drooling in his mind.

"We have to go shopping tomorrow!" the dark haired beauty exclaimed to her friends. "Jeff just asked me to the Charity Ball," she continued gaily.

"You go, girl!" Courtney said enthusiastically. "But, didn't you already buy a dress last month?"

"Duh," she replied. "That was before Jeff asked me. Now I need something more glamorous if I'm going to have paparazzi on my back. I was thinking a backless gold forties inspired dress…"

Lukas and Sean gave each other a look that conveyed their loss in this mindless estrogen-charged chit-chat.

"Uh," Patrick cleared his throat when he finally came to, "I'm Patrick and this is Luke and Sean and you are…?"

"Oh silly me," Courtney said. "This is my sorority sister Lanie. She was the one I told you about, the one who's dating Jeff Ackerman and she happens to be playing Mary…"

At the sound of that familiar name, Sean, Patrick and Lukas looked at each other, hardly believing their ears and more to the point, their eyes. Lukas felt his blood rush to his face and could feel his heart slamming in his chest. Amidst the deafening roar of his heartbeat, a million thoughts raced through his head: homeschooled, lover of Mary, GP-wholesome, casual, beach loving, Pedro Calderon dela Barca fan, pop-culture snob… *Her? Could it be? It couldn't be.* He had to know, but he couldn't speak. While his thoughts swirled about a mile a minute, his mouth had gone dry.

Thank God, Sean had the sense to ask the question Lukas needed an answer to. "Lanie is an unusual name. It's not Hawaiian is it or could it possibly be Spanish…"

Lanie gave him a small smile. "It's both actually. My mother is Filipino/ Spanish/Hawaiian and we're from Hawaii. Lanie is just my nickname. My real name is Alana O'Keefe."

"I see," Lukas said, swallowing hard. "Are you a performance art major or something?"

"Oh no," Alana answered airily. "I'm majoring in communications journalism, minoring in English. Oops, I have to go now, Jeff's here. Toodles, can't wait to go shopping tomorrow."

Faye resentfully observed the three men's reactions to Alana. She chose her next sentence deliberately. With a feigned affection, she said "That Lanie, she can be so self-absorbed. She didn't even ask you guys anything about yourselves. So where *are* you from?"

"She is *not* self-absorbed, Faye," Courtney said loyally. "You would be as excited as she is if you were going with Jeff, too. Now maybe we can all go to the ball together unless Luke or Sean already have dates..."

"I'm not going," Sean replied and before Lukas could say anything, Patrick answered for him. "Luke and I would love to join you if you can save us a table."

"Alright then, we'll see you there and I'm sure we'll talk again soon," Faye said a little too cheerfully, dragging Courtney by the elbow.

Lukas was immensely relieved at the ladies' hasty exit. He had so much to think about. He wanted to be alone but Sean and Patrick hovered around, waiting for him to speak.

A few minutes later, Lukas finally said, "I guess that's her. I'm not sure if I'm glad she's so beautiful or disappointed that she's so – so..."

"Superficial?" Sean finished.

"Well, it may seem that way but she was just here for two seconds, Luke and she's really hot. You've got to give her a chance and you've got to tell her who you are! The Charity Ball is the perfect opportunity to reveal yourself," Patrick suggested.

"No, I'm not telling her. Not yet anyway and I'd appreciate if you didn't breathe a word to anyone until I figure all this out. Especially not her friends."

Sean looked worried. "Yes, especially not her friends. If I know the Alpha Lamdas, this could all blow up in your face and hurt you, Luke."

"What do you mean? What kind of sorority is that?" Lukas asked.

"The Alphas pride themselves on being the most popular, most beautiful and exclusive sorority in SILU. I don't mean to generalize them but I know for a fact that their parties are wild: booze, drugs, sex. Let's just say, they need a lot of prayers for conversion."

Lukas' heart fell when he heard that. How could he have misjudged her? The Lanie he thought he knew seemed so different, so perfect but this supermodel clone was seemingly so vain and shallow although granted Patrick had a point: He only talked to her for two seconds. That was not enough to draw conclusions. Didn't she deserve a chance? Wait a minute, she was dating Jeff Ackerman and everyone knew about Jeff Ackerman's reputation with the ladies in Hollywood. If she associated with him and the sorority, didn't that say something about her, too? What was that old English saying "Birds of a feather flock together"?

Patrick spoke. "Well, I won't tell anyone if that's what you're worried about. This is Luke's business but let me know if you need anything, lad. Remember I've got your back, even if it means tap dancing."

Lukas appreciated his friends' concern but he really needed to be alone right now. Lukas wanted to run outside, straight to Church, to his room or anywhere but the auditorium, but he had to stay for rehearsals.

Try as he might, he couldn't stop staring at Lanie all night. Worse, he couldn't stop thinking about her long after rehearsals were over.

Chapter 10

Alana found it hard to concentrate on school the following day. As she walked out of her last class for the day, her thin dainty eye brows were frowning, her mind was in deep in thought.

It was not just her mediocre grades that bothered her. She had come to accept that media communications was not her expertise, but something else entirely was upsetting her. Jeff was making sexual advances at her that she was not ready for. It began at the concert, on their first date. She didn't like that he was so aggressive. At least the frat boys she dated were always so awestruck by her that they let her lead the dating game. But Jeff was older of course and he was used to taking the lead obviously. But did he have to be so touchy feely, really all over her, at the concert, on their *first* date? She didn't like that at all, which was why she was skittish for the entire concert instead of being able to enjoy it. Sure Alana liked Jeff, found him very attractive, but this was going way too fast. She was unsure about losing her virginity at this point in her life.

Alana realized that she was behaving and dressing in a manner that encouraged his advances but it wasn't like she advertised that she wanted sex. Or did she?

With a shake of her head, Alana tried to clear the thoughts away from her mind. Maybe playing the Virgin Mary was getting to her. She felt as if someone was watching her and that someone was watching her sadly. She had not given heaven any thought at all in the last two years at SILU, but lately, she could almost sense all of heaven thinking about her a great deal. Her conscience weighed heavily on her for the first time since Lukas. *Lukas? Where did that blast from the past shoot from?*

Unnerved, Alana forcefully pushed her thoughts aside once more. With a defiant upward tip of her chin, she convinced herself into feeling as giddy as she was the first time Jeff asked her out. Jeff was more mature than the clumsy college guys she had dated. Jeff was just used to a different world of dating, that's all. Jeff was hot and he would look so distinguished in a black tux. She was going to the Charity Ball with the most sought after director in Hollywood. She was going to be the envy of all her sorority sisters. She was going to have a good time, wherever this relationship was going to take her.

Alana stopped in her tracks. She looked up to find herself standing outside the Church of Jesu. The Church of Jesu was located at the center of the entire University. Since it was built in the early twenties, it formed the shape of a cross and was decorated by stained glass windows. All the major roads of the university surrounded the Church. The Jesuits who built the university envisioned that the university student life would revolve around the life of the Church that Jesus' started. Hence, the Jesuits insisted that there would be three daily Masses celebrated everyday: early morning at 6:30, 12:00 noon and 5:30 in the evening. Despite the declining attendance, the Jesuits maintained the tradition, hoping that the students could never make inconvenience an excuse for missing Mass.

Alana peeked inside and saw that some people were still there, clearing up the pews and putting away the equipment. *The 12:00 Mass must have just finished*, she thought to herself. She glanced up and saw a sign that said, "Adoration Chapel now open Monday, Wednesday and Friday." Adoration Chapels are holy grounds where the Body of Christ is exposed on a monstrance for adoration purposes.

Alana realized that what she wanted most right now was to be alone with her thoughts instead of heading to a gaggle of girls in the sorority house. Mentally recalling her mother's teachings, she tried to remember whether or not she had to be in a *state of grace* to adore the Eucharist or if that was required only for Holy Communion. She ran her lessons in her head:

"State of grace is the state of being free of mortal sin, predisposed to receiving graces from heaven. Mortal sin has three requirements: serious sin, full knowledge of seriousness of sin and deliberate commission. State of sin causes blockage of the soul from receiving graces." Alana was relieved to remember that one didn't need to be in a state of grace to adore the host. *Whew!* She thought to herself, as she began looking around for the entrance to the chapel.

Alana tentatively slipped into the Adoration Chapel. It had been two years since she had adored the transubstantiated body of Jesus Christ but she knew enough to genuflect before the true presence of Christ. Alana bowed as her mother had taught her early on. She sat in the front of the church as she always did so that people wouldn't see her if she cried before Jesus, as she sometimes did.

Alana stared straight at the altar. The white host or the Blessed Sacrament, was encased in a two foot gold monstrance with gold and silver rays. To the left side of the monstrance was a four-foot statue of the Immaculate Heart of Mary, dressed in a white gown accented with delicate gold embroidery and crowned with a gold grown. She was depicted holding her heart, surrounded by roses, enflamed with fire. To the right side of the Blessed Sacrament was a four-foot statue of the Sacred Heart of Jesus, clad in a flowing white garment, with a red tunic draped across it. With His left hand, Jesus held his heart, enflamed with fire, surrounded by thorns and topped by a cross.

Kneeling down, Alana buried her face in her hands, unsure of what to say.

"Jesus, it's been a while, I know. I shouldn't be here at all. I feel so unworthy to be talking to you. But I can't talk to anyone who will understand the issues I'm facing, not Courtney and hardly, Faye. You probably already know my relationship with dad and mom has been strained. So that really narrows down the list of people I can talk to. So here I am. I hope you can stand to listen to me right now."

"Anyway, do you remember the vow of purity I took before you? Do you think you can release me from that because the guilt is sure weighing me down and it's getting in the way of my happiness? It might ruin any future with Jeff and any future with news reporting on TV. Thank you."

"Umm, I'm going shopping in a bit. Can you help me pick out a fabulous dress to wear on sale? Also, I'm going to play your Blessed Mother at the Christmas program next weekend. Can you please help me remember my lines and do a fantastic job? Oh, I've got finals coming up, too. Please help me get better grades. I miss my straight A's."

She sat down and became fidgety in the silence. Alana decided to pray the rosary. Once again, it had been a long time but one never forgets the rosary although one might fumble through the mysteries. Alana finished the rosary.

"Blessed Mother, are you here? I suppose you can still hear me. I wanted to ask you something: What is the big deal about preserving one's virginity, anyway? Everyone's having sex and having a good time. I don't understand anymore why I took that vow of purity but I still can't bring myself to you know, let it go. It's like I've jinxed myself or something. Can you help me out here? I'm struggling and I can't talk to anyone about anything anymore. I guess I don't know what to ask from you. Please, please, just pray for me. Whatever your intentions are for me, Jesus will grant you what you ask. Don't ask Jesus to take Jeff from me though ok? Not until I decide I'm ready to give him up. And don't ask Jesus... Well, I guess you can pretty much ask Jesus to change things. I need change. I'm not happy anymore and I want to be. Amen."

~ ~

"Are you on your way to lunch?" Sean asked Lukas as he was putting away the song sheets and closing the piano shut.

"No, I need to be alone today."

Sean didn't need to ask why. With a wave, he left the church, leaving Lukas to put away the last of the songbooks back into their pockets behind the wooden pews.

After seeing Lanie last night, Lukas decided to pay the Blessed Sacrament Adoration chapel an hour long visit after daily Mass. He turned the corner and headed straight into the chapel at the back of the Church of Jesu.

The chapel was located at the head of the cross-shaped Church. There were ten rows of wooden pews to accommodate the adorers. Lukas noted that there were two other people in the Adoration Chapel today: a dark haired woman up front and another woman in the far left corner. Lukas picked the farthest corner on the back of the chapel. He knelt down and prayed:

"Lord, I've been wanting to talk to you so much. I'm confused, agitated, afraid, fascinated... Where do I begin?"

Then Lukas realized that this was no way to start a conversation with a beloved friend. "Forgive me Lord, I have been self-absorbed. Thank you for the gift of the Eucharist, your Blessed Mother, your Church, your priests, my family and friends. Thank you for brining me to America and for giving me the opportunity to study here. Thank you...."

Lukas' grateful words soothed his soul somewhat. He began to realize that he had so much to be joyful about. Calmly now, Lukas began to pour out his heart and soul.

"Thank you Lord for letting me find Lanie. She is a surprise to say the least. What do I do now? Should I tell Lanie who I am? Should I spend time trying to get to know her? Is she worth it? What is your will, Lord? Speak and I will do it. You know I live only to serve you."

A moment of silence passed. Lukas then felt the Holy Spirit rousing his heart. He was strongly reminded of the book of Tobit that he had read the night his heart broke. That Lanie was meant to be his from the beginning of creation.

Lukas wanted to believe that, but all evidence pointed to the contrary. She was just so beautiful, too popular, too worldly, too different from what he thought he fell in love with.

"Lord," he prayed. "I have preserved my heart for so long, I don't want to make another mistake and have it broken again."

The silence stretched. Lukas knew that silence meant he had all that he needed to know for now. The rest of the instructions would come later. With a deep sigh, he understood he would have to wait and see how things would unravel before doing anything concrete like revealing things to Lanie or anything hasty like asking her out. Waiting was always difficult, but waiting was what he had to do.

"Lord", he prayed intimately, "You sure can speed things up as fast as you want them or take your sweet time. I'm praying for you to move things along because it seems like I've waited too long already but in the end, I'm going to let you take the lead and wait for your initiative."

More silence followed. The more Lukas sat there in the presence of his Lord and beloved friend, the more he grew astounded by what he heard. Imagine that: the most beautiful woman he had ever met and who barely acknowledged his existence was destined to be his wife. Impossible, unbelievable, ludicrous! Lukas was tempted to ask for a sign, but he did not dare. Pure faith did not require signs.

Suddenly, he heard a rustle from the front of the chapel. He glanced up surreptitiously and received the shock of his life when he recognized the woman who was sitting up front and who was now leaving the adoration chapel. The dark hair, olive skin and green eyes were unmistakable: Lanie, his supposedly future wife, had come to Jesus.

She barely paid any attention to him of course, but Lukas' felt his heart soar for a minute. If Alana was here, there was something in her that still connected with the source of infinite love. Her presence at the chapel removed all doubt from Lukas' mind.

Lukas turned to the statute of the Immaculate Heart of Mary. He remembered that Our Lady's messages at her apparitions in Medjugorje, Croatia were always to pray, fast and seek conversion. Supposedly, she had once told the visionaries that the self-discipline of fasting had the power to even stop wars.

When Lukas gazed into Our Lady's eyes, he could almost hear her sweet voice, urgently imploring him, "Fast, Lukas. Fast. There is a lot at stake here."

If fasting could stop wars, then it can do anything for Lanie, Lukas thought to himself. He made a firm decision to take Mary's advice. While he waited for Jesus to lead him, Lukas vowed to fast every Wednesday and Friday on bread and water. He could almost hear his stomach groan in anticipation.

Sand and Water

Lukas left the Adoration Chapel feeling reassured and placated. Once again, he wished that everyone knew of the powerful graces that heaven poured out during Adoration of the Holy Eucharist. Lukas contemplated that if more people knew that secret of sitting with the Sacred Heart of Jesus, it would probably solve half of the world's problems.

~ ~

The night of the Christmas program finally arrived. A flurry of activities was going on in the backstage as the audience started piling in. Sound and lights crew were testing equipment, make-up artists were doing touch ups, stage hands were making sure everything was in place, the choir was assembling, the dancers were putting on their costumes, and the cast was receiving last minute instructions from the director.

"...You all know what you are supposed to do and where you are supposed to be. I'm going to be sitting up front this time to watch you, not direct you so it's all up to you to wow this audience. I know this is cliché but try to put yourselves on that very first Christmas in the manger. So, don't just break a leg, knock 'em dead."

Jeff motioned to Alana. When she came closer, he wrapped his arm around her waist and gave her a kiss on the cheek. That was the most affection he had ever shown her when they worked together. Jeff prided himself on being professional on set and he had a rule against drawing unnecessary attention to himself from his cast, which was fine with Alana. She was still having mixed feelings about Jeff. On the one hand, he was so handsome, it was so easy to fall in love when she looked at him. On the other hand, there was the issue of her virginity, which she was still struggling with.

Alana smiled up at him. "What was that for?"

"For looking so hot in your virginal dress and veil."

She wrinkled her nose in distaste. "I don't know if those are appropriate words for Mary," she said.

"Well, you're hardly the Virgin Mary, so I'm going to say that again. You are hot," Jeff said.

Alana frowned at the comment. She resented being called "hot". Of all the words in the dictionary, she thought men could be more flowery with words to describe their loved ones. That was probably the English literature fanatic coming out of her.

Seeing her frown, Jeff gave her a smack on the lips and said, "Now run along to Bethlehem. You have a baby to pop."

The kiss did not escape Lukas, who could never take his eyes off Alana when they were in the same room. Lukas was devastated. He looked away and prayed that he could go through tonight's performance after seeing what he just saw.

Lukas climbed up the steps of the stage along with the rest of the choir. He felt the adrenalin rush as he took his place. By the time the curtains rolled up and the choir sang their opening song, he forgot about Alana. Lukas was singing for Jesus.

When the applause died down, the choir descended the stage to make way for the play. Patrick was busy moving the props and the set around. As soon as he was done, he pulled Lukas aside and told him, "Luke, one of the light technicians said he could sneak me into the booth if I wanted to catch the rest of the show from up there but I have to be backstage all the time. So I asked him if you could sit there instead and watch until the choir comes on again at the end of the show."

"Sure. Thanks."

Lukas followed Patrick up the backstage staircase, around a long narrow hallway until they reached the best seats in the house.

The scene opened with the Annunciation of the angel Gabriel to Mary. Lukas had seen the rehearsals quite a few times, but there was something about tonight that made it special. He watched Alana gracefully portray Mary and studied the conflicting emotions that flickered across her lovely face. As the play progressed, Lukas was so drawn by the look of innocence, kindness, gentleness, humility, and love of the character she played. It was almost as if he could see the person that Alana was meant to be: a replica of Mary. Throughout the play, Lukas was riveted to his seat, hanging on her every word and gesture.

To say that he was enthralled by the end of the Nativity scene is an understatement. Perhaps it was because he had become personally attached to the actress or maybe it was because the mood and lighting had captured the poignant birth of His savior. Whatever it was, as the angels sang their "Gloria", Lukas felt like jumping off his seat, bowing to the infant Jesus and offering his life to Jesus' mother. He almost forgot he had to be back on stage once more, until he heard the announcement of a ten-minute intermission.

Meanwhile, on stage, the curtain fell on the Holy Family, the shepherds and three wise men to a hearty round of applause. Alana exited the stage while the choir members got ready to climb back into their places. She paid no attention to Lukas as he brushed past her, nor did she pay any attention to Courtney who had approached to tell her she did a wonderful job.

Alana was deep in thought. During the play, as Alana enunciated the words from Luke's gospel, "How can this be since I have no relations with a man?," she felt a startling shot of current run through her veins, yet another reminder of her virginity. Then when Alana said the Magnificat, she barely heard herself as she felt her goosebumps rise. It was almost as if she was transported to the scene of the Annunciation when Mary said her yes to the God. And after that, she found herself completely moved by the way Joseph had treated his wife... with such tenderness, respect and love.

Alana dashed out of the auditorium and sought solace in a secluded spot under a huge comforting tree. She sat down on the soft ground and placed her face between her knees. Alana's heart thumped wildly. She didn't know how it happened but she knew there was a message here for her tonight. Three things became absolutely clear to her: Mary's virginity was essential to the plan of God. Mary was blessed with the most loving man for a husband. And Mary's yes to God's plan was crucial to the birth of Jesus.

Mulling it over, Alana came to the realization that her virginity and purity was part of God's plan, even though she didn't know why yet. Alana also grasped that more than anything, she wanted a husband like Joseph, not a man like Jeff. She did not want to be just another girl on his endless string of girls. Finally, Alana comprehended that her yes to God's plan for her life was crucial to bringing Jesus into the world.

Alana broke down and sobbed. She knew what she had to do now. She was going to remain a virgin until her wedding day. She was going to go out with Jeff one last time tomorrow night at the ball and say goodbye. She was going to get her life back together: switch back to major in English, go home for Christmas and reconcile with her parents and, most of all, return to the Church and the Sacraments. Then she would renew her vow of chastity.

Chapter 11

For the last five years, the SILU Annual Charity Ball was celebrated at the posh Hotel L'Triumph. The Hotel L'Triumph was a five star hotel built by a hotel mogul in the heart of Boston. It was a forty story building situated in the center of a man-made lake and waterfall. The outside structure was designed in ornate gold and white columns, to resemble a palace fit for a king. Consequently, it housed dignitaries, royalty, politicians, movie stars and other celebrities.

Once inside the hotel lobby, guests were welcomed by the ostentatious wrought iron stairway. The entire second floor was dedicated to the Grand Ballroom, an intricately designed multi-function room that resembled a Victorian palace. The crystal and gold chandeliers, plush red carpet and chocolate brown velvet drapes of the grand ballroom provided a tastefully extravagant venue for SILU's biggest night. Since 5:00 that night, the band played an assortment of sounds. There was classic, pop, jazz, and ballad tunes for every kind of music taste.

Each elegantly decorated table was topped with a small ice carved centerpiece. The dinner plates and silverware were elaborately laid out in a setting that only Emily Post would appreciate. Champagne was flowing and regal bow-tied waiters were stationed to serve the seven-course meal.

On the night of the Charity Ball, everyone who was anyone in SILU was there and naturally, everyone who was anyone wanted to talk to the director Jeff Ackerman. Ordinarily, this would perturb Alana, being left at the table with Courtney and Faye but tonight she was all radiant with her recent discovery and her resolutions. Alana's golden toned skin practically glowed with the rest of her gold dress.

To Lukas, who had just stepped into the grand ballroom with Patrick, Alana looked more dazzling than

Anabelle Hazard

ever, even though he was of the opinion that she should have picked a less revealing gown.

As Lukas and Patrick strode through the ballroom, Courtney and Faye enthusiastically waved them over to their table. Lukas inhaled sharply before he sat on the seat Faye had saved for him, right next to her and right across Alana.

"That was some program last night," Patrick began jovially.

Courtney agreed. "They say every year is better than the previous one. Next year's cast and crew sure have their work cut out for them."

"They certainly have big shoes to fill, if I do say so myself," Faye said smugly.

"This calls for a toast," Lukas declared, raising his champagne glass. "To our big shoes and big feet!"

"Hear! Hear!" They laughed, raised their glasses and clinked them together.

After they sipped their champagne, Courtney noticed Alana absentmindedly fiddling with a ring on a chain around her neck.

"Why Lanie, is that an engagement ring I see on your neck?" Courtney asked knowingly.

Her question caught Alana off guard. "No. Its my, uh, purity ring. My dad gave it to me when I was 12, when I said my vows to remain pure until my wedding day."

Faye's jaw dropped. "You're kidding, right?"

"Nope," Alana answered, her voice unsteady. Despite her empty stomach, she took a huge gulp of champagne.

"So, like, Jeff's not going to get a congratulatory token from you tonight?" Faye asked, with a sneer.

Alana was starting to get uncomfortable, as were Patrick and Lukas who overheard the entire exchange.

Alana answered slowly. "He's not, but he doesn't know it yet so don't say anything about it. Now can we please not talk about my sex life... or lack thereof... in public?"

"Well you're the one "outing" yourself by wearing that ring *in public*," Faye retorted.

Alana blushed. "I'm wearing it to remind myself. I didn't expect it to be the dinner table's conversation piece!"

"I wonder what the Alpha Lambdas' are going to say?" Courtney mused.

Alana was growing unsure of herself now. She downed the entire glass of champagne and quickly grabbed another one from the table setting next to her.

Lukas sensed her anxiety. Before thinking, he said outright, "Well, I'm no Lamb, but I think your purity ring is a cool idea."

Faye gaped at him while Alana managed a weak but grateful smile.

Courtney rolled her eyes and said, "Its LambDA, duh."

Patrick cleared his throat. "Well, if this was a movie we'd be in a hysterically awkward scene right now so I suppose I'm the comic relief and I have to think of something funny to say... I wish I had my script right about now and that the director was here."

They laughed, mostly out of politeness. Everyone turned their attention to something else, to the ceiling, the band, the next table, anything else but Alana's ring. Although Lukas tried to pay attention to Faye, he couldn't help but be utterly impressed by Alana's vow of chastity. He had not known that about her. At that moment, Lukas looked at Alana with new eyes: his respect for her deepened and his admiration for her heightened. *What a precious jewel she is*, he thought silently.

Lukas' spirits had just begun to lift when Jeff Ackerman slid into the seat next to Alana and put his arm around her shoulder. A crestfallen Lukas turned away quickly.

"Care to dance?" Jeff asked Alana.

"Love to," she said. The pair left the table and danced to three fast songs. The next song was a slow ballad. Roughly, Jeff pulled Alana close.

Alana put her hand on Jeff's shoulder tentatively. Just when she began to relax, he whispered in her ear. "You know I've got a room upstairs. Do you want to slip out of this ball for a few minutes?"

Alana's back stiffened. There went her bubble. She looked deep into Jeff's eyes and spoke. "Jeff, I'm not that kind of girl. I'm not sleeping with you if that's what you have in mind."

Jeff gave her a bewildered look that plainly said *"Could've fooled me."* Shrugging, he cajoled her one more time, "Listen, I've signed up to direct a new movie with a role that would be just perfect for you so we can hold a private audition up at the suite…"

Alana was furious. "Are you dangling a movie offer in my face to get me to bed?!?! How pathetic! The answer is no, no, no."

Jeff was taken aback at her burst of temper. He dropped his arms and stopped dancing. Then he glowered at Alana.

Once Alana saw Jeff's cold hard face, she couldn't believe that she ever thought he was handsome. There was nothing in his eyes but venom.

Jeff deliberately turned his back to her and walked away. He left her standing by herself, stunned, right in the middle of the dance floor.

What was the matter with her? Jeff asked himself crossly. If she was playing a game, he was not interested. There were plenty of women who would sleep with him and who would jump at the role he offered.

Knowing that Alana was looking on, Jeff purposely walked up to Faye and asked her to dance. He thought Faye was pretty enough. She would do for tonight.

Lukas and Faye were engaged in quiet conversation at the table when Jeff touched her on her bare shoulder and charmingly asked her to dance. Faye said yes without batting an eyelash.

Lukas whirled around, almost frantically. His gaze fell on Alana in the middle of the dance floor staring at all of them. Her face was flushed in humiliation. She narrowed her eyes, spun on her heel, walked across the dance floor, and headed straight for the bar. Lukas couldn't move fast enough. In five seconds, he had crossed the dance floor and took the only empty seat at the crowded bar. He wasn't next

Sand and Water

to Alana but he quietly observed her from the corner of his eye.

One tequila shot. Two, three tequila shots. A vodka currant. That was enough. He made his way next to her and stood beside her.

"Lanie, are you ok?" he asked with concern.

"*I* am tickled pink, thank you very much." She giggled, obviously drunk. "My date and my best friend are dancing while I am having a good time with Jose Cuervo here," she said holding up her drink. "And tomorrow I am going to be the laughing stock of my sorority sisters. Isn't that the funniest thing?"

"I think it was brave of you to stand up for your faith. And I think you are terrific for making a vow like that. What I think is funny is that your best friend is glaring at me like I was a four-year-old."

She giggled even more, then whispered. "You've committed an unforgivable *faux pas* you know, by associating with a totally uncool twenty-year-old virgin. There goes your repu...burp...reputation."

"Lanie, virginity is something to be proud of, not ashamed of. It's so ironic that Joseph considered divorcing Mary because she wasn't a virgin and at the time, it would have been considered perfectly appropriate behavior, but now it seems like virginity is worse than a crime. I'm surprised no one has stoned you to death."

She nodded laughing, and asked "Are you a math major, Luke?"

"No. Why?"

"Cause if forty is the new thirty, does that mean I have one or two decades to go before my wedding day?" Her eyes widened. "That's like forever!"

Lukas said seriously, "Virginity is a complete gift of yourself to God or your husband. The man you marry should be so honored that you are giving him something so valuable and so beautiful on your wedding night."

"Thanks. Hey, you know, you are like, so mature, unlike my date. You remind me of someone…"

Lukas' heart skipped a beat. "Who?"

"Aha! I've got it," Alana snapped her fingers together. "You know who you sound like? You sound like my father giving me a lecture. So very wise, you are. Are you old?"

Lukas laughed despite himself. "Not old, just happy. Proverbs 3: 13 says: Happy the man who finds wisdom, the man who gains understanding! For her profit is better than profit in silver, and better than gold is her revenue."

"Ahh," she slurred, poking him on the chest. "Now there's a poetic man for you. But I am sorry to tell you that your lines won't get you lucky tonight." She held up her ring to his nose and declared loudly, "Virgin, remember?"

Lukas laughed so hard that Alana was poking fun at herself. She never failed to surprise him. "That's the spirit, girl. Say it out loud. Virginity is an asset, not a drawback."

"Look, Luke.... Look, Luke....Hey, I'm a poet too. Hahahaha. Look, Luke... She leaned closer and said, "How come I never noticed how good looking you are?"

"You better stop feeding me lines or my head's going to fill up this ballroom and if it poops the party, then your friend Faye will really have something to glare about," Lukas joked, secretly pleased by her drunken candor.

Alana pealed into laughter. "Ok. You're good looking, wise and funny. Tsk, tsk. Faye should have kept a tighter leash on you."

He smiled. "I wasn't aware that I belonged to her."

"I'm sure glad you don't cause between you and Jose here," she said, holding up her glass, "I feel so much better."

"Thanks. Us Latino men are chivalrous to boot. Salut!" he said holding up his drink.

Alana looked at him and pursed her lips. "Luke, the thing is... thing is.... you're getting blurry. Please stop moving around, you're making me dizzy."

With that, she collapsed into his arms, her eyes closed, a slight smile on her lips.

~~

Lukas effortlessly carried a lifeless Alana out of the Hotel L'Triumph and onto a taxi.

When Faye continued to glare at them, Lukas figured she wasn't going to help her friend get home safely. Since Courtney and Patrick were nowhere to be found, Lukas decided bring Alana to her sorority house. He assumed that she lived there but if not, she could probably find a sympathetic sister to keep an eye on her or Alana could simply find her way home when she came to.

While the taxi waited by the driveway, Lukas rang the doorbell to the Alpha Lambda's yellow and white colonial style sorority house. A sorority girl answered the door and let them both in. She showed Lukas where Alana's room was. He laid Alana on the bed, pulled the covers over her, and tenderly brushed her dark hair off her face. Then Lukas headed back into the taxi.

Lukas would have wanted to stay with Alana to make sure she was alright. But it was hardly appropriate to stay with her in her room, considering that they were both barely acquaintances. Besides, he had to pack as he was going to catch the early flight tomorrow to be home for the holidays and for Stephen's birthday. That meant he wouldn't see Alana again until the next semester, which was over a month away.

Lukas sighed deeply. He wished he had asked for her number or email but he didn't want to take advantage of her clouded judgment. He wondered if she would remember him, tonight and everything in between. He supposed there was nothing he could do but leave everything in God's hands.

Chapter 12

When the sun was at its noon peak, Alana woke up with a throbbing headache. She gingerly descended the stairs, walked to the kitchen and grabbed a glass of water to down her pain reliever. As she groggily walked away from the refrigerator, the three sorority sisters who were eating lunch at the dining table immediately stopped talking.

"Morning," Alana greeted them hoarsely.

The three girls completely ignored her and decided to keep whispering amongst themselves.

Misconstruing their lack of response for a failure to see her, Alana joined them with a piece of toast and fruit.

Annette Owens, the sorority president, gave Alana a pitiful look and derisively remarked for all to hear, "Well, it looks like the blondes last night had more fun and have more brains in them than the brunettes of the house."

The other two bottle blondes giggled obnoxiously. Alana had expected some sort of reaction to her escapade from her catty sorority sisters, but she hadn't expected it to come so viciously – or so soon. Courtney and Faye probably couldn't wait to spread the latest gossip.

Alana remained silent. The headache, bordering on migraine, kept her from thinking or saying anything clever.

Faye, who overheard the remark from the living room, shot back, "Not all the brunettes are a disgrace, Annette. Just those who play the Virgin Mary."

"Now hold on girls. Don't be too quick to jump on Lanie's throat," said Courtney, who was lounging by the living room with five other girls. "Maybe she got lucky with that hot Spanish guy. I tell you these European students are dreamy!"

Alana felt her cheeks grow hot. She didn't remember everything that happened last night. The last memory she had was of walking to the bar and someone joining her. After that, her mind was a blank. *Did she sleep with him, whoever he was?*

Anabelle Hazard

"Lanie obviously didn't get lucky. She was passed out all night," snorted another sorority sister named Linda Gianini. "Did you, Courtney, get lucky, I mean?"

"Nah, that Irish guy was just a tease. I should have made the moves on his friend if Lanie passed him up, too. He was way cuter to begin with. Oh, did you see what Erika McCleary was wearing last night?"

"You mean Erika Mc*Tacky* in her size one hundred and sixteen red velvet Santa Clause suit?" Chelsea Watterman remarked snidely.

"More like Santa Clause's stuffed and shapeless sack!"

"Well at least the sack got lucky with her toady date which is more than I can say for our fuddy-duddy Lanie..." All the sorority girls roared with laughter, just like Alana had predicted they would.

Alana couldn't take it anymore. How did she put up with mindless chatter on boys, sex, gossip, slander and *convoluted values* for too long? She threw away the rest of her breakfast and climbed the stairs. On her way up, she passed by another sister who mocked her with malice, "What's the rush, Lanie? On your way to Church?"

Alana shut the door to her bedroom and held back her tears. She had nowhere to go for the day, but she could not stand to be in this house anymore. She got dressed and headed for Church.

Alana was late for Mass. She had arrived in the middle of the homily and just stayed behind when everyone else went to Communion. Despite her newfound resolution for change, she knew she was not worthy to receive Jesus until she went to confession. She decided to ask the priest to hear her confession after Mass.

When Alana knelt down inside the confessional, her tears began to flow freely. "Bless me Father for I have sinned. My last confession was about three years ago. I have been so selfish and unkind. I don't even know how many times. I've not gone to Mass in two years. I have disrespected my parents and fought with them over everything. I've been smoking, drinking, tried drugs and although I've never had sex, I have been going too far with some guys and obviously, I've caused them to sin in the way I act and dress. I've been envious of my friends and caused them to envy me. I have been proud, vain..."

The list of sins was seemingly endless. By the time she was done, Alana was sobbing.

Fortunately, the priest who heard her confession was kind and understanding. Fr. Tim Chatman, S.J. spoke to Alana in the most benevolent voice he could muster, "Thank God for the grace of a good confession and the grace to ask for forgiveness in the confessional after such a long absence. My dear child, Jesus always extends his mercy to his children who are deeply sorry for their sins. Today, Jesus lovingly embraces you and assures you that he died for your sins already and washes you clean with his own blood. Do not sin anymore and hurt the Lord, your God."

Then he added, "I know it is a challenge to remain pure in this world. I encourage you to ask the Blessed Mother to help you. Chastity is not about how far one can go without breaking the rules but keeping your mind, body and soul pure and free to present before Jesus on your wedding day. For those of us who are celibate, our wedding day is when we experience the resurrection, a complete union with God. When you become a bride, your wedding day is a foreshadowing of your resurrection and union with God. The joys of marital intimacy is simply a foretaste of the wedding feast of the Lamb. As a bride, your marital consent means to commit to give yourself to your groom totally, faithfully, fruitfully and with openness to life. Won't you want to totally give yourself to your husband as you do Christ?"

"Yes father, absolutely. But, does that mean I have to be submissive to him, too?"

Fr. Tim blinked at the question. It was rare to be asked about this topic in the confessional but being a seasoned marriage counselor, he knew the traditional Church teachings inside out. More importantly, since he had much experience dealing with the adverse reaction it caused on modern women, he knew how to approach it diplomatically. "Yes, it does. The bible says so countless of times. The most prominent one under Paul's controversial letter to the Corinthians: Jesus Christ is the head of the

Church and since the family is the domestic Church, the husband represents Christ and the wife, the Church. Hence, the wife must obey her husband as the Church obeys Christ."

"But Father, my history professor passed around a quote from Pope John Paul's letter to women: that both husband and wife must be subject to each other, that is, mutually submissive to each other."

"Oh yes, I like that one. But mutual submission is not the same as headship and role definition. Mutual submission deals with both spouses being called to work for the best interests of the other so much so that the pope reminds the husband that he is supposed to lay down his life for his wife. Essentially, husband and wife are both to be submissive to the *good* of the other not so much as to each other. In reality, the pope's words state that husband and wife are subject to Christ. On the other hand, the issue of headship means that the husband's role is to lead and govern his family as the head of the domestic church, the household."

"Hmm. It sounds like splitting hairs to me."

"It might. But you sound like a smart girl so you should be able to understand the fine line if you really study it. You see, Pope John Paul didn't overturn centuries of Church teaching which is grounded in truth. If the pope wanted to do that, he would have paved the way for women to become priests. But he has emphatically stated that women are not to take on the priestly role. Women's roles are different, special and he affirms that too in his letter to women. Note that the pope never once stated that the wife is to be disobedient to her husband so a wife shouldn't make mutual submission as an excuse to disobey her husband."

"If you really want to know the truth, read John Paul II's papal document next to the first papal document written by Pope Pius XI when he quotes from Casti Connubii:

'Domestic society being confirmed, therefore, by this bond of love, there should flourish in it that "order of love," as St. Augustine calls it. This order includes both the primacy of the husband with regard to the wife and children, the ready subjection of the wife and her willing obedience, which the Apostle commands in these words: "Let women be subject to their husbands as to the Lord, because the husband is head of the wife, as Christ is the head of the Church." (*Casti Connubii*, 30).

"Also read Pope Leo XIII's Encyclical on Christian marriage which teaches: *"The husband is the chief of the family, and the head of the wife."*

"In the light of all these teachings, you can see that what the Pope meant to do was to clarify the husband's leadership role, not as one of domination rather, one of service. Ultimately, it is a challenge for the husband, as the head of the family, to place himself in the service of his wife."

"Thank you, Father. I don't think I'll need to read all those. You explained it quite well so that my little brain can wrap itself around it. The only problem is now letting my heart accept it."

Fr. Tim chuckled. "Maybe you can pray a decade of the rosary as penance and ask for the grace from the Virgin of Virgins to embrace that teaching. Now listen as I give you absolution…"

Alana felt a weight lift off her chest when she heard the words straight from Jesus' mouth: "I absolve you from all of your sins."

She stayed in the church long after everyone had gone home. Alana's appreciation for the Sacrament of Reconciliation increased tremendously. She had been the recipient of such mercy and grace today. It was no doubt Jesus with his healing powers who was in that confessional with her because only He had the authority over the unclean spirits that had departed from her side that day. Alana knelt down before the cross, profoundly grateful that she could be forgiven and could now begin anew.

Alana drove back to the sorority house and packed everything she owned. She would not be returning to this house next semester. It was never her home. She didn't know where she was going to live and who she was going to hang out with yet, but she knew her life here was over.

~ ~

Sand and Water

Christmas day at the O'Keefe household was merrier this year. Joe and his wife Maria were overjoyed that Alana had returned to the Sacrament of the Holy Eucharist. Alana's younger brother Jack was ecstatic that his older sister started spending time with him again. He didn't even mind that she dragged him shopping or brought him to the Adoration Chapel. But nobody was more glad that she was home than Alana herself.

After they watched Jack open all his Christmas presents, Maria took a present from under the tree and gave it to Alana. "This is from your dad and me," she said, smiling.

An intense feeling of gratitude for her mother flooded Alana. Alana had always considered Maria the most patient and helpful woman in the world. Maria was a child of a Spanish-Filipino war veteran who had instilled in her a gratitude for all of life's blessings and a compassion for the least fortunate. It was Maria who had passed on her sympathy for the poverty-stricken third world countries of the world to her daughter and an admiration for the lively Spanish culture. It was thanks to her mother's patience that Alana had been ingrained with uncompromising moral values.

Alana tore open the wrapper and uncovered an exquisite gold and diamond encrusted pendant of the Holy Family. She took it out of the box, gently ran her fingers over it and put it on the chain around her neck. She took off her purity ring from the chain and put it on her ring finger. "I love it. Where did you get this from?"

"From Rue du Bac, Ireland," Joe replied. "We got that when we were on pilgrimage early this year and waited for the right moment to give it to you."

"We hope you'll always wear it to remind you that your true family is in heaven. God is your Eternal Father, Mary is your Blessed Mother, and Jesus your brother. St. Joseph should be the patron of your future husband and father to your kids," Maria explained.

"Awww mom and dad. I know that and I sure am grateful that God gave me to this holy family."

Sand and Water

"Well, we're not always going to be around, Lanie and things aren't always going to be the same, but we wanted you to remember that we love you so very much and though we're not perfect, we do try to love you as best as we can. I wonder if you still think we've been too hard on you? I've kind of blamed myself for your leaving the Church. Was I too much of a disciplinarian?" Joe asked, his voice breaking.

Alana ran to give her mom and dad a hug. She was so moved that her own parents had shown her selfless, unconditional love despite her unfaithfulness and rebelliousness. "Oh you two! I may have blamed you when I was an angry, immature and self-absorbed brat, but I now see that you are *not* responsible for my own choices. It is *I* who owe you an apology. I have dishonored you when you have given me nothing but love and faith, the two most valuable presents parents can ever give their children. I am so sorry. Please forgive me."

Maria patted Alana on her cheek before kissing her. "Of course we do. Jesus doesn't put a limit on the number of times He forgives, neither should we."

Suddenly, Jack's buzzing remote control operated helicopter hovered raucously above them, circling their heads. Jack cupped his hands around his mouth and made a sound that mimicked a police megaphone. "This is the police," he announced. " We've got you surrounded. Why are you punks standing around with your arms around each other?"

Maria looked at her eight year old son dotingly and stretched her right arm out to him. "You're welcome to join the family hug, Officer Jack."

"Freeze lady. Hands on your head. You're under arrest. Now I'm taking you to jail where you will have to make brownies for lunch and dinner everyday."

"Oh yeah?," Joe challenged him. "Why don't we punks gang up on the good officer here and tickle him?"

With a yell, Jack made a run for it. Alana caught him trying to climb the stairs. She grabbed her brother, kicking and giggling, brought him to the couch and laid him on his dad and mom's legs. After a few minutes of tickling frenzy, Jack finally screamed a breathless "Uncle!"

Alana collapsed on the carpet, laughing. Looking at how they all got along despite the misunderstanding and bickering, one would never suspect that she and Jack were adopted as babies. They were both every bit as part of the family as her parents were.

Alana had always known she was chosen as a child. Her parents never hid it from her. As soon as Alana was old enough to understand it, they had always offered to help her track her biological mother if she was ever interested. As a child, Alana had not been intent on searching for her roots as she was content with her family and considered them her true parents. However, lately she had to admit that she was starting to become curious. She made a mental note to mention it to her parents when she got the chance.

"Say, mom, how many more days till the St. John Bosco Christmas Party?" Jack asked.

"Let's see… three days to go, Jack."

"Aw man, that means 3 times 24 equals 72 hours away!?!"

Alana looked at her mother quizzically. "Since when is he so excited to go to a party?"

"Since he got his Christmas presents and wants to show them off to the other kids. You're coming with us to the St. John Bosco's Academy Homeschool family party, aren't you, Lanie? You haven't been there in three years. I'm sure your old friends would love to see you."

"Wish I could mom, but I've got nothing to wear!"

"Aha! That sounds like a classic Lanie line which translated always means "Can I have more shopping money, dad?" Joe said teasingly.

"No really, dad. All my dresses are kind of inappropriate for a family party or church for that matter. They're all too short, too tight, too bare, too skimpy… I need to change my wardrobe. They're totally embarrassing."

Maria gave her daughter a fond smile. "I think that's a compelling argument. I'll take you shopping tomorrow, Lanie. It's on me."

"You mean it's on me as I have to pay for every credit card bill around here," said Joe, wryly.

"That's right. That's the beauty of marriage, Lanie. What's his income is mine and my bills are his. You better go thank your dad for your new wardrobe."

~ ~

Laura ran over to Alana as soon as she arrived at the party with her parents.

"Lanie!" she cried, throwing her arms around her. "It's been ages, girl! We've all missed you."

Lanie returned the hug warmly. How did she ever think she could replace her childhood friends with the sorority girls? "You look fantastic, Laura. Where is everyone else? I can't wait to see them."

"They're by the table at the end but I want to get two minutes with you first. So do me a favor and walk very slowly to the table before they pounce on you. Now, what's new? The mommy grapevine has told me little bits and pieces but not everything, of course. Let's see... no boyfriend, no kids, majoring in media communications..."

"Actually, that will soon change."

"What!?! You have a secret boyfriend and you're having kids?!?!"

Alana laughed. "No silly. I'm going to switch my major back to English next term. I've talked to the department heads about it and they've agreed to let me credit some of my communication media classes but I have to almost overload on my credits. That means, I won't have a social life and probably won't have a boyfriend. So you'll have kids way before I do."

"Nonsense! Jimmy wants to go to med school so that means I have to wait before we get married and figure everything out financially."

"Wait, you and Jimmy Lawrence?!?!" Alana shrieked. "Tell me everything."

"Well, we went to the UNH together, joined the campus ministry, spent way too much time together and then last summer, at the Spirit Ministries annual camp, we

Sand and Water

got lost in the woods and when nightfall came, he confessed that he liked me, always has, he said."

"Wooohooo! I always thought he did have a bit of a crush on you. So he finally got up the nerve. Way to go Jimmy!"

"Yeah, it only took him ten years to say it," Laura said sardonically.

"I've no right to be maid of honor for dropping you both like hot potatoes when I thought I was cooler than you all, but can I at least be a bridesmaid? Flower girl? Guest?" Alana asked.

"Naturally, you're going to be maid of honor but you're going to have to earn your keep. You have to get him to ask me to marry him, *mi amiga*. While you're at it, kindly mention that my biological clock will rust with age if he has to wait for another ten years to get up the nerve."

"I'll get right on it," Alana said with a wink. "Now you have to promise me that when its time to throw you're bouquet, you wont bother turning your back on the girls. Just aim straight into my catcher's mitt."

"Sure, I'll put Velcro on the bouquet and you can put Velcro on the mitt, too. We'll stop at nothing to get us both married, right? Isn't that our motto?"

They both giggled like little girls, just like the old days. Then a few of the homeschooled kids they used to hang out with spotted Alana and descended on her as Laura predicted. Alana was delighted to be in such familiar company. She loved her old friends, they were just like her extended family.

When dinner was over, the DJ played a song that was guaranteed to get the older generation, led by Joe and Maria, dancing on their feet. While Alana sipped her punch, she heard the strains of a song she had not heard in a long time. The lively beat of Dancing Queen by Abba came on the loudspeakers.

For a split second, Alana was transported back in time. She was eighteen again, living with her family, hanging out with her closest friends, and the night would be complete when she turned on the computer to chat with *LSAbba*.

LSAbba or Lukas. Why was he suddenly on her mind? Alana remembered clearly that they would keep each other laughing the whole time they chatted. Maybe that's why no guys had ever kept her interest long enough in college. They never measured up to *LSAbba*'s sense of humor and the chemistry they shared was totally unsurpassed. He sure could make her laugh, and he was so full of sweet words the last time they chatted.

Alana wished that just for tonight she could switch on that computer and find Lukas there. He wouldn't be there, of course. She felt a pang of sadness at that thought. The poignant memory of their goodbye played back in her mind like a movie: Alana had switched off the computer one final time. She sat and sat and sat. She tried to go to sleep but couldn't. After four hours of tossing and turning in her covers, she sat up and logged into the chatroom. *LSAbba* was nowhere to be found.

Chapter 13

Spring in Massachusetts was always a welcome change from the cold, snowy winter. Lukas peered outside the only window in the Church of Jesu that wasn't made of stained glass. As he prepared the vestments, the cruet, chalice and ciboria for the priest prior to the noon Mass, he couldn't help but appreciate the birds perching on the mulberry trees right outside the sacristy. He was inordinately pleased that spring had sprung. He had looked forward to biking again during the weekends.

Fr. Tim Chatman, S.J. motioned to Lukas that Mass was about to start. Lukas took one last glance at the bird when his eye saw the familiar figure of a dark haired, olive skinned girl walk past the tree. Everything inside him wanted to run outside after her and he would have if only he didn't have to serve as a sacristan and cross bearer for the Mass. With his eyes, he followed her figure as she entered the side door which led to the Adoration Chapel. He couldn't wait for Mass to be over.

As he walked to his place by the side of the altar, a distracted Lukas barely missed his cues. The only thing he managed to pay attention to at the Mass was the first reading from the book of Ecclesiastes chapter 3, verse 1 through 11. Lukas always counted this bible passage as his favorite.

There is an appointed time for everything,
and a time for every affair under the heavens.
A time to be born, and a time to die; a time to plant,
and a time to uproot the plant.
A time to kill, and a time to heal;
a time to tear down, and a time to build.
A time to weep, and a time to laugh;
a time to mourn, and a time to dance.
A time to scatter stones, and a time to gather them;

Anabelle Hazard

a time to embrace,
and a time to be far from embraces.
A time to seek, and a time to lose;
a time to keep, and a time to cast away.
A time to rend, and a time to sew;
a time to be silent, and a time to speak.
A time to love, and a time to hate;
a time of war, and a time of peace. ...
He has made everything appropriate to its time, and has put the timeless into their hearts, without men's ever discovering, from beginning to end, the work which God has done.

As soon as Fr. Tim gave his final blessing, Lukas moved like a hunter on the prowl. He swiftly put everything away in the sacristy, asked Sean to manage the worship book return on the pews and bolted out the Church of Jesu.

Silently, Lukas entered the Adoration Chapel. His eyes rapidly scanned the people who were praying. There were about five students today, three of them had just come from Mass and the other two were people he didn't recognize. No Alana in sight.

With a sigh of defeat, Lukas knelt by his usual place and began his prayerful conversation with "*Why?*"

"Why, Lord? Why?" he prayed. "I know I am not supposed to ask why and just have faith but... why couldn't have Lanie come ten minutes before Mass so I could have talked to her? Why couldn't I run into her when I wasn't serving at daily Mass? Why couldn't I just find her sipping coffee at the café? Why is she so hidden from me still after I thought I found her?"

Back in late January, when Lukas returned from Spain for the second term, he resolved that he would visit Alana at the sorority house on the pretext of asking how she was after he left her there on the night of the Charity Ball. However, to his surprise, the sorority sister who answered the door coldly informed him that Alana did not live there anymore and had been "disowned" by the sorority. When he pressed on and asked where he could find her, the door slammed in his face.

His second attempt met with a contemptuous Faye at the door. Sheepishly, Lukas lied to her.

"Oh, pardon me," he had told her. "I thought this was the Alpha Omega Rome house."

Faye arched her brows and replied haughtily, "There is no Alpha Omega Rome sorority or fraternity. Maybe in Italy, but not here. Incidentally, Rome is not in the Greek alphabet."

After that blunder, Lukas didn't bother the sorority house anymore.

All throughout February, Lukas repeatedly tried to search for Alana at the Arts and Communications Department. There was no sign of Alana O'Keefe anywhere. He occasionally struck a conversation with some students and casually asked about Alana O'Keefe. The only lead he had gotten was that she had switched to another major.

By March, Lukas' search grounds extended to the library, the cafeteria, the gym and other common areas. Since there were twenty six dorms and about fifteen sorority houses, he hardly had time to systematically stake out all the student's living quarters. Other than that, he did not want to alarm the security surveillance cameras all over the place.

Lukas had just about given up when he saw Alana today outside the Church of Jesu. However, the momentary ray of hope that sparked fizzled as quickly as it came.

Lukas did not know what to pray that day. All he could ask was why. After his thirteenth variation of why, Lukas felt drained and concluded that Jesus probably was exasperated with him, too. His shoulders slumped, Lukas sat inside the Adoration Chapel very quietly.

Lukas' mind returned to the first reading. He recalled Fr. Tim had mentioned in his homily that it is "God who sets the time for everything. He is never a moment too early or a moment too late." Lukas reflected on this over and over in his head until some light of understanding dawned on him.

It wasn't time for him and Alana to meet again. Simple as that. God was working something out in him, in her and in everything. Lukas came to accept that he was back to waiting on God. Again.

Sheesh, he thought to himself, *I have a lot of work to do tempering my impulsiveness and determination with patience and prudence.*

Lukas' stomach gurgled, reminding him that he was still fasting.

~ ~

"I'd say we're just about ready to join the Tour de France, lads," Patrick said, as they parked their bikes by the side of the road to rest on the grassy park area.

"Speak for yourself. My back and legs are sore from that mountain," Lukas complained. "As much as I like biking, I can't wait for the winter. Are you guys going to be on the Christmas program again?"

"Sure I would love to but this time I'm going to be a star in my own right. Playing stagehand was not the road to superstardom," Patrick responded with a playful grin.

"You know, I heard the new director is planning to showcase local school talents by holding a talent competition before the play. The winners get to perform on the program and the prize money is pretty hefty," Sean announced.

"Interesting," mused Lukas. Briefly, he wondered if Alana would be performing this year.

Patrick came up with an idea. "Hey, Sean, if you can play the keyboards, Luke can sing and I play the guitar, we just need another guitarist, a drummer and we'd be a band. Those Gingerbread Men ain't got nothin' on us."

Sean gave it some thought. He could certainly use the money. "You might be on to something, Patrick. I can ask some of the guys from last year's orchestra if they're willing to play rock music this year."

Lukas started to get excited. He had not played in a band since he began his Catechism classes. The very idea of singing songs and playing the guitar about Christ or Christmas was appealing. He may even compose a song here and there. "I never thought I'd say this Patrick, but you are a genius."

Patrick raised his eyebrow mockingly. "Don't you forget that joining the World Youth Day was my idea. Not to mention the spring break in Florida..."

"Yeah where you almost maimed us on that boat ride," Sean remarked.

"Who would have thought driving a boat could be so dangerous?" Patrick said defensively.

"Normally, it's not if you've had some practice, if you haven't been drinking and if you're paying attention to driving instead of paying attention to the half-naked girls on an oncoming boat," Lukas retorted.

"What's the big deal? We're alive and well, all twelve arms and legs are intact, on our way to winning something better than the lottery so there's no use whining over spilled milk... er, boat." Patrick said cheerfully.

"Ok, so you've had one proven success and one established disaster to your name," said Sean. "I'm curious. Does going to last year's Charity Ball, which was entirely your idea, credit you in the Hall of Fame or discredit you in the Hall of Shame? That will tip the scale and determine whether I'm in or out of this band business."

"Definitely one of the best evenings of my life," Patrick exaggerated, stretching his legs out from under him in a nonchalant pose. "I had a great time dancing with what's her name- Cindy or Courtney. She's an awesome dancer, that one. Wouldn't mind taking her dancing again except she probably won't want anything to do with me."

Sean snorted. "Yeah, you're definitely in Courtney's hall of shame alright for ditching her for another blonde at the end of the evening. And I find your judgment a little truth-impaired, considering you got champagne dumped on your head at the strike of midnight. I want to know Luke's opinion."

Lukas considered the matter for a minute. "There were highlights and lowlights to the Charity Ball, I guess. We got to eavesdrop on a very interesting conversation and all in all, I had a hilarious time with Lanie even though she was uh--tipsy. My only regret is that I didn't get her phone number or email. It's like she's completely disappeared since then except for one surreal random apparition."

"Are we back to looking for her again? I believe the French have a term for this you know: *déjà vu*," Patrick said, yawning.

"Well, I'm not exactly looking, anymore. I believe God will bring her to me when the time is right," Lukas said with conviction.

"Wish I had your faith," Patrick commented.

"What are you talking about? You do have my faith. You're Catholic! With a little fine-tuning, a bit of practice voila! you will turn out just like-"

"Sean?!? No thanks." Patrick guffawed.

"Dude, I was going to say the Pope. But you know what, I know what your problem is. You're afraid if you give God enough attention, He might ask you to give up something, such as --God forbid-- women!"

Patrick shrugged.

Sean's eyes grew wide as the idea come to light. "You're afraid God's going to make a priest out of you so you're subconsciously trying to sabotage a priestly vocation by playing Don Juan," he said in an accusing tone.

Patrick didn't bat an eyelash. "It's working so far, right? I don't hear any call to the priesthood. I've successfully drowned out God's voice." Patrick folded his arms on his chest.

Lukas could hardly believe his ears. "Patrick, St. Ignatius teaches us that God can sometimes make us desire what He desires for us. You don't see anyone tying up Sean and dragging him to a monastery, do you? He's actually happy that he's following his calling. Who knows? Your desire for marriage may also be God's desire for your life."

"Hmmm. I always thought the Divine will is opposed to our human will because of the effect of original sin," came his response.

"In some cases, the Holy Spirit can inspire us into doing something that we are predisposed to doing. In other cases, the self-sacrifice required of agape love requires us to let ourselves die which causes us pain. But in the latter case, God always equips us with the grace to do His will so that we will actually want to do the sacrifice required. Our task is to discern which will is Divine or human," Lukas explained.

"Guys, there's a Retreat based on the Spiritual Exercises of St. Ignatius that I'm attending over the Christmas break. It teaches about discernment. It will be held in a Jesuit Retreat House in Cape Cod for about thirty days but some participants stay longer if they want one-on-one spiritual direction in discerning a priestly vocation. You are more than welcome to attend. I'll share a room with either or both of you... even you Patrick."

Lukas eagerly accepted the invitation. "Count me in, Sean. I need to find out where God is leading me 'cause the one thing I do know is that I didn't find happiness when I ignored God's voice for twelve years."

"I'll think about it," Patrick said. "Now, are you in on St. Ignatius' hottest new band or not?"

Sean clapped him on the back. "I'm in, 'lad'. But what would set us apart from every other band, singer and act?"

"Easy," Lukas answered. "We'll play nothing but original worship music. I can start writing some songs tonight."

"Say goodbye to your social lives then," Patrick said smugly. "I'm your new slave driver talent manager."

Chapter 14

Ringggg. Alana's alarm clock rudely interrupted her dreams of a blonde knight in shining armor rescuing her from the pits of over studying. The clock read 5:30 am. Since she had stayed up until 2:00 am studying for her English midterm exams, Alana computed that she only had three hours of sleep. Oh how she'd love to skip today's 6:30 am Mass, just this once.

With a groan, Alana turned off her alarm clock. After a quick debate with herself, she decided she needed more sleep than prayers this morning. She would just stop by the Adoration Chapel at noon before lunch and try to make it to the evening Mass. Alana shut her eyes and obtained another two more hours of sleep.

As soon as she woke up, Alana headed straight for the English Department to take her midterm exam on Classic Books. She loved all of her new subjects. Despite her lack of sleep and absence of a social life, or precisely because of, she was doing exceedingly well on her grades.

I should have pursued this course a long time ago, she mused regretfully. *I should never have let my sorority sisters talk me out of it.*

When Alana was finished with her exam, she turned in her paper and walked back to her dorm to get ready for another exam on Philosophy Writings of the Saints, another subject she loved. The first thing that greeted her when she walked in was the sight of her bookshelves crammed with books from top to bottom. Lately, Alana's life revolved around books now for she soon realized that majoring in English literature meant that she would be reading books every time she could spare: while waiting in lines, eating lunch, in between classes, before bedtime. Not that she minded at all. It was easier to bury her nose in a book rather than catch the eye of someone she knew from the sorority circles or engage in small talk with someone who wanted to get her phone number.

Anabelle Hazard

As Alana gazed at her books, she felt a twinge of loneliness. The books, as engaging as they were, were not a good substitute for human company. Alana needed friends, maybe even a boyfriend. *Not just any boy though,* she thought. *Someone like Lukas, kind, funny, sweet... but Oh dear Lord, not quite like Lukas because he has to be a faithful Catholic. You know I couldn't bear to marry someone who would have such a hard time loving you or your mother.*

There, she prayed it outright. She was clear on what kind of a man she wanted. She could only hope it was what God wanted for her too.

After Alana did some eleventh-hour studying, she ate lunch by herself and spent half an hour at the Adoration Chapel. Just when she headed out the door, someone lightly touched her on the arm.

Alana looked into the kind brown eyes of a female student. She had honey blonde hair and her petite 5'3 frame was dressed in simple, elegant and modest clothes.

"Hi there," she drawled in an unmistakable Southern accent. "I'm Kerry Lancaster. I see you here every once in a while and was wondering if you'd be interested in joining some ladies for faith sharing every Friday night. Usually we alternate between bible study or book club discussions on books written by saints."

That sounded like music to Alana's ears. She could study and socialize at the same time! "I'd love to. Where do you meet?"

"We take turns. Sometimes at someone's apartment, quiet coffee shops, school function rooms... Our next meeting is tonight at my place."

"Oh, I was going to attend the 5:30 pm Mass."

"No worries. We have dinner at 5 and the discussions don't usually start till an hour later, so you can come anytime after you're done "supping with the Lord." One other girl, Melanie, goes to the 5:30 Friday Mass too and she's always comes in just before we officially start."

Alana smiled gratefully. "Thanks Kerry. I'm Lanie."

"I know who you are. I tried to pledge in your sorority last year but was blackballed. No offense, but it was the best thing that ever happened to me."

"I'm so glad you approached me today, Kerry. I'm out of the sorority loop nowadays. I'm badly in need of some "un-normal" company, if you know what I mean."

Kerry laughed. "I like "un-normal" as opposed to abnormal. Very counter-cultural. Here's my address."

Well, Lord, Alana thought in her head, *I didn't exactly meet a man today but a friend. Thanks.*

~ ~

In order to graduate timely, Alana had to take summer classes and catch up on her English credits. However, she managed to fly home to Honolulu for a week at the end of June. Although June was always crazy in Hawaii, thanks to all the wedding honeymooners, Alana was able to take an unimpeded stroll on the sandy shores of a local beach, where tourists didn't visit as much.

Alana's favorite moment of the entire day had always been the dawn. It was so still and promising and it was usually at this time when she heard the quiet voice of the Holy Spirit. Alana didn't have that many things to say to God today but she was hoping to catch God's voice.

She walked down the length of the beach on her bare feet, holding her shoes in her hands. As she passed by an empty area with a volleyball net draped across it, Alana could almost hear the familiar sounds of a volleyball game: the "thwack" of the ball bouncing on a wrist, the slap of a spike, the cheers from the spectators, the voices of the players calling out "my ball!" and the referee's whistle... Looking longingly at the court, Alana recalled a sound from her younger days: a heated argument with Laura that boys should play against the girls instead of having coed teams. Laura believed that boys and girls should be allowed to play together in one team as she regarded women as "weaker sex." Alana vehemently disagreed. Alana had believed she was every bit as tough, as agile and dexterous as any boy and she wanted to prove it. This was a sore point between them.

Alana left the volleyball net and walked further down, closer into the ocean. She touched the wet sand with her toes and gauged the water as fairly warm. She put both feet into the sand, allowing the waves to lap up to her ankles. Oh she loved the mixture of water and sand. Even though some people thought it was messy and sticky, she liked looking at the thousands of fine grains become enmeshed and yet remain completely separate from the saltwater.

She stood in one spot, feeling the wet sand sink underneath her feet as the waves came up to the shore. Alana looked at the peeking sunrise. The sun's rays were golden, magnificent as they came out of the sea. She noticed that the sun and the water seemed to come from the same place and yet they were distinct from each other.

God began to speak to her as she admired His creation. "My child," God seemed to whisper. "Look at the sun and the water, how they are both created lovingly by the same hand, made with the same love and yet they both serve different purposes. The sun warms the earth and provides nourishment for plants to grow. The sea provides a home for animals and becomes life-giving water for men and women. So it is with men and women. Men and women are absolutely equal in dignity before me. They were each created in love and each formed with a different purpose. But men and women have different roles to fill in the order of creation."

Alana looked down at her feet. "Now look at the sand and the water. They can become one, yet remain separate. This is my plan for man and woman. They are uniquely different from each other and they have the capability of becoming united while still maintaining diversity."

Alana was almost in tears at the tender, loving voice of God who had stooped down to her this morning to explain a mystery that had plagued her mind for many, many years. She was truly awed at God's wisdom that formed the plan of creation.

Alana remembered full well the story of creation from the book of Genesis. On the sixth day, God created Adam and took Eve from his rib. She understood now that woman was supposed to be under the protection and guidance of Adam's arm. Woman could not lead man, wife was not meant to lead husband. And woman could not lead the Church of Jesus Christ. If Jesus intended it otherwise, He would have made the most perfect of creatures, His mother, a priest.

Thank you God, she whispered. *Thank you for making me see the light, for giving me a glimpse of your infinite wisdom and understanding my place in this world. Yes, there is a spot for me but it is not on a self-made pedestal. It is where You decide to place me. Guide me that I may always seek Your will, Your plan, know it with certainty and live it for eternity.*

Alana gave her reflections further thought. She could of course become a fine editor or writer if she wanted to or even an excellent English teacher. But if God should call her to stay at home, with her kids, home school them and become involved daily in the education of their souls, this would in no way diminish her dignity as a woman. Such an important role of co-creating and raising future saints would in fact become the supreme fulfillment of her role as wife and mother. This role was and still is Mary's.

The sun was almost fully up. That meant Alana had to head back to her home, pick up her mother and brother so they could go to weekday morning Mass together.

Alana was unusually quiet during the ride to Church. She was still mesmerized by the humble way that God taught her humility. The first reading for the Mass was very appropriate. It was taken from the book of Job where God decided to give Job a lesson along the same lines. Basically, God had told Job the exact same thing He had told Alana: *I am God, you are not.*

Job 38: 4-20
Where were you when I founded the earth? Tell me, if you have understanding.

*Who determined its size; do you know? Who stretched out the measuring line for it? Into what were its pedestals sunk, and who laid the cornerstone, While the morning stars sang in chorus and all the sons of God shouted for joy?
And who shut within doors the sea, when it burst forth from the womb;
When I made the clouds its garment and thick darkness its swaddling bands?
When I set limits for it and fastened the bar of its door,
And said: Thus far shall you come but no farther, and here shall your proud waves be stilled!
Have you ever in your lifetime commanded the morning and shown the dawn its place For taking hold of the ends of the earth, till the wicked are shaken from its surface?
The earth is changed as is clay by the seal, and dyed as though it were a garment;
But from the wicked the light is withheld, and the arm of pride is shattered.
Have you entered into the sources of the sea, or walked about in the depths of the abyss?
Have the gates of death been shown to you, or have you seen the gates of darkness?
Have you comprehended the breadth of the earth? Tell me, if you know all:
Which is the way to the dwelling place of light, and where is the abode of darkness,
That you may take them to their boundaries and set them on their homeward paths?"*

After receiving Holy Communion, Alana prayed to Jesus in all humility: "Truly God, you are God and I am not. Jesus, you are my master. I am your servant. Bless my future husband, that he may lead our household to heaven."

~ ~

The one thing Alana looked forward to when school resumed for her senior year was spending time with the Friday faith sharing group. Since she joined the group during the spring, she had never missed a single meeting. The girls she met there were amazing—so full fervor for their faith and genuinely nice.

Over the summer, Alana was sorely deprived of her sisterly companions. Hence, Alana was incredibly delighted that they were meeting up again on this crisp Friday night in September. Tanya Hastings and Michelle Shaw were hosting the meeting at the apartment they shared.

"Mmm that sweet potato dish was delicious, Tanya. What's your secret ingredient?" Kerry asked.

"Its marmalade and tadahhh-- Liquor!" Tanya said with exaggerated flair.

"Are you trying to get us drunk or something?" Michelle, an African-American sophomore, asked in mock anger. "Between the blood of Christ wine and this, we'll be as wild as those sorority houses tonight." Then she shot a guilty look at Alana and said, "Sorry, I didn't mean..."

"Who me? Wild?" Alana feigned incredulous surprise. "I don't know what you're talking about, sister. I was always in the library when they had those crazy parties. FYI, I was the token misfit of the house."

Michelle laughed. "I hear you *sistah*. I'm the token misfit of the track and field varsity team. You know they're all trying to get me to try steroids for the meet? When I said no they all rolled their eyes and called me "goody-two-running-shoes".

A few ladies giggled at the joke, while some expressed sympathy.

"Well some rich kid called me 'Polyanna' with disgust when I told him I wouldn't write his thesis for him," said Danielle Evertts, a brainy dean's lister in her junior year who had planned on proceeding to law school. "I have to say though it was so tempting to accept the money. I could use that to pay some of my law school tuition." Danielle did not enjoy the privilege of most of SILU's students. She was on part scholarship and had to work to earn her degree.

"Good thing you didn't, Dani," Amanda Gerber, of the famous political Gerber family, a senior majoring in political science, cheered on her friend. "I myself get so tired of being labeled a "conservative" like it was some form of disease. We're all going to have to remind each other that God's enemy has convinced the world to follow his way and we just have to keep on the narrow path."

"Hey Dani, if you need some money you should try competing in that talent show prior to the Christmas Program. Supposedly, the top five winners will perform at the program after the play and the champion, as voted by the audience, will get the reward money."

"Really?! I'll have to think of a talent, quick. I think I was overlooked when heaven was handing them out," Danielle said.

"Is anyone interested in forming an a capella singing group?" Kerry asked.

Five or six girls said they were. Suddenly, there was a charge of excitement about competing in the winter talent show.

Danielle looked downcast and tried to make light of it. "Can I lip-sync? I don't have your beautiful singing voice, Kerry."

"Oh Dani, I'll give you my share of the reward if we win it," Amanda offered generously.

"Mine, too," Jean and Kerry offered in unison. Jean Chan was a foreign exchange student from Hong Kong.

The rest of the girls all nodded in agreement.

"Oh, I couldn't possibly accept that," Danielle protested, her voice choking with emotion. She was obviously touched at the gesture.

"We insist. You deserve to go to law school and become the lawyer who will be responsible for reversing *Roe vs Wade*. But if it makes you feel better, you can earn the money by praying novenas for us from now until December," Jean suggested.

"Sisters, you've got yourselves a deal," Danielle said, smiling broadly.

Alana couldn't help but smile at this latest demonstration of true sisterhood, so different from the false sisterhood she witnessed where everyone tore everyone else apart and fought each other in pride, jealousy and anger. They really all were adopted daughters of God, sisters-in-Christ, belonging to the same family. They even shared the same goal of working for the reversal of abortion in the United States, a fight that Christians have fought since 1973. It was a sad day in January 22, 1973 when the precedent case of *Roe versus Wade* legalized the woman's so-called "right to choose" to terminate the life of innocent babies, babies that would have been blessings to the world had they been allowed a chance to be born and to grow up into adulthood.

~ ~

A slow September rolled into an uneventful October for Alana. October whizzed past, turned into a frenzied November and all of a sudden, the holidays were right around the corner. On Friday night the week before Thanksgiving, Alana was happy to be in the presence of her lively faith sharing group. This time, they were at Coffee Mugs, an out-of-the way, quiet coffee house located in the suburbs of Boston.

"Well ladies, how were the first round of auditions?" Alana asked her friends conversationally.

"You should have seen the number of talented people this school has!" Kerry answered. "I was so intimidated by all of them. I thought we'd never get a call back. It must have been Danielle's prayers that pulled some strings up there for us."

"Congratulations then. So, how does this all work?" Michelle asked.

Amanda explained, "There are five judges and five rounds of auditions. They eliminate five or six acts a week. You really should go to the auditions. They're open to the public and highly entertaining."

"I would if I didn't have my evening classes," Alana replied. "I remember how much fun it was practicing for the play last Christmas."

"Oh but you'll be at the final program if we make it right, Lanie?"

"Wouldn't miss it for the world," Alana answered warmly.

"I hope that one band *Psalm 96* makes it to the final five, too." Tanya said. "You should hear them play. They are awesome, probably our biggest competition."

"Did you say awesome? The word I'd use is handsome," Jean giggled. "The drummer and the guitarist are so cute they remind me of those boy band posters I had all over my bedroom walls..."

"But that singer is all man. He looks like he should be in the movies," Frances Dupaix finished. Frances was an outspoken junior. Being a performance arts major, she had the most experience onstage than all the other girls.

Kerry tapped her forehead in concentration. "Oh I know who you're talking about. I see him at the noon Mass all the time and I've worked with him at the campus ministry several times. He *is* good looking but I just figured he'd be a priest since he serves as a sacristan all the time."

"Well if he is, what a waste of good genes that would be," Amanda added, shaking her head.

"Ok, listen up. Those who can't go to the auditions will have to go to the noon Mass to check out our potential faith sharing group heartthrob," Michelle declared jokingly. "We'll take votes on the next meeting, which will be in two weeks since Thanksgiving is coming up."

Even Alana was now curious. "I'll make sure I go before the 'elections' then," she said.

The door to the coffee shop opened. A slightly overweight junior named Melanie Grates waved to her friends before ordering her coffee.

"Oh Melanie's here," Kerry announced. "Means its time to officially start."

"Good. I've been dying to discuss "*The Mystical City of God*' since we started," Frances said. The *Mystical City of God* is an account of the life of the Blessed Virgin Mary as revealed mystically to the Blessed Mary of Agredu.

"Me, too. I didn't realize that Mary's life was lived in complete surrender to the Divine Will. How inspiring she is."

"Totally," Danielle agreed, vigorously nodded her head. "Do you remember that part where she says in the Magnificat: 'He has scattered the proud in the imagination of their hearts. He has put down the mighty from their thrones, and exalted those of low degree.' Gives me goosebumps. I mean, if you think about it, God chose his son to be borne by a humble Jewish girl and to be raised by a poor carpenter. Jesus first manifested himself at lowly stable to underprivileged shepherds. Then Jesus picked uneducated apostles to preach the word. Now, He's chosen virtual unknowns hidden in the convent to glorify His name: like St. Therese of Liseux, Mother Teresa, Mother Angelica."

St. Therese of Liseux was a Carmelite nun who wrote a widely read spiritual autobiography, was hailed by Pope Pius as the greatest saint of modern times and declared the thirty third doctor of the Church. Mother Teresa, the Nobel peace prize awardee, was a nun who founded the worldwide order Missionaries of Charity that takes care of the sick and the dying. Mother Angelica is a cloistered nun of the Order of the Poor Clares who single handedly started the largest Catholic cable network, the Eternal Word Television Network.

"Yeah, it makes me want to be so concealed, far away from the spotlight the world has to offer," Alana said with a hint of regret.

"It must be difficult for you to go unnoticed looking like you do," Melanie commented. Melanie was shy and unassuming. She always wondered what it would be like to be the center of attention but neither faulted nor envied Alana. Alana secretly thought that Melanie had the most melodious singing voice she had ever heard and she was extremely impressed that Melanie's talent never got to her head.

Alana's cheeks turned red in embarrassment. "Don't remind me, please. I loved the attention for a while but I quickly filled up like a hot air balloon and I thought I was royalty or something."

"I have to confess that I like being in the limelight," Amanda confided. "When I'm onstage singing, I feel such a powerful adrenalin rush…"

"Well, just make sure you don't hog that microphone on the next audition, ok, or heaven help me, I'll wrestle it from you," Frances joked.

"Geez, we have a diva situation here!" Jean teased.

"What's Mary of Agredu going to say about that?" Kerry chimed in.

"What I liked most," said Alana, "is the obedience of Mary to the head of her household, St. Joseph. Even though she knew that they were supposed to leave for Bethlehem to have the baby there before he did, she waited for him to come to that decision and followed his lead. I was also surprised that Mary sought Joseph's permission on many things."

"Meanwhile, St. Joseph was looking for ways to keep his pregnant wife safe and sound and trying to keep her from making the journey which completely showed that he loved his bride as his own body.

"This particular slice of their life showed me so much about the relationship between spouses as enunciated by St. Paul: '*Wives should be subordinate to their husbands as to the Lord. For the husband is head of his wife just as Christ is head of the church, he himself the savior of the body. As the church is subordinate to Christ, so wives should be subordinate to their husbands in everything.*'"

"You know, as a former feminist I thought we were equal to men and we are in some sense equal in dignity but absolutely not equal in role. That was a very tough pill to swallow but by the grace of the Holy Spirit, I can now understand my role as a woman and future wife."

"Yes, Mary was through and through a handmaid of the Lord as she called herself in her Magnificat. She lived in supreme obedience to those that God put as authority in her life: her parents, her church teachers, her husband and most of all, Jesus her son. She has rightfully earned the title Queen of Heaven," said Michelle, sipping her cappuccino from her mug.

"I think the greatest obstacles to sanctification are pride and disobedience, which means the fastest way, as shown by Mary's example, is humility and obedience," Kerry said.

"Personally, I think we're in the wrong school to be learning about humility and obedience," Frances offered her opinion.

"On the contrary, we're exactly in the right school to teach our peers about humility and obedience," Amanda countered.

"Two words that feminists need to learn," Jean said pointedly.

"Actually," Danielle said thoughtfully. "The feminist movement is not altogether evil. It began as a good thing by advocating for women's right to work, equal pay and opportunity. It was just twisted in the later years by pro-abortionists to make it seem like women have a right to murder the souls that God entrusts them with."

"You're right, Dani. I just don't understand how the Supreme Court of the United States failed to consider that God bestows the life of the soul as early as the moment of conception and not three months during pregnancy as they seem to think and how they overlooked that the Constitution guarantees everyone the right to life."

The girls nodded their assent sadly.

"Hmm, I like the word handmaid. Can we interrupt this discussion to vote on whether the acapella group can change our name to *Handmaids of the Lord?*" Kerry asked.

"I don't think we're quite worthy of holding Mary's title," Danielle quipped.

"*Handmaids of the Handmaid?*" suggested Melanie "and we can wear a blue dress, white apron and tie a white scarf over our hair."

The choir unanimously loved the idea.

"How about *Handmaids of Psalm 96?*" Amanda giggled and so did the rest of the sisters.

"Ok girls that's enough swooning for tonight," Michelle said. "You might work yourselves up to hyperventilation at Mass tomorrow."

Alana was more than curious now. She was *very interested* to see the mystery guy, whoever he was.

Chapter 15

While Sean played the piano to the entrance hymn, Lukas held the cross above his head for the processional, walked up the aisle in front of the priest, bowed before the altar, and settled in his place by the side of the presider's chair.

Lukas felt a chilly draft sweep into the Church of Jesu, alerting him that fall was slowly changing into winter. Lukas absolutely loved this time of year. Even though he never went home to Spain for Thanksgiving, he liked being with Sean's family. The Speigel's were your typical large Catholic homeschooling family of ten. The four older ones had moved out of the house and married but they lived close and came over with their children often.

Lukas wanted a large, happy family like theirs someday. He hoped he would be able to provide for his wife so that she could stay home and teach their children spiritual lessons alongside academic excellence. He imagined that he would work at a scientific laboratory all day and come home to a wife like Alana, his boisterous children jumping into his arms to greet him. Lukas dreamed that one of his children would have a priestly or religious vocation. He would certainly foster that.

Then an unsolicited thought sprung up in his head quickly: *What if he was the one who had a priestly vocation?*

Lukas stirred out of his reverie just in time to join the Gloria. Lukas paid close attention to Jesus for the rest of Mass to make up for his wandering thoughts. He performed the sacristan's duties alongside the priest, assisting him as he prepared to celebrate the Sacrifice of the Holy Eucharist. Lukas was always grateful that he had a vantage point at seeing the Mass. He had read Our Lady saying somewhere that if one knew the value of a single Mass, they would never turn their back on it. Since then, Lukas always treasured the moment of consecration, when the priest held up the body of Jesus. To him, this was a grace-filled occasion and he could almost picture the entire communion of saints kneeling in awesome reverence to the Savior.

The communion of saints was a concept that Lukas eagerly accepted. He cherished the teachings of the Catechism of the Church that the Church is made up of a body of saints in various levels: those on earth earning their heaven; those in purgatory, being purified before the reward of union with God; and those in heaven, who had been purified and earned the recompense of standing before God and living joyously with the entire heavenly court. Lukas hoped his grandmother and mother were heavenly residents and he anticipated the joy of their reunion when he earned heaven, someday. Wherever they were, during the consecration of the Eucharist, Lukas knew he and his mother and grandmother were united in worship of Jesus, praying for one another and the rest of their family members.

As the priest lifted up the body and the blood of Christ inside the gold chalice, Lukas bowed in deep adoration and said nothing. He was usually at a loss for words when he reflected on the Savior, who humbled himself to take on a species of bread and wine so he could remain on earth. Lukas received communion in his tongue and walked back to his kneeler, deep in prayer.

As soon as he finished praying the Anima Christi, Lukas looked far out into line of people receiving communion. There were the usual 12 o'clock churchgoers: students, faculty, staff. But there were also the sporadic churchgoers that he had never before seen: the teacher who came especially for his birthday, the visiting student from a neighboring non-Catholic college, and the random SILU students who felt like dropping in at Church for the day. He saw them go up the front of the altar, around the front pew and down to the side aisles. As he watched the communicants closely, there was one particular student that seized his interest. This time, Lukas knew it wasn't an apparition. There was Alana, her dark hair cut shorter in layers, just touching her shoulders. She wore a long elegant black skirt and a green turtleneck, long sleeve sweater, which seemed to highlight the green in her eyes, eyes that were looking straight at him.

Hardly believing his vision, Lukas blinked. He would have rubbed his eyes if he was a cartoon character but he knelt perfectly still, hands folded in prayer.

Once she realized Lukas was staring at her, Alana timidly looked away. From where she sat at the middle of the pews all throughout the Mass, she couldn't make out his features. She thought he vaguely looked familiar, but she couldn't quite put her finger on it. As she walked up to communion, she stared and stared, willing him to look her way so that she could see his face fully. When he finally did, Alana was taken aback. Undoubtedly, he was as handsome as the girls had said: dark hair, deep blue eyes with eyelashes that should have belonged on a woman, tall, slim but fit, smartly dressed in his khaki pants and navy sweater …and thoroughly engrossed, unbelievably enamored, incredibly enraptured with Jesus. But what held her gaze more than his appearance was because he looked… looked like someone she had met at a sorority party or something. Alana associated his face somewhat with Faye or Courtney and then -- she remembered.

Good heavens! she thought, *he was Faye's date for that awful and embarrassing Charity Ball.* Alana panicked for a split second. *He's going to remember what I've done if I don't hurry out of here!*

Alana was relieved that she had to slip out of the Mass right away to get to her next class. After the priest blessed the congregation, Alana did not wait for him to walk down the aisle. She mouthed a "see ya later" to Kerry and literally ran out of the Church of Jesu as fast as her legs could take her.

Lukas did not realize that he was holding his breath the entire time he walked down the aisle. The heavy cross still in his hand, he cornered Kerry as she stepped out into the foyer of the Church.

"Kerry," he called out. "How are you today?"

"I'm fine thanks. And you?"

"Not bad. Hey listen, I've been meaning to tell you that you and your acapella group are pretty impressive so I wanted to wish you luck on tomorrow's auditions."

"Oh thanks. You, too. You and the band are very inspiring."

Lukas tried to be suave, but he did not want to stall for time in case Kerry was in a rush. *Besides*, he thought to himself, *this cross is starting to weigh my arms down.* "Was that girl you were with part of your singing group, too?" he asked aloud.

Kerry hid a smile. *Ahh,* she thought to herself, *so this is what it's about.* "No," she said. "I know Lanie from our Friday faith sharing group, along with the rest of the acapella singers. She goes to the 6:30 am daily Mass, you know."

Lukas cast her a lopsided grin. He could tell she wasn't born yesterday and had caught on to his inquiries. He answered, "With late night practices and auditions, I can't wake up that early. Do you think she'll be at the auditions tomorrow?"

"Lanie has evening classes but she said she'll definitely go to the Christmas program. I can subtly arrange an introduction for you," she offered, her eyes twinkling.

"Um, thanks. I think I'll wander over to you after the program is over. So I have between now and then to come up with a smooth line," Lukas mumbled.

Kerry smiled. "She doesn't need lines, Luke. Despite what it looks like, she's a real nice, down to earth, approachable girl."

Lukas returned her smile. "Can you do me a favor and not let the cat out of the bag? It'll be bad for my machismo."

Kerry said in a sober, conspiratory tone. "This conversation never happened."

"Thanks Kerry. See you at the auditions."

She winked, and reproached Lukas with a shake of her head, "And I thought you were a candidate for the priesthood." With that, Kerry exited the double doors, thinking to herself how neat it would be if one of her sisters

Sand and Water

in Christ would become a bride to a Godly man such as Luke.

Lukas placed the cross back at the altar and almost danced out of the church in exhilaration. He wanted to scream, wave his hands in the air, jump up and down, or race a cocky Patrick in his bicycle. Instead, he walked into the Adoration Chapel and tried to be still. He couldn't even bring himself to talk. He was just smiling, silly smiling at Jesus for at last bringing Alana back into his life.

Lukas knew that Alana's presence today was not a coincidence. He understood that Kerry's words confirmed that a remarkable change had occurred in Alana—she was out of the sorority house, in a faith sharing group, a daily communicant and occasional adorer of the Blessed Sacrament. What more proof did he need that the full year of prayer and fasting had borne their fruit?

Lukas continued to sit for another forty minutes, soaking in the happiness of letting God take care of his love story.

But Lukas' happiness proved to be short-lived as he started to be plagued by the persistent idea that emerged from the back of his mind: that he might be called to the priesthood and have to give up Alana. However, he brushed it away determinedly. Right now, he only wanted to revel in the bliss of having found Alana and the exhilaration of getting to meet her all over again.

When the holy hour was over, Lukas genuflected and walked out of the chapel. He thought about what to say to her, how to casually bring up the subject of internet chat rooms, how she might react and what it would be like to finally reveal himself. Would she laugh, be embarrassed, pass out again (he hoped not!)? Then Lukas stopped himself from planning it out too much. *God will take care of it*, he assured himself. Jesus once told his apostles, "Do not worry about what you are to say. The Holy Spirit will come upon you and teach you what to say." Lukas absolutely trusted in that same Holy Spirit.

Chapter 16

Alana leaned back against her seat, entirely content to be in the audience instead of the stage this time. Seated beside her were Danielle and nine other girls from the Friday faith sharing group. They were all on hand to cheer on Kerry, Amanda, Jean, Tanya, Frances and Melanie. The lights to the Gonzaga International Center soon dimmed and the stage curtains parted.

As expected, the Nativity play this year superseded the previous year. It was partly a musical, with a poignant solo of Mary's Magnificat. In addition, the play was told from the perspective of an angel, hence, the birth of the Savior was seen through the eyes of heaven. The play closed with the three wise men offering their gifts of frankincense, gold and myrrh.

After a ten minute intermission, the curtain rose to reveal a beautiful manger scene suspended in mid-air. Then the narrator angel announced that on this special night, St. Ignatius Loyola University would present their gifts to the Savior through their multi-talented students who had been screened from over 1,000 hopefuls.

The opening act showcased a skilled dance group that engaged the audience in a graceful mix of multicultural dances, honoring the child Jesus. The second act consisted of a lively musical repertoire of a string quartet and male and female choir. The third group presented a sleek but not too original combination of a ballet and modern dance using classical music.

Finally, the fourth group to come onstage was the *Handmaids of the Handmaid*. Alana and her friends sat upright, anxious to see their friends' performance. Melanie led a solo aria of the "Ave Maria" which was followed by a chorus of what sounded like the voice of angels. From where she sat, Alana could tell that Melanie's beautiful voice held the audience spellbound. Then Kerry and Amanda took turns with "A King is Born," while the others provided the perfect backdrop of humming. The fourth song was a divine operatic pop version of "Do you hear what I hear?" once more led by Melanie and interwoven with the sounds of a heavenly chorus. Their last number was "Gloria in Excelsis Deo," the climactic finale to the story of the Child Jesus' birth.

When Alana stood up in ovation, she couldn't resist hooting a catcall. The *Handmaids* music had moved her and as she looked around, she was convinced that the audience was completely wowed by their performance as she was.

The final group called onstage was *Psalm 96.* The angel narrator explained that Psalm 96 is a song giving glory to God and that accordingly, this group's goal was simply to worship their King. The band began with an original signature song entitled Psalm 96. By now the audience had become familiar with this catchy tune. As the band played, the young audience got up, danced and sang the chorus along with the group. Alana noted that the group had already established a rapport with the audience, probably because the females were ready to swoon at their every song and the males genuinely appreciated exceptional musical talent when they saw it. When the song was over, the fans expressed their admiration for the band with an extended heartfelt applause.

"Thank you! It is such a pleasure and honor to play for you SILU," the lead singer acknowledged the fans' positive reception with a huge authentic smile. The mention of SILU brought on catcalls. He proceeded to introduce their next song. "Our second number is an original Christmas pop/rock song written by the keyboardist Sean and myself. While the song is original, the idea of interweaving Spanish and English in a song is copied from one of the most celebrated ballad singers of all time, Julio Iglesias. Now not all of us were born when he made it to the top forties (except for the University President Fr. John Williams over here) but I have it on the highest authority that Mr. Iglesias is cooler than his pop star sons. Here goes…"

The audience swayed along with the soothing melody and some of them took out their lighters, as if in a rock concert. Those who had been to the *Gingerbread Men* performance a year ago could not deny that singing for God with *Psalm 96* was infinitely better and far more meaningful than singing aimless songs with just another pop band.

Danielle nudged Alana with her elbow. "He's so cute! If he was a rock star, I would so be a groupie!"

Alana nodded her head giddily. "I don't understand a word of Spanish, but I don't care. He could be singing about throwing snowballs but his romantic voice sounds like he's asking me to marry him, and I'd say yes in a heartbeat."

The second song ended to a warm applause. The lead singer described their third song. "Our third number is another original song that I wrote back when I was younger. I thought I wrote it for a girl but as I read the lyrics, I realized that I really was writing for God because it is Him that my heart longs for and it is heaven with Him that I dream of. I guess if one really loves God, one would realize that every love song is about Him."

Alana settled comfortably in her seat as the pianist began a slow introduction on the piano. When the lead guitar joined him, Alana's ears picked up on the familiar haunting melody and she was surprised to find that she recognized it from somewhere in her memory. Mesmerized, she watched the lead singer turn his back on the audience and croon to Jesus on the manger. With growing incredulity, Alana listened to a song she thought she would never hear again:

Where are you? Who are you?
I've never seen you, but I know you exist.
Deep into the night, I think of you and long for you
I wonder if you are thinking of me, too.

Where are you? Who are you?
I have to believe that someday destiny meant for us to meet.
What do I say when we finally cross paths?
What will you say when I chase after you with words you think aren't sweet?

You are here, you are real.
I've found you and my heart at last begins to heal.

*But still I don't know where you are, who you are
And yet my soul knows you are my home.*

*I am here, I am yours.
I will follow wherever you go.
I will love you as long as I live
I know now that love is true and true love is only you.*

As the audience got up on their feet in a rousing applause, Alana enthusiastically got up along with them. She clapped her hands passionately, each clap growing more intense than the previous one. Her eyes were wet with tears, as were most people's eyes in the audience. She didn't know why they were crying but her tears were an overwhelmed reaction to her discovery: that Luke was Lukas, and all along he was breathing the same air that she was, walking along the same paths, sitting in the same classrooms, praying in the same Church pews.

His former blonde hair had become a dark rich brown, the glasses were gone, but the kind blue eyes and the accent were there. *How could I have not known who he was?* she reproached herself.

Suddenly, Alana's heart raced and she felt her stomach do a somersault. In a mad rush, unstoppable thoughts raced through her mind, making her almost dizzyingly breathless: *Does he remember me at all? Does he know I'm here? Does Lukas know who I am?*

One after another, Alana mentally recalled flashbacks of times they had been together in close proximity ... Courtney pointing out Prospect #2 at the start of rehearsals...Courtney introducing him as Luke while Alana went on and on about Jeff... Lukas and his friend asking her if she was from Hawaii...Lukas watching her intently at the practices...Lukas overhearing the entire conversation at the Charity Ball... Lukas -- oh dear Lord, was it Lukas?-- coming to console her at the bar when Jeff humiliated her...and then Lukas returning her stare at noon Mass a few weeks ago...

He knows, she thought to herself, drawing an exuberant breath. *Surely, he knows. He's mentioned Julio Iglesias and possibly alluded to me as the highest authority on Julio Iglesias. Did he deliberately sing this song, thinking I would be here? Oh, I dare not hope!*

Alana could not wait for the fourth song to be over, for this whole program to be over. She and Kerry had agreed to meet backstage after the show but now she was indomitably resolute to track down Lukas in the jungle of performers backstage.

Alana inwardly groaned when the audience requested an encore. Her eyes were transfixed on Lukas as he sang an upbeat worship song, leading the crowd in exultant praise of God. His stage persona was electrifying. She could not help falling in love with his zealous faith, his charismatic voice, his feral energy, his raw emotion and his gorgeous, now familiar, face. Lukas' singing held her engrossed in amazement, more so now that she knew who he was.

Alana had always known that there is always something about watching a good-looking performer onstage that makes women naturally fall in love with him, but when the performer is someone a woman has fallen in love with in the past, someone she thought was lost forever, and resurrects with a faith and undying devotion to God, it is a completely different story. The entire picture changes, the world shifts, and it is the soul, more than the heart, that is enraptured. With a single song, standing fifty feet away, Lukas erased every reservation Alana unknowingly held against him. In that one decisive moment, Lukas managed to sweep her off her feet. Alana wanted to stay exactly where she was, flying high in the air, and in the same instant, she wanted to land on the ground and run into his arms. Oh, it was bittersweet torture to watch him perform so masterfully and not be able to talk to him! Now, she wanted him to keep singing, to sing for *her*.

Everyone was sorry that *Psalm 96's* last performance had to end. Alana's applause was unbound, inexorable and then unconsciously she kept her hands together folded in prayer, and brought it to her smiling lips, in thanksgiving to God for bringing him back into her life again, this way. It was a moment she knew she would always remember for the rest of her life.

"That caps tonight's performance, folks," the emcee declared. "Thank you all for being here. You know tonight's proceeds are donated to charity. Now, I'm going to call on the Dean of the accounting department to give us the results of tonight's votes. Dean Robert Fulton will announce the winner while our distinguished --and ancient--University President Fr. Williams will award the winner a check for $25,000 from our generous benefactor and alumni association. Come on up, Fr. Williams --and please do it before Kingdom comes."

Fr. Williams hobbled up the steps to the stage with his wooden cane. He gruffly grabbed the microphone from the emcee and joked, "I may be old but I can still dance. I'll give those ballerinas a run for their money next year."

Everyone laughed. Then the drums rolled to further build up the tension in the auditorium, succeeding fully in building up the tension in Alana's heart.

Dean Fulton made a dramatic show of opening the envelope results and announced to the spectators poised in suspense: "The winner of the talent show is... *Psalm 96!*"

The audience went wild. Even Danielle and the other girls cheered in standing ovation. They had hoped that their friends would win, but they had to admit that *Psalm 96* was on fire with the Holy Spirit and the band had absolutely captivated the crowd.

Alana watched enthralled as Lukas and his band members hugged each other. Lukas received the award on behalf of the group and accepted a congratulatory handshake from Fr. Williams.

Lukas raised his hand to silence the audience. Then he addressed the crowd, "First of all, *Psalm 96* praises and thanks God for our talents and we thank you all for voting for us. Our band has already agreed that the prize money will be donated to the Students for Life movement. Our keyboardist Sean has been an active volunteer since he was a Freshman. He brought up the idea to us during practice and we all thought that was the best thing to do..."

The audience spontaneously clapped their approval. Danielle leaned over and spoke into Alana's ear, "I truly am glad they won."

"Me, too," she said, trying to keep her voice modulated. Inside her, her organs were still dancing in worship and her knees felt like they were going to buckle underneath her. *Hurry up, Lukas, get off the stage,* she pleaded urgently.

As soon as the cast and crew took their final bow, the audience departed the theatre, still talking about the performances that night. After bidding her friends a quick goodbye, Alana made her way out of there as fast as she could. By the time Alana reached backstage, she was breathless with anticipation.

On seeing Alana, Kerry waved her friend over to the dressing rooms, where she was standing. Alana walked to her, frantically looking to her left and right, searching for any sign of Lukas. She saw the dancers, the choir, the cast members, even the director but no Lukas. Slowly, Alana became disheartened. *"Of course,"* she thought, *"he's probably fighting off the legions of female fans."*

Trying to forget about her predicament, Alana hugged Kerry. "You did such a terrific job out there. I'm sorry you lost."

Kerry dismissed her apology with a wave. "Don't be. Those guys deserved it. Besides, a talent scout from a Christian recording company approached us tonight and asked if we would be interested in a demo. That's more than we prayed for."

"Oh, that is good news. I'm so happy for y'all," she said, mimicking Kerry's Southern accent.

Kerry laughed. She motioned to someone behind Alana to come over. Alana turned, expecting to see the rest of the acapella group. Instead, she found herself face to face with the man who captured her heart back in high school and once again, tonight.

For a brief moment, Lukas and Alana held each other's gaze wordlessly. Kerry took that as her cue to disappear.

Sand and Water

Neither of them moved. Finally, Alana broke the silence. She gave Lukas her best smile and said shakily, "Lukas, It's me -- Lanie."

Lukas returned her smile and replied, "I know."

Alana's heart slammed in her chest at the confirmation. "How long...when...how did you know?" she stammered. Alana fought the nervous impulse to bite her nails.

"Your orange hair gave you away," Lukas joked, referring to one of their old running jokes.

Alana was thrilled that he remembered their conversations. "I had no clue you were right under my nose! I'd like to know everything! I have so much to ask you..."

A cute brunette, whom Alana recognized as the school paper's editor in chief, came up to touch Lukas on the arm. "Luke," she said flirtatiously, "we're ready for that interview and the photo ops with the band."

Alana felt a pang of jealousy. But Lukas quickly chased it away when he spoke to Alana as if she was the only one in the room. "Can I see you tomorrow, Lanie? You can ask me anything you like, but I just have to take care of some things tonight."

"Yes! All my finals are over. My big plan for the day was just to pack."

"Do you want to meet me at the noon Mass and have lunch after that?"

Alana nodded, happily. "I'll be there," she promised.

"Can't hardly wait," he said sincerely.

Lukas gave her another smile and this time, she noticed the dimple on his right cheek. Alana nearly swooned. She watched the two of them walk away and could not wipe the silly grin on her face, all the way to her dorm.

Chapter 17

Lukas did not have to serve at Mass the following morning. He had foreseen that a late night after the program would mean he would have a late start the next day. However, despite the late night, Lukas still got up the usual 7:00 time. He awoke with an air of cheerfulness. The lack of sleep could not ruin his mood.

Despite his indifference to fashion and vanity, Lukas paid more attention to the clothes he picked out today. He wanted to dress nicely for Alana. He noticed that she now picked out classic and feminine styles, as opposed to the trendy and skimpy clothes of last year's freezing winter.

Lukas arrived at the Church of Jesu fifteen minutes before Mass. He chose a seat in the back row so that he would not miss Alana when she entered. When Alana came in five minutes before Mass began, Lukas beckoned her over to sit next to him. Alana genuflected on the aisle and sat down beside Lukas.

"I thought you'd be serving at Mass today," she whispered.

"Jesus gave me the day off. I told him I have a long overdue date." He winked, laughter in his deep blue eyes.

"Oh," she said, her tone teasing. "Your 'Boss' is very considerate. Mine demands to tag along on all of my dates, so you'd better be on your best behavior."

Lukas stifled a laugh. "I will. Now be quiet or He might fire you."

Alana had to put in the last word. She whispered, "Jesus can't afford to fire me. He barely has enough on his staff as it is. Too many employees are taking days off."

Lukas' shoulders shook with laughter. He opened his mouth to say something but the bell sounded, signaling the beginning of Mass. Despite sitting next to each other, Alana and Lukas managed, with supreme difficulty, to concentrate on the Holy Sacrifice of the Eucharist. In the silence after communion, each of them prayed in joyous thanksgiving for the gift of this day and each other.

Once Mass was over, they decided to have lunch at a café place in the mall because Alana needed to do some last minute Christmas shopping for her friends in Hawaii. Lukas asked her if he could tag along and Alana happily acquiesced.

As soon as they paid for their lunch, Lukas and Alana took their trays to a secluded table for two. They took a seat by the bay window, which overlooked the busy street. Neither of them paid any attention to their surroundings.

"So," Alana began, sipping her lemonade, "you, my friend, have been very busy since we last chatted. You want to tell me the whole story?"

Lukas gave her an impish grin. "Let's see... After we said our dramatic goodbyes, they put me in a mental institution for the broken hearted. I escaped with the help of a janitor who smuggled me out of there in his cleaning cart..."

Amused, Alana played along. "Ahh, no wonder you still have a distinctive smell on you — like garbage or something." She sniffed his sleeve and pretended to gag.

"Oh that explains the flies swarming over my head all the time." Lukas joked back, feeling a little nervous about telling his story.

"Seriously Lukas, I want to know where you've been. I've always wondered about you and can't wait to hear how you wound up in the sacristy... in SILU no less!"

"Wait, really? You wondered about me? I thought you'd have forgotten by now." The little boy in Lukas had to ask. He wanted to hear Alana say that again.

"No, Mr. Iglesias. You are a difficult man to forget. Now, please, tell me your story before I die of suspense."

Lukas was exceedingly pleased that Alana had not forgotten him and that she was truly interested in hearing about him. It made it easier to recount the personal details of his spiritual life. "Ok. In a nutshell, when you broke my heart, I prayed on my knees for the first time since I was a child. I know I told you I didn't believe in God but that night, I wanted to believe in God because I wanted to be with you again. I guess it was very selfish to use God to get to you but it turned out that God, being a wise God that He is, even used my selfish motive and turned it around."

Lukas then related the entire story of how he returned to the Church he was baptized in. "The funny thing Lanie is that just when I fell in love with Jesus and the Church he founded, the need to be with someone – even someone as wonderful as you—was gone. And just when I thought I'd forgotten you and God had healed me, He led me to try to find you in Massachusetts. I only knew three things about you, but I had to trust that God would drop you out of the sky into my arms someday."

Alana wanted to hear more. She was enthralled by Lukas journey home to the Church. It sounded like her own return to the Church: a waiting, patient, loving and forgiving God welcoming a contrite soul in the folds of His arms. "Go on, please."

Lukas decided to keep some things private from her for now so he reserved some details to himself. "So then, I joined this Christmas program, met Courtney and Faye, and voila! you sauntered up talking about Jeff and the Charity Ball..."

Alana turned bright red at the mention of that. She waved her hands in her face, fanning herself to get some air. "Can we fast forward that part? It's a little embarrassing."

"Alright," Lukas said sympathetically. "Hey, are you going to the Charity Ball tonight?"

"No, I wasn't planning on going."

"Can I convince you to come with me?"

"Boy, you're the king of last minute dates, aren't you?" Alana grumbled good naturedly. "Actually I'd love to, except I have nothing to wear. I threw away last year's gown."

"Good thing you did. You looked beautiful but it was too revealing for me. Oops, I'm not embarrassing you now, am I?"

"No, siree. You know what?" she said impulsively. "We're in a mall today. Let's go shopping for a modest dress so I can be the worthy date of SILU's newest rock star."

Sand and Water

Lukas smiled. "Great. I get to be with you the whole afternoon and tonight as well. Are you saying goodbye at midnight, too like the last time?"

"My curfew is at one. I have to leave for the airport early tomorrow morning."

"Ok then. Now, can we talk about what you've been up to the last three years?"

"Oh, you won't want to hear my story. It's pretty sad."

Lukas shook his head. "No fair. I told you my three-year autobiography, now you have to tell me yours."

"Umm... I've never had a sister so I thought I'd find one in the sorority. It turns out I was invited by the wrong sorority. In short, I became involved in the typical college lifestyle: drinking, partying, boys, popularity contests, gossip... Yuck! Every capital sin in the book. Except the one thing I surprisingly maintained was my purity and it is only by God's grace that it's happened."

Lukas looked deeply into Alana's eyes. "I remember that conversation on the purity ring at the Ball last year. I thought you were the bravest, most noble lady I've ever met."

"Thanks, Lukas. Frankly, at that time, I really didn't know who I'd become. I was like my evil twin. I think the turning point for me was when I played Mary. It's like Our Lady sent me conversion graces straight from heaven. From that moment on, I felt that things had to change, they just had to. I couldn't stand myself or my life anymore. The sorority sisters weren't very supportive of my new resolve, to say the least. I've never felt more persecuted for my faith than when I came home from the ball so I packed up, left and never looked back."

She continued. "When I returned home, things just fell in place. I reconciled with God, the Church, my parents, my old friends. Then I returned to English as my major. When I got back into SILU, doors opened for me. God led me to the right kind of sisters this time and those sisters unwittingly led me to finding you."

"Well, I helped them along," Lukas confessed.

"What do you mean?"

"Kerry and I schemed to bring you backstage after the show and Sean and Patrick convinced me to reveal myself to you onstage like that."

Alana was so delighted, she couldn't stop smiling. "Really?! How long have you planned that? How long have you known I was me?"

"I found out when Courtney introduced us at the rehearsals. I didn't mean to judge you but I was truthfully disillusioned at my first impression."

She nodded. "I don't blame you at all. I would never be impressed with me, either!"

"So anyway," Lukas continued, finishing up his last bite of sandwich, "in prayer, I sensed that I should give you space and in due time, I'd know when to bring it up. Do you think I was I wrong in bringing it up only now?"

"Not at all. I'm so glad you sang that song. It's so romantic. I mean, I know you said it wasn't for me anymore but still, you had every girl in the audience wanting to be a groupie especially me!"

Lukas waved his hand in the air in a gesture of indifference. "I don't care much for all the hype and attention. My ambition is just to live a simple life, raise a holy Catholic family."

Alana flashed him a grin. "So neither of us is Hollywood bound. I'm glad we got that straight then."

Lukas turned his eyes away from her dazzling smile. A shadow crossed his features. *I have to tell Lanie the truth before I lead her on*, he thought ruefully. But he just wanted to enjoy this date, he argued with himself. *I'll do it when the right time comes*, he promised.

Alana's next question made Lukas wonder if she read his mind. "So what was it that made you decide now was the right time to reveal yourself?"

"Seeing you at Mass with Kerry. She told me just the things I needed to know—that you were going to the 6:30 Mass regularly and you really are as nice as I hoped you were. I think I was waiting for a sign that you wouldn't laugh at me for falling in love over the internet and following you all the way to your college."

"Why that Kerry was in cahoots with you the whole time! I'll have to get her an extra special present now," she said gleefully.

"Should we shop away, Lanie?" Lukas asked, deliberately changing the topic.

"Let's and please tell me your favorite color so we can pick out a dress." They both got up and strolled around the boutiques.

Something caught Alana's eye on one of the display windows. She grabbed Lukas' arm and asked him excitedly, "What about that white one?"

He gave her a lopsided smile. "I think white would look great on my bride but since it's just a Charity Ball, let's pick your favorite color."

As soon as the words were out of his mouth, Lukas mentally reprimanded himself for bringing up the subject of weddings and marriage. Somehow, he just couldn't help but think of weddings when he was with Alana. But he had no right to bring it up, not yet anyway.

Alana gave him a sideways glance. "I'm partial to black so we'd be going for the widow look."

Was it her imagination or did he look disturbed when she said that? Maybe she was jumping the gun by joking about weddings and marriage. Maybe he wasn't even thinking that far yet. Or maybe she had crossed the line over into dark comedy by joking about death. Embarrassed, she covered up the blunder with humor. She pointed to an obnoxiously pouffy orange and yellow spring dress. "Would orange be a bit much with my orange hair?" she asked in an effort to regain the bantering mood.

"A tad," he said with a small smile. "Let's do a compromise and look for something in black and white. Look over there, the answer to our prayers."

Alana turned to where Lukas had pointed. *Not bad*, she thought. She tried the dress on in the dressing room and had to agree that it was perfect for tonight's party. Quickly, she purchased it and gave Lukas a light smile on their way out. "Where to, next?"

"The ball, of course, Cinderella."

Chapter 18

Alana carefully applied make up on her eyes and touched her lips with lipstick. She had not put on make-up in ages. Ordinarily, since her reversion experience she skipped make up because she had read that in one of Our Lady's apparitions in Spain she disapproved of the young girls' use of nail polish and other vain applications. But tonight, Alana made up her mind that she would dress and accessorize appropriately, just as one invited to a wedding feast would pay their host due respect. It was, after all, *Jesus'* Christmas Charity Ball. Or so she told herself.

Alana picked up her barely used curling iron and spent another fifteen minutes doing her hair. She was out of practice with the styling products and some of them were probably past their expiration date. On any other day, she rushed out of the door with a haphazard ponytail or with a few strokes of brushing. But once again, today was an exemption. She put her hair up elegantly and left some tendrils to fall around her face. She had to admit that she was very excited to spend time with Lukas tonight. She very well felt like Cinderella going to a once in a lifetime ball.

Thinking of Lukas, Alana put on her dress swiftly and checked the clock. He would arrive in five minutes so she had to be ready to open the door and get into his car in a jiffy. They had spent too much time in the mall, leisurely shopping, talking and laughing that they were now running late.

The doorbell rang just as Alana put on her left sandal. She put the right one on and zoomed past the full length mirror to the front door without giving herself a chance to do a final once-over.

When Alana opened the door, Lukas' breath caught in his throat. He took it all in: she looked like a dream in her long black and white gown, with her upswept hair and dramatic make up. Her enigmatic smile put the sweetness in an otherwise cosmopolitan image. He didn't know how

Anabelle Hazard

she pulled it off but Alana managed to look at once sophisticated and yet very demure.

Lukas finally tore his eyes away from her face and drew down to where the gown ended on the floor. From underneath the folds of her dress, he spotted something amiss.

Alana was just enjoying Lukas' reaction to her appearance and also admiring how dapper he looked in a black and white tux when she noticed that he was now suppressing his smile and his eyes were crinkling with amusement.

"Lanie, you are the epitome of the word stunning," Lukas began. "But I don't know how you'll be able to dance when you've got two different shoes on."

Alana looked down at her left foot clad in a black strappy high heeled sandal while her right foot had on a dirty tennis shoe. She howled with unbridled laughter. "Ah, no wonder I could barely walk to the door. I must say these sneakers are far more comfortable to dance with. Should I wear them in case I have to run for my life when your female fans come after me with brooms?"

"You are the only female I care about. C'mon hop into my getaway car," he said, holding his arm out to her.

Alana hobbled to the closet and slipped on the matching sandal. Then she and Lukas climbed into his seven year old second-hand Ford Taurus. Lukas turned the ignition on but it wouldn't start. He switched it on again and the engine coughed, sputtered and died. He looked at Alana worriedly.

"Well, we're a fine pair you and I," she quipped. "Me in my fashion forward shoes and you in your get-caught car. We both managed to make wonderful first impressions on our long overdue date, didn't we?"

Lukas laughed despite himself. "I'll give it 5 minutes. She usually comes around."

"Um, Luke, since we're sitting here. Do you mind if we pray the rosary? I promised my mom and dad that everyday I would pray it after dinner like we always do so that we're still in some way praying together as a family. But since we'll be at the ball and everything..."

Sand and Water

"Say no more. I would love to pray with our boss's mother but you'll have to take the lead, I don't exactly remember how to say it."

They began saying the rosary. Soon after it was over, Lukas turned on the ignition and the car came back to life.

"Just like magic, eh?" Alana said, patting the dashboard. "That rosary sure is powerful."

"I have to confess I'm not much of a believer in repetitive prayer but I heard someone say—I suspect it was my *abuela*-- that next to the Mass, the rosary is the most powerful prayer. Do you know why?"

"I'm not sure. I mean I'm no theologian but I think the Hail Mary is an act of loving trust. It's asking Our Blessed Mother to pray for us without any thought of our own intention but just asking God for whatever her intentions are. She only wants God's will so when she prays, it is always for the good of our souls so it's the best non-self interested prayer there is. And when we trust her with our souls I think that pleases Jesus because He himself gave us His mother at the foot of the cross and He wants us to love and trust her just as He did by choosing her to become his own mother. Besides, it's hard for him to refuse her request."

"I guess I have to work on my relationship with the Blessed Mother a little since I don't remember too much of my own mother," Lukas answered, his breaking voice betraying his emotion.

Alana gave his arm a squeeze. "I'll bet its her prayers in heaven and the Blessed Mother's prayers that are responsible for making you turn out so wonderfully," she said.

"Thank you, Lanie," he said softly. "How do you do that?"

She gave him a puzzled look.

"Make me laugh and cry and feel great about it?"

She shrugged and then laughed. "I guess you can thank my mother for that—er mothers --all three of them."

Lukas laughed along with her. "I know you think highly of your adoptive parents. Do you know much about your birth parents?"

Sand and Water

"Nothing at all. Like any adopted child, I wonder who they were, why they gave me up and what it would have been like if they raised me but I have never seriously wished for a different life. My life's not been perfect but all in all, its been good. My parents have taught me to be insanely grateful to God for what I have and I am. Their trick was to take me to the Philippines and Latin America several times to make sure I knew how blessed I was to have a roof over my head, comforts and other privileges."

"Your parents could have taken you to Spain too and you would have seen a family like mine, with more than enough money, without a mother, without faith. You are indeed blessed, Lanie."

Alana nodded. "Yes but being blessed means that I have more responsibility. As the gospel goes: 'to whom much is given, much is required.'"

"So what exactly is it that God's asking you to do?"

Alana narrowed her eyes and looked around suspiciously. Then she whispered, "I'm an under cover student. Any day now I'm expecting the package from heaven containing my highly classified, extremely dangerous mission impossible instructions."

The rest of the drive was spent in more thoughtful conversation, some teasing and more than enough laughter.

~ ~

Lukas and Alana were fashionably late for the ball. Luckily, they had reserved seats waiting for them along with Sean, Patrick and some members from the band and their dates. Alana thoroughly enjoyed talking to the band members, particularly Sean. She thought he was a very mature and wise man and had no doubt he would make a fine priest. She especially admired his uncompromising ideals, even when he spoke straightforwardly about it. Alana also took to the boyish Patrick. She couldn't help but be utterly charmed by his entertaining comments. As diverse as Patrick and Sean's personalities were, Alana almost wondered why they were friends. But then again she realized that the best of friendships, like any successful

Sand and Water

marriage, were not bound by common character traits but a mutual choice to work on building and maintaining a relationship.

Lukas also had fun joking around with the rest of the band while they ate dinner, but he wanted Alana to himself again. Strange as it seemed, he missed her attention, even though she was right next to him, giving him a secret smile here and there. He asked her if she wanted to go out for some fresh air in the balcony as soon as she put down her desert fork and wiped her mouth with a napkin. She complied.

Lukas pulled out Alana's chair and helped her up by gently holding her arm. The slight touch was enough to make Alana shiver. Her reaction was not overlooked. Mistakenly blaming Alana's response on the cold draft, Lukas draped her shawl over her shoulders and around her arms. Alana's spine tingled with the sensation of his fingers accidentally grazing across her jaw line and neck. But far more than that, what really affected her was his intuitive show of sensitivity to her needs.

Casually, as if it were the most natural thing in the world, Lukas took Alana's hand and held it in his. It was the first time he had done that and Alana thought she was going to faint with delight. Although her cheeks flushed at the simple romantic gesture, Alana tried to hold her composure.

Lukas had been wanting to hold Alana's hand the entire afternoon they were together but he wondered if she would consider it disrespectful and too forward for him to show his affections. Every time his hand wanted to touch her back or hold her hand, he put them back awkwardly in his pockets. Now, he couldn't contain himself any longer. He let his hand find hers and was glad he did when he saw her shyly smile up at him.

As they wended their way around the tables, hand in hand, Alana accidentally bumped into Faye and Courtney, who were coming from the bar.

"Oh hello, Courtney and Faye," Alana said apprehensively. She clutched Lukas' hand a little too tightly. "How are you two doing? I haven't seen you since—"

Sand and Water

"Since last year's Charity Ball when you passed out at the bar and Luke carried you back to the sorority house."

Alana's surprised expression told Lukas that this was the first she'd heard of that incident. "Oh, I assumed that you or Courtney must have brought me home," she replied feebly.

"Of course not," Faye said in her frostiest voice, "I spent the night with Jeff in this hotel and I meant to thank you for that awesome chance of a lifetime. It's nice to see you two *losers* are still getting along fine." She said that intentionally to remind them that they were both ditched by their "dates" the previous year.

Instinctively, Lukas freed his hand and put it around Alana protectively.

Alana's eyes were flashing. She could bear whatever insult Faye threw her way, but Lukas did not deserve her ire. She opened her mouth, intending to hurl back a nasty remark but something inside stopped her. Instead, Alana found herself saying kindly, "It's nice to see you look beautiful as usual Faye. Please give Jeff my best."

Faye walked away in a huff, leaving Courtney behind her.

Courtney took Alana's hand and gave it a squeeze. "Lanie, you have to forgive Faye. She and all the other sisters have always been jealous that you've had all the cutest guys eating at your hands and even more so now that you have the newest school celebrity as your date while Jeff dumped her on that same night."

Alana was glad that she had bit her tongue. "Courtney, I harbor no grudges against any of you. Believe me. I can only hope that you and Faye and everyone else can forgive me for all of my shortcomings too. I was the most self-absorbed, prima donna who ever lived in the Alpha house."

"Oh Lanie, you are priceless, you know that? I hope we can hang out again soon."

"Me, too. My number is the same if you need to find me. Take care, Courtney."

Although Lukas remained silent the entire time he watched the exchange between the three women, he was far

Sand and Water

from impartial. Initially, he wanted to jump to Alana's defense by saying some corny line like "I feel like more of a winner with Alana as my date that winning that talent show" or some mean-spirited one like "I didn't realize I'd lost something valuable" with a double intended meaning at Faye leaving him last year. But as Lukas watched Alana's temper turn into compassion, he grew amazed at Alana. Then when Alana humbled herself and apologized to Courtney, his respect and admiration for her became unparalleled. He had always known she was no ordinary woman but turning her left cheek at her worst enemy made her that much more Christ-like in his eyes.

As they continued walking to the double doors leading outside, he discovered that ironically, Alana's angry, very angry, eyes were now turned at him. "So, what exactly happened last year? You got me drunk on that bar, took me home and then what? What else are you hiding from me?" she asked through clenched teeth.

Lukas almost smiled at the irony of it all. Just when he thought her a saint, her Irish temper flares up at the most unlikely target.

"Whoa," he said defensively. "First of all, you ordered all of those drinks. We had a conversation at the bar because when I saw you on the dance floor with your eyes practically launching missiles like they are now, I only wanted to make sure you were ok after your "friend" and date publicly humiliated you. You passed out and if I didn't catch you, you would have probably ended up inside an ambulance. I took you straight to your sorority house, put you to bed and left for the airport to spend Christmas with my family. When I came back to the sorority house in January, I was told, very icily by your friend Faye, that you no longer lived there. That is the truth, Lanie." Lukas couldn't help but look hurt.

Alana was immediately apologetic. "I'm sorry. I didn't mean to take out my anger on you. I'm really mad at myself because I don't remember what happened that night. I'd always wondered if someone took advantage of me and all you did was save me from my stupidity. Lukas, thank you. You are so my hero. Can you tell me what we talked about that night? I just need to know if I made a fool of myself."

Lukas instantly forgave her. "Let's see... You said it was a social *faux pas* to be hanging out with you and that even though I was wise like your father, funny and good looking I wasn't going to get lucky because you wanted to remain a--"

"-A twenty year old virgin! I remember saying that. Oh my gosh, I remember everything! I did call you funny and good-looking. I think I wanted you to kiss me, but you never did." Alana covered her mouth in total shock. "I was terrible! Shameless! And what a brazen thing to say right now!"

Lukas laughed, relieved that she remembered and that she was no longer upset and elated that she had wanted to kiss him. Right now, he wanted to kiss her too but he didn't. He told her the truth. "Lanie, I want to kiss you right now but I've promised God that the next woman I kiss will be my bride at the marriage altar, when the priest says I now pronounce you man and wife."

"Oh wow! That sounds so romantic and beautiful. Your wife will be so lucky," Alana declared, impressed.

"As will your future husband, Lanie," Lukas said sadly. *Tell her now, you idiot*, he told himself. *Tell her the truth before this gets out of hand.* But he couldn't bring himself to. He promised himself that he would tell her on the way home. He just wanted to be with her for now.

Alana sensed Lukas' discomfort again. *Secrets*, she thought, *more secrets. What is he hiding from me now?*

They stood there, silently, for a few minutes until an Abba song came on.

Lukas grinned at her. "Should we try out your dancing shoes?"

She giggled. "Definitely!"

They both made a run for the dance floor and danced their uncertainties away. Next, a slow song came on. Lukas couldn't resist pulling Alana close to himself. He smelled her hair and drank her scent in. He wanted to remember this night forever. He didn't know if it would happen again.

Alana lay her head contentedly on Lukas' chest. She didn't know it was possible to fall in love so quickly. Well then again, she did because Lukas had just as quickly captured her heart a long time ago, too. It seemed to Alana that Lukas had absolutely no faults. He was gorgeous, wise, smart, funny and so in love with Jesus. He was so unlike the cyber *LSAbba*, whom she had so many reservations about. Alana took a moment to thank God that Lukas followed her here and prayed that this thing between them would last forever.

"This sure beats cyber dances, doesn't it?" Lukas whispered in her hair.

"Mmm hmmm."

"Lanie, in case I haven't told you, you are better than I ever dreamed of."

She sighed, not looking up. "You too, Lukas."

"Lanie?"

"Shh… since you're not going to kiss me, just let me enjoy being in your arms, ok?"

"I was just going to say that the soft spot you're stepping on—it's my foot."

Alana got off his toe, gave him playful kick on his shin, and kept on dancing. "You better not stop till the clock strikes 12."

~ ~

Lukas and Alana left the ball at 12:15. The ride home was less jovial than the ride going to the Ball. Neither of them wanted the night to end but Alana had to leave for the airport the next day and Lukas had to leave for the Jesuit retreat house in Cape Cod, too.

Lukas pulled his car up to the parking lot of Alana's apartment.

Alana turned to him and spoke. "Luke, I have a confession to make, now… There was one time during the spring when I went to the Adoration Chapel while the Mass was going on. I was there for fifteen minutes or so and then left. When I got to class, I realized that I forgot a book so I went back to get it. I think I saw you praying in there. At

Sand and Water

least I'm pretty sure now it was you. I retrieved my book quietly and looked at you. I saw your sad face but you didn't notice me. I wondered what would make you so depressed and for a minute there, I said a prayer for God to make you happy. Are you happy now?"

This was the opening Lukas had been waiting for and putting off. *It was now or never.* "Yes and no. Lanie, if you don't know it already: I'm in love with you. I always have been and it never went away. I'm even more in love now that I've actually been with you. But..."

Oh great, she thought to herself with dismay. *It figures that there's a 'however' part that's bound to break my heart.* She braced herself mentally.

"...I'm going on a 30 day St. Ignatius Spiritual Exercises retreat tomorrow. It's a silent retreat so I can't call or write to you."

"Oh is that all?" she smiled, momentarily relieved.

"No. There's more. When school resumes, I officially start a discernment process with Fr. Tim Chatham. It means I'm discerning whether I have a religious or marital vocation. During the six month period, I'm not supposed to date anyone because that will interfere with discernment. That means, I can't deliberately contact you or arrange to see you. If we bump into each other, which is unlikely considering you and I never go around the same circles, I of course will say hi like old friends do but I cannot get involved or anything like that. I'm – I'm sorry if this hurts you but I have to ask you to keep your distance from me."

Alana found herself angry for the second time that night but this time her anger was more forceful. "Why in the heck didn't you wait to reveal yourself to me until your discernment was over? What was the purpose of leading me on and making me fall for you now when you are not free to give me your heart entirely?!?!"

"I don't know, Lanie. I thought it was the right time but maybe I made a mistake. I don't know why I thought the Holy Spirit was leading me to tell you the truth now instead of later."

"Don't you dare drag God into this! Quit being a coward by letting Him take the blame. Oooooh, I am so livid...enraged by your poor judgment and for saying all the things that you've said to make me hope of...of...a future together!"

Lukas hung his head. "I don't know what else to say."

Alana's chest was heaving in her fury. "Tell me one thing though, Lukas, if you are in love with me, how can you be in love with the idea of being a priest, too?"

"To be honest, I thought I was surely headed for the marital life but a few months ago, my brother Tomas announced that he was going to get married in the summer after graduation. When he offered my grandmother's engagement ring to his fiancée, she refused it because she wanted to choose her own. That ring came with a letter from my mother before she died. She gave us strict instructions to read it only when one of us was going to ask a woman to marry him.

"Apparently, the letter says that one night when mama was ill and on the verge of dying, she dreamed that a voice from heaven told her that one of her sons was going to become a fine Bishop and another one would marry a fine Catholic woman to raise saints. Since our youngest, Stephen, is autistic and speech impaired, we assumed that the prophecy did not refer to him and he could be whatever he would be. At the back of my mind, I hoped that Tomas would experience a conversion and become a priest, leaving me to marry. But since Tomas is still engaged, I have doubts that it will happen so that leaves me with the future of priesthood as predicted by heaven.

"I know my mother offered her illnesses for at least one of her sons to become a priest and I just wanted to make sure she did not suffer or die in vain, you know. Now, I'm not saying I will be a priest solely because of that which is why I need proper and formal discernment but I only want to know God's will, His plan for my life. Please don't hate me. I just feel as though God is calling me to do something and I have to figure out what it is."

Despite her rage, Alana understood where Lukas was coming from. It was actually a virtue to seek God's will instead of one's own, she grudgingly admitted to herself. She did not speak for a long time.

"I am sorry, Lanie. I would ask you to wait for me but there is no guarantee you're waiting for something so it wouldn't be fair to you."

Against her better judgment, Alana's wounded pride surfaced on top of her anger. *Now he thinks about fairness? How could he? It's really his fault we're in this mess, again.* Blinded by her wrath, Alana wanted to lash out at Lukas, to lacerate his heart over and over again, just as he did hers.

In a steely tone, Alana's final words to Lukas were, "It's unbelievable that things would end this way again. I hope you'll understand if I stay away from you completely in the future, Lukas. I cannot have you break my heart again. It needs to be whole for the man I am going to marry someday and I hope it won't be you."

Alana got out of the car, ran up the stairs, unlocked her door and cried herself to sleep.

Chapter 19

Lukas was miserable during the entire ride to the Jesuit Retreat House. Sean and Patrick tried to lift his spirits by poking fun at each other but Lukas' mood remained dismal. They just decided to leave him alone with his thoughts.

Lukas kept repeating Alana's harsh words over and over his head. That was not how he wanted last night to end. It was worse than his worst case scenario. He hoped Alana would say "I'll wait forever for you" but that was unrealistic, he supposed.

Did she really mean that she hoped it wouldn't be him she would marry or did she say it in the heat of the moment? Above all things, those were the words that hurt him the most because in his heart, if he ever got married, he wanted to marry only her. If that happened, he swore he would spend the rest of his life making amends to her and never break her heart.

Who was he kidding? He was not worthy of Alana and probably not worthy of becoming a groom of the Church, either, if he was so in love with a woman. With his palm, Lukas wiped a tear that threatened to roll down his cheek.

Lukas stared outside his glass window aimlessly. The pain of Alana's words had not been dulled by the countryside scenery covered in a white layer of snow. He might as well become a priest now, he thought, that way he'd never have a broken heart or break anyone else's.

Lukas prayed desperately, "Lord Jesus, please take me. No one else will and no one else should."

The tires crunched on the gravel as Sean drove up the black iron gates of the Sacred Heart Retreat House. Since 1672, when Jesus first revealed His heart to a French nun named Sr. Mary Margaret, the Sacred Heart became a popular name for many churches and retreat houses. Not long after, the Sacred Heart statue and pictures made its way to homes and more recently, to Lukas' bedside.

Though his own heart was breaking, Lukas had the sense to offer up his suffering to the Sacred Heart of Jesus. He repeated his daily morning offering:

"*O Sacred Heart of Jesus,*" he prayed in absolute sadness. "*Through the Immaculate Heart of Mary, I offer you the prayers, works, joys and sufferings of this day in union with the Holy Sacrifice of the Mass, for the intentions of your Sacred Heart, in reparation for my sins and for the intentions of our Holy Father. Amen.*"

When the car pulled up into the driveway, Lukas saw a huge cross erected in front of the retreat house. The three men got out of the car and took in the breath taking view of the ocean. Gradually, the peace and serenity of the place settled on Lukas. He felt his morale slightly improve. When he looked closely at the body of Christ nailed to the wooden cross, he saw the outstretched arms welcoming him eagerly. As always, running into Jesus' arms was the best place to heal a broken heart.

~ ~

The Spiritual Exercises is a month long program composed of a series of meditations, prayers and contemplative practices as written and developed by St. Ignatius of Loyola, founder of the Jesuits, or the Society of Jesus. Over a period of time, in Lukas' case thirty days, retreatants are given presentations or meditations on the key topics of God's generosity and mercy and the complex reality of human sin; the life and public ministry of Jesus, Jesus' passion and death; of Jesus' Resurrection, his Ascension, and finally the pouring-forth of the Holy Spirit at Pentecost. Throughout the retreat, the retreatants meet regularly with a spiritual director to discuss their experiences of prayer and reflection, and to receive guidance in praying with the Exercises, in thinking about what they are doing, and in the interpretation of what is happening to them.

On the fourth day of Lukas' retreat, he learned a lesson that seemed tailor made for his situation. The reflection was about detachment from one's hopes and dreams, goals and preferences and to seek only what God's purpose is for one's life. At this point, Lukas was still hurting from their last date and still pining away for Alana. He knew that if it were entirely up to him, he would never get over her. But Lukas had faith and he relied on the grace of God to detach himself from his own will. Lukas prayed for the grace of "indifference" as St. Ignatius liked to put it, for his own desire of marriage, more particularly marriage to Alana. God did not fail Lukas' plea. Seeing this young man's desire to serve only the Divine Will, God blessed him with a liberation from his own human will.

On the eleventh day of the retreat, Lukas received God's invitation to use the talents and gifts he had been given to serve Him. Lukas thought long and hard about his passion for science and his aptitude for biochemistry. Lukas had always been driven with the desire to find the cure for cancer. But the more he worked on his projects and experiments in the laboratory, the more hopeless the situation seemed. The only cures and remissions Lukas had seen were those that had been hailed as miraculous, attributed by the faithful to God's power but condemned by the scientific community as flukes. Lukas began to wonder if there was some other purpose he had to serve. Were there other diseases out there threatening the lives of humans and tearing apart families? What other causes could benefit from his aptitude? Was God leading him to keep trying to find the cure for cancer or did He have a new plan for his life?

Lukas dwelled on this lesson longer than the others. There were so many unethical issues in the scientific world these days. First there was the issue of cloning, the use of aborted fetuses on vaccines and medicines and more recently the up rise of embryonic stem cell research. The newest discovery made Lukas sick to his stomach. Stem cell research deliberately merged a female's egg with a male's sperms to conceive life. The new living being was then used for research and heartlessly discarded when they served their purpose. Lukas detested knowing that some of his peers played God in this way.

What a complete disregard for the sanctity of human life there is in science and medicine and how ironic that it has destroyed the very life it was made to serve, he thought to himself regretfully.

As Lukas sat in silence, reflecting on the so-called "progress" of science and medicine, his thoughts took him to his mother and father. When his mother Monica became pregnant with Stephen, she had been told from the onset that there was a problem with the baby. The doctors tried to convince her to have an abortion to save her life. In Spain, the laws allowed for a woman to terminate her pregnancy if her physical or mental health required it. His father, Frank, an experienced obstetrician, did not have the heart to tell Monica what to choose—he left the choice entirely to her. Monica chose to carry her baby to full term even if he or she would be handicapped and prayed that God would give them both their lives. However, Monica died while giving birth to Stephen.

Lukas couldn't imagine what his father must have felt at that time. Lukas certainly didn't blame him for losing his faith but he was disappointed that he and his brothers were deprived of knowing the faith his mother died for.

Lukas smiled, reminiscing about his mother, a devout Catholic, who insisted on making her life and even her death a testimony to the belief that God held all of sacred life in his hands: He could create it, give it and He could certainly take it away.

Monica Swenson was a saint in Lukas' eyes. He had no clear memories of her but she left him a legacy of faith. Thinking about her brought a pain in his heart, the pain of a child who grew up without a mother. Suddenly, Lukas recalled a memory that he had long ago buried in his mother's grave.

When Lukas was seven years old, Monica Swenson was lying in her hospital bed, her stomach round and ready to bring forth a child into the world. She was weak physically, but her spirits were higher than Lukas had ever felt them.

Faintly, she called Lukas to her bed and he came over right away.

"Luke," she said. "I am about to deliver your baby brother or sister. Please take care of the baby in case mama is not around."

Lukas nodded sadly. At seven years old, he couldn't articulate his emotions but he knew she was saying goodbye in case something happened.

"You are a good son, Luke. You will grow up to be a wonderful man, I know it. I just know it. Tell mama now, what do you want to be when you grow up, *mijo?*"

Lukas stared transfixed at the IV that ran medicine into his mother's arm. "Ummm, a scientist, mama. I will help you find the cure for your illness."

Monica smiled at her little boy. "That would make me happy indeed. Have you figured out if you are going to work in a laboratory or a hospital like your papa?"

"I don't know, mama. You can tell me what you want and I will do it."

Monica held Lukas' hand and kissed it. "It isn't about what mama wants, *mijo.* It is always about what God wants, God's will. Now think about where you can serve God the most, alright, because that is what you should grow up to be. And if you keep serving Him as He asks then someday we will be together again in heaven. I promise it. *Te quierro mucho.*"

Lukas had almost forgotten those final words his mother had spoken to him. But remembering them now released him from a burden that he had been carrying for a long time. He was free to choose whatever God led him to do.

If God asked him to work as a professor teaching ethical science, he would pursue it. If God called him to work in a pharmaceutical company researching medicinal cures, that's what he would do and he would work for no less than a principled company. If God invited him to work in a non-profit laboratory serving indigent patients, he would do it willingly, untiringly making sure that he did not compromise the Catholic Church teachings.

Lukas almost broke his silence at this startling discovery. *This is better than finding any cure,* he thought to himself. *Because apparently finding the cure for one's soul is infinitely better than finding the cure to one's body.*

That night, Lukas thought of his grandmother, too. Elena Monteverde had died in her bed peacefully when Lukas was only fifteen. His grandmother knew that her death was coming and she was looking forward to it because she was going to be reunited with her husband, her parents and her only daughter.

Elena Monteverde's final day when she still had her speech control was spent with her three grandchildren. She talked to all three of them cheerfully, as if death was not at her door and as if pain was not wracking her cancer-ridden body. Elena had refused the option of euthanasia, offering up to heaven every pain that she could endure. Elena's agonizing days were spent waiting for God to take her earthly life and for the Blessed Mother to help her be "born into eternal life."

"Tomas, I just saw your report card!" she called out to her oldest grandchild, the reproof in her voice unmistakable. "When are you ever going to take your classes seriously?"

"Never *abuela*," Tomas replied without apology. "There is so much to do outside of school that studies waste my time."

"Don't say that or the seminary will never take you in with your poor grades!" Abruptly, Elena turned to Lukas and gave him a piece of her mind, too.

"Lukas, be careful who you marry, ok? Do not be deceived by looks. She has to be a lover of the Virgin Mary. You do know Our Blessed Mother, don't you?"

Lukas gave her a lopsided smile. "Yes *abuela*, you only have 30 pictures and statues in your home of her many different faces."

"Good. Remember that face well. Your bride will be as beautiful as her outside and inside especially. I have prayed to Our Lady of the Pillar to make sure of that."

Stephen, who was only eight years old then, brutally frank and curious as always, asked her, "But what if Lukas becomes a priest, abuela? He cannot marry anymore."

Elena closed her eyes. "Then he will have Mary for a mother-in-law...Now, that doesn't sound right. I suppose if you become a priest Lukas that would indeed make your mother very happy..."

Those words Lukas remembered very well. But now, placing it beside his mother's dying words, he realized that Monica wanted only God's will for him and he was free to make a decision on his life. The only voice that was worth paying attention to was God's voice.

This was the breakthrough of Lukas' retreat. He was free to be whoever God called him to be: whether it was in a seminary in Europe or a laboratory in America.

Lukas returned to SILU with a renewed sense of freedom. He was free from whatever held him in captivity: his past and all the bondage that came with it. And, by God's grace, he was even free from the irresistible longing for Alana. He learned that this feeling of liberation was a common experience on most retreatants who undertook the Spiritual Exercises.

In the silence of thirty days, broken only by his conversations with the spiritual director, Lukas experienced a deeper conversion in his spiritual life. In the light of God's love, Jesus passion, death and resurrection, and the Holy Spirit's power, Lukas' broken soul was profoundly transformed. He emerged not only a liberated man but a man with a mission. He now knew that God had a master plan for his life, to follow in the footsteps of Jesus Christ. He wasn't sure yet if the plan involved marriage or the priesthood as following Jesus is possible in both vocations. But he would have to figure that out for himself in the ensuing months, with Fr. Tim Chatman's help.

Chapter 20

A disconcerted Alana lingered at the family room after the family rosary was over. Joe and Maria knew there was something troubling her so Joe had ushered Jack out of the room to give Maria and Alana some privacy. Alana's story tumbled out of her lips in a rush.

"Oh mom," Alana sobbed. "I can't believe I said that to him. Those were very hurtful words. I want to apologize and tell Lukas I'll wait, but I'm afraid it'll complicate his discernment and make him wrongly choose me over God. I don't want to do that because if God wants him as a priest in the Church, that's where he should be. I shouldn't be the block standing between him and God's will."

It had been three days after the horrific Charity Ball. Since Alana had had ample time to reflect and pray about it, she was more rational now and completely remorseful.

Maria gave her daughter a sympathetic hug. She knew that a heart break was the worst thing imaginable to a young woman. Maria searched her mind for what to say to console her but the home schooling aids did not equip her for this moment. If Alana was a child with a scrape on her knee, Maria would know what to say or do but seeing Alana was now a grown woman, she felt at a loss on how to handle the situation.

Maria thought long and hard before answering. Pop culture bombarded mothers with the advice to be "friends" with their daughters. On the surface, that sounded like the most fail-proof discovery of the century but Maria was wary of such advice. Although Maria did feel like the grown-up Alana had become a friend to her when they did fun things together, Maria liked to maintain that she was still a mother with years of wisdom to offer her daughter. And judging by her daughter's quest for advice, Maria surmised that Alana had deliberately turned to her instead of her friends because she trusted her mother. Thus, Maria junked the pop culture's take on the family life. She let her strong, sensible, maternal side do the talking.

Caressing Alana's hair, Maria pointed out the obvious. "Well, you can't contact him anyway right now, honey. You just have to wait and see what happens and trust that God is ministering to him as He is ministering to you. You can also pray and fast for Lukas, you know."

Alana mulled over the suggestion. "That sounds like a worthy project mom. It's about all I can do to love him from a distance. Did you and dad ever go through this? I need to know there's a possible happy ending out there for me."

"Well your dad and I went through tough times for sure when we had to wait. It took us three years to wait to adopt the perfect baby. We both knew that we couldn't have one biologically so we always thought it was God's will for us to adopt. We kept looking and searching and temporarily housed foster children but nothing ever worked out. Finally, we went on a pilgrimage to Fatima, Portugal to plead with Our Blessed Mother for some motherly interference. On our first day, one of the sisters from a convent nearby gave us the best news, that there was a baby waiting to be adopted. When we saw you, we knew at once you were our long awaited God's gift from heaven. There is always a happy ending to every story that comes from God. You are ours."

Alana had heard that story so many times in slightly different versions but she never got tired of hearing it and her mother knew it. Already, her agitation had turned to calm acceptance of her predicament.

Alana rested her chin on her hands and asked her mother, "Do you think things happened the way they were supposed to, mom, as part of God's plan or did we goof it up?"

"We can't look back and change the past, Lanie. We can only live in God's will in the present. As for the future, Romans 8:20 says that "we know that in all things God works for the good of those who love Him." Speaking of the future, do you want to hear some exciting news?"

Alan perked up. "What?"

Sand and Water

    Maria called her husband back into the room. "Joe, we need you in here."

    Joe popped his head in the doorway, a concerned smile on his face. "So did the both of you solve all of the world's problems or did you need your hero to do that for you?"

    "We took care of everything, superman. Or rather, God's taking care of it," said Maria. "You're here as the bearer of good news."

    "I see." Joe smiled broadly, walked over to Alana and took his daughter's hand. "Well Lanie, since you told us last year that you were interested in finding your birth parents, we contacted the convent in Portugal. Sr. Mary Margaret, who helped us facilitate the adoption, had been assigned to another convent in Africa. However, five months ago, Sr. Mary Margaret called to tell us that she was back in Portugal and would love to speak with us if we wanted to visit them for the summer. We hired a lawyer and he took care of the legalities of getting an approval to open your records."

    "Oh my gosh! Really and truly? Didn't Sr. Mary Margaret tell you everything you needed to know though when you first met her?"

    "Sr. Mary Margaret told us what was necessary to process the adoption but she said that your birth mother gave her specific instructions to reveal certain things only if her child wanted to know. So what say we head off to Portugal for the summer, after your graduation?"

    Alana leapt up from the carpeted floor and ran over to hug her father and mother. "Oh you are the best set of parents ever! Let's go now!"

    Maria laughed. "You have to graduate first Lanie as this *is* your graduation present."

    Alana got ready for bed that night, feeling that her spirits had vastly improved since she woke up that morning. The thought of finding information on her history was exhilarating. She could never change her past, that she was sure of and she had the maturity to accept things as they were but who knows if it could possibly have answers to her future?

Sand and Water

    Alana desperately wanted to share her news with someone. No, scratch that-- she only wanted to talk to Lukas about it. Alana sighed deeply. He probably did not want to see or talk to her again and she didn't blame him. After all that he had done for her– audaciously seeking her notwithstanding the odds, his faithfulness in waiting despite her indifference, his chivalry in the face of her drunken stupidity, his complete love for God as opposed to her love of self-- she had some nerve to angrily hurl cruel words at him that she never meant. Oh if she could only undo what she said and tell him… tell him what?

    I'm sorry. I'm so sorry. Sorry that I said what I said, mostly sorry that I can't have you, Lukas. When the God of the Universe, infinite and powerful decides He needs you, I can't compete with that.

    Alana was back to feeling stinging pain once more. She took out her laptop out of its black traveling case and played her favorite CD but even Julio Iglesias couldn't soothe her wounds tonight.

    She badly wanted to apologize to Lukas for her burst of anger and pride, to assure him that she didn't blame him for what he did and that she did not mean anything she had said. At the same time, Alana wanted to respect his request to keep her distance, to keep his discernment free from interferences from her. Fasting and prayer were good, but she felt she had to do something more. But what?

    Alana picked up the phone to call Laura. Laura answered in one ring.

    "Can I call you right back?" she whispered excitedly. "I think Jimmy just might propose tonight and I want to stick around so he doesn't lose his nerve!"

    "Sure. You can call me whenever, its not important," was her reply.

    Alana hung up quickly. She felt happy for her friend and wanted her to enjoy the night. Alana did not want to drag Laura down needlessly by going on and on about Lukas. She had already burned Laura's ears the past two days. She was probably tired of hearing the same old mantra.

Sand and Water

Alana scrolled down the numbers on her phone book, looking for Kerry's number. She began to dial it but realized that the time difference between Hawaii and Georgia would likely catch Kerry at a bad time.

Alana decided to email Kerry and maybe Danielle, too. She was better at writing than talking anyway. Alana checked her email before she got down to composing one. She had one message in her inbox since this morning when she last checked it. It was from Danielle addressed to all the girls in the Friday faith sharing group. She wrote:

Hey Ladies,

When we get back for the second semester, there's something I need your help with. The Students for Life SILU chapter is part of a massive campaign on the anniversary of *Roe vs Wade*. We need volunteers to do some work for Saturday, January 21st[th] and on the day of the anniversary itself Sunday the 22nd to create flyers, letters, postcards, stuff them in envelopes and send them out for the Sunday Masses at all the local parishes. Since most of the staff and usual volunteers have decided to head out to the March for life Rally in DC, we're short staffed to do the logistics for our local activities. Can I count on you? Any form of help is welcome. Your big or small acts may save a life. Thanks.

P.S. In case you're worried about working on a Sunday, I think this counts as an exception — Remember Jesus said that we shouldn't hesitate to take out an ox that's stuck in mud. So feel free to think of me as the dumb ox.

Danielle

Alana had to laugh at that. Of course, she wanted to help out Danielle. The pro-life movement was very close to her heart since-- since Lukas had made her aware of it at the Christmas Program. She sighed. Everything always pointed her back to Lukas.

Am I ever going to get over him, Lord? How? ...I suppose I can just keep my distance like he asked and let You take over.

With that, Alana simply poured out her heart on an email. When she was done, she glanced at a prayer card of Our Lady of Sorrows. It showed Mary with seven swords piercing her Immaculate Heart. Alana knew that her pain was nowhere near Mary's but she also knew that even the littlest offering to the Immaculate Heart of Mary could make a remarkable difference before the throne of God.

"Blessed Mother, I offer up my heart ache to your Immaculate Heart. May it comfort you in your pain for the loss of the unborn and bring peace to their mothers and fathers who grieve their sins."

Chapter 21

From the distance, a flash of lighting lit the dark, overcast morning sky. Five seconds later, thunder clapped. The three day thunderstorm in Boston wreaked havoc on the first week of classes for the second semester. Car and human traffic was everywhere in the campus. Slushy mud with snow lined the walkways and seeped into the slippery hallways.

The awful weather almost deterred Lukas from meeting Sean at the Conference Rooms of the Student Activities Center. Almost, but the cause was too important to skip. Besides, Sean was counting on him for some help lugging boxes around.

Lukas stepped out of his car into the pouring rain. He sprinted to the building, almost tripped on the entrance steps and literally slipped into the four conference rooms that Students for Life- SILU had reserved especially for the campaign.

Lukas wiped off his muddy boots and took off his rain coat near the doorway. As soon as Lukas was done shaking off the wet outdoors, he scanned the room for Sean or Patrick. Patrick wasn't there yet but Sean was over at the far corner of the room, by a table across some girls he recognized from the Handmaids a capella group. There was Frances, Amanda, Jean, Kerry and ...right beside her was Alana.

Every instinct in Lukas felt like bolting out of the room when he saw Alana, but at the same time, he wanted to see her, too. His heart pounding in his ears, Lukas walked at a snail's pace over to Sean. None of them had noticed him coming in so he overheard some snippets of the conversation as he slowly made his way over to them.

"Jeez Lanie," Frances had scolded her in jest. "Just lick those envelopes instead of wasting your time with the glue, will ya?"

Anabelle Hazard

"Yuck! They taste awful and I wouldn't want to receive an envelope that someone licked," Alana replied, making a face.

Jean giggled. "Oh, I'd want to receive an envelope that *someone* sealed with a kiss." She looked at the table across from them, at the drummer from the band *Psalm 96*, Cole Yencheck. Cole was a business graduate student.

"Jean, you've read one too many romance novels," Danielle rebuked her. "Guys like that don't exist anymore. They email or text nowadays."

Alana chuckled, as she sealed another envelope with glue. "Yeah, take it from this English lit major, guys today aren't like the romantic heroes of fiction." *The men today run off to seminary and break your heart,* she added silently.

"Oh hey, there you are Luke!" Sean called out, seeing Lukas approach.

At the mention of Lukas, Alana's back stiffened. She didn't need to turn around to know that he was there. *How much of the conversation had he heard?* she wondered. *And what does he think about what I just said?*

Lukas heard every word Alana had said. He didn't see her face when she made her comment so it made him wonder: *Did she say that with sadness or with sarcasm?*

Lukas avoided the ladies table and went up to Sean. "What's my assignment?"

"Here, take some of the boxes from the hallway and bring them in here."

Lukas did as he was told. He walked back out into the hallway, causing Alana to release the breath that she had been holding. She did not know what to say to him, how to act around him, couldn't even look at him with her heart beating so violently in her chest.

Lukas carried about twenty boxes in silently. Each time he came through the door, he thought about what to say to Alana. A casual 'hi' didn't seem right. He bided his time thinking of and waiting for the right opening. Maybe she would acknowledge him or say something to him. But twenty minutes later, Alana showed no sign of paying attention to his coming and going. She chatted gaily with her friends, but not once looked his way.

Maybe, he thought to himself with regret, *she did really mean what she had told me that she wanted nothing to do with me in the future.* He decided to keep his silence.

Alana could hear Lukas' footsteps every time he left the room and every time he came back. She had unbelievably distinguished his muffled, even footsteps from all the noisy racket in the room. She could even smell that masculine after shave that he wore during the Charity Ball above the pungent odor of glue in front of her. She couldn't bring herself to look at him though, fearing that she would lose her heart all over again.

Gradually, over a span of twenty minutes, it began to bother her that he acted as though she didn't exist. The more she noticed his silence, the more she found herself growing angry. He was the one who told her to stay away and now he wanted to completely ignore her presence. *He was acting like a...a...jerk!*

"The boxes are all in here, Sean. What next?" Lukas asked.

"Hey Dani, do you need help in your assembly line?" Sean called out to Danielle.

"Sure. Sit over there by the girls," Danielle yelled back. She pointed to the table where Alana was unthinkingly, then realized her mistake. She shot Alana a look that conveyed *I'm sorry.*

Alana threw her a look back that plainly accused *How could you?!?*

Lukas missed Danielle's look as he kept his penetrating gaze on Alana. Hence, he only saw Alana's scornful one.

How can she go from being in love with me a month ago to hating me? Lukas couldn't be this close to Alana and not feel anything. He believed he was over it, over her, but she still got under his skin. Since he did not want to see that scowl on Alana's face again, he tried to finagle his way out of the assembly line.

Lukas cleared his throat. "Um, is there anything else I can do?"

Sand and Water

Sean looked up from his charts. Then he realized what was going on. The tension was so thick he almost suffocated in its fog. "Oh, here, Lukas, make some phone calls for me and coordinate with the parish volunteers."

Alana's perceptive ears heard that exchange above the girls' chatter. *Now he can't stand being with me?* she thought, incredulously, painfully.

Lukas ambled over to the phone lines. He didn't want to make any calls at all. He wanted to sit across from Alana, look into her eyes and make her smile. He looked at her briefly. She was smiling at one of her friends. She was smiling at everyone and everything else around her but him. Lukas sat down and made his first call.

Making phone calls wasn't so bad once he got the hang of it, he thought. Lukas was actually starting to enjoy talking to people on the other end of the line. He almost forgot about Alana's presence. Almost, but not quite. She was still there, looking beautiful in her blue sweater and dark denim jeans.

Alana caught Lukas laughing over the phone. Though she tried excruciatingly to smile and catch up with the conversation around her, all of her senses were attuned to Lukas. *What's so funny over there? Who's making you laugh?* she wondered with a twinge of jealousy.

Lukas hung up the phone, still chuckling. He turned to the direction of Alana's table and saw her give him a strange, puzzled look. *Can I ever make you laugh again?*

Alana saw Lukas' smile fade into a thin line of seriousness. *Oh, he was still so handsome even when his dimple was gone.* More than anything, she just wanted to...to hold his hand again and hear him say *I'm not going to be a priest, Lanie. I want to marry you!*

Alana looked away angrily. He should have done his discernment before sweeping her off her feet like that! Her old wounds resurfaced.

Lukas was beginning to feel some hope when he first caught Alana looking at him. Then he saw the temper flicker in her eyes. He knew that temper very well. *I've lost my chance*, he concluded sadly.

Sand and Water

From her seat, Kerry noticed almost everything that went on silently between her two friends. She wished she could do something about it. They were both in so much pain over nothing, really. Kerry believed God would work everything in due time but that these two were just so impatient and headstrong that they could not see past their own feelings.

Kerry softly asked Alana, "Would you like to go to the restroom with me?"

Alana arose from her chair and followed Kerry inside. "Oh Kerry! He hates me! He does! And I hate him back! No, I don't. Why won't he say anything to me? Is he still upset with me?"

Kerry guessed as much. "How would you feel if I intervened?"

Alana gave her a sad smile. "He's going to become a priest Kerry. I'm afraid there's nothing you can do about it."

Kerry rolled her eyes and drawled, "I don't mean *that* kind of intervention. I'm not God. I just meant maybe you can leave with a little bit of peace if he talked to you, that's all."

Alana shrugged, "He won't, but you can try."

Kerry and Alana left the rest room together. Alana settled back on her seat while Kerry joined Lukas near the phone. Kerry gave it another fifteen minutes before initiating the topic with Lukas.

"So... while you're in discernment, are you under pain of mortal sin if you talk to Lanie or something?" she asked in a joking way.

Lukas looked at her, suspiciously at first. Then at seeing her sweet smile, he told her the truth. "No, I can talk to her. I just didn't think she wanted to talk to me so I'm being respectful of her wishes."

Kerry rolled her eyes at him. Using a honeyed voice to balance the harshness of her words, she crooned, "C'mon Luke. You told Lanie to scram so she's just trying to be invisible."

"But I didn't mean..." he protested, then stopped himself when Kerry walked away. With a resolve to be more amiable, Lukas got up from his seat, and walked towards the girls' table.

At that moment, Patrick came strolling into the conference room, late as usual.

"Reporting for duty, Sir Sean," he said with a mock salute. Patrick didn't wait for a reply. As soon as Patrick spotted Kerry, he grabbed a chair and plopped himself right next to her. "Well hello, ex-competitor, haven't seen you since the talent show. How have you been?"

"Busy," Kerry replied matter-of-factly. She was aware that Patrick had been trying to get her attention since the start of the talent show but Kerry was not impressed. Although Patrick wasn't bad looking and the other girls in fact thought he was cute, Kerry did not care for his devil-may-care attitude. She thought him too asinine, and his red hair was totally not her type.

Patrick was not daunted by Kerry's lack of interest. Patrick in fact liked the challenge she presented. "All work and no play makes Kerry a... busy girl," he joked, a twinkle in his eye. "You should've taken my offer to go to the Charity Ball. It was a blast."

Kerry didn't glance away from her stack of flyers when she answered him. "Yeah, it's not my thing. I was curled up that night with a good book... a *history* book," she said pointedly.

"Aww, you should have come with me. I could have changed your mind about parties. Lanie had a great time, didn't you, Lanie?"

Amanda and Jean gave Alana a bewildered look.

Frances demanded, "I thought you said you weren't going, Lanie. Who did you go with?"

"She went with me," Lukas answered quietly. He had snuck up to the table while they were absorbed in the engaging repartee between Kerry and Patrick.

Amanda and Jean exchanged another look with their mouths open. Kerry glared at them and shook her head, willing them not to ask anymore questions.

Frances deliberately ignored her. "Well?" she persisted. "Did you have fun?"

Lukas and Alana answered at the same time.

"I did," Lukas said.

"I didn't," Alana said.

Alana stared at Lukas. *Of course you had fun, your date didn't tell you to jump off the cliff when the evening was over,* she thought. *You knew how the evening was going to end, unlike me who unfortunately had the rug pulled out from underneath.*

Lukas stared at Alana. *Why would you say you didn't have fun? Are you deliberately trying to hurt me again?*

Alana gulped at the hurt look on Lukas' face. She stood up abruptly. Alana could not take her mind and emotions wreaking havoc on her any more. "I have to get going. I have work to do at *The Magis* office."

The Magis was the English Department's quarterly publication, a collection of writings consisting of short stories, poetry, essays and photo essays from the contributing students. The term *Magis* literally means more. It was coined from the Latin motto *Ad Majorem Dei Gloriam,* which stands for 'for the glory of God'. Pursuant to St. Ignatius philosophy, *magis* refers to the philosophy of doing more for the greater glory of God.

Alana had served as an editor for *The Magis* since she shifted her majors. Although she did not have to be there today, Alana needed an excuse to leave and *The Magis* provided a convenient alibi.

Lukas watched Alana push her chair away and leave the table. His heart sank. *Oh Jesus,* he prayed. *Doesn't it just figure that when I search for Lanie, I can't find her? But when I don't need to see her, she shows up? If I weren't so miserable, I'd find this whole thing so amusing."*

Alana shrugged into her coat, tied her scarf around her neck and opened the door.

From his seat, Cole overheard Alana's announcement and saw Alana leaving. Quickly, Cole assessed this as his chance to talk to her alone so he grabbed his coat and umbrella and called out to her, "I'm heading that way. I'll walk with you over there."

Lukas saw everything. His eyes followed the two of them leaving under Cole's umbrella. With a shake of his head, he thought: *Lanie's already moved on. Please Jesus, have mercy on me, don't let me see her again so that I can forget her.*

Chapter 22

Although Alana needed the umbrella as a shelter from the cold hail and rain, she was not exactly ecstatic to have any sort of company, even if it was someone as nice as Cole. She really wanted to be alone, but Cole had something in his mind.

"Hey Lanie, I'm actually about to turn in my first poetry to *The Magis* so I was just hoping to get your opinion on it."

Alana looked at Cole's eager face and could not refuse his request. "Sure, let's get into the ed's office and take a look at your work."

They walked in silence the rest of the way. It was hard to talk anyway with the sound of the rain and thunder. Besides, they were trying to concentrate on avoiding the puddles.

As soon as they reached the English Department building, which housed *The Magis* office, Alana led Cole into one of the editor's rooms in the back. Alana sat on one of the editor's desks and Cole took the seat across from the desk.

Cole took out a piece of paper from his jacket pocket and slid it across the table to Alana. Alana read every word slowly, carefully. She could not help but be moved by the tender romantic love articulated in his poetry.

"Cole, this is absolutely perfect! I didn't know business grads were so poetic," Alana gushed.

"Thanks, Lanie. If you'll consider publishing it in the next issue, can I ask you for a small favor? Can you put just before my name the dedication: 'To my partner Joshua, with love'?"

Alana's mouth dropped open. *Cole was Frisco—er, gay?* She suppressed a gasp and said calmly as if she was making small talk about the stormy weather, "Are you gay?"

"I'm not sure yet. I like both men and women. But now I feel I might be totally gay with my intense feelings for Joshua."

Anabelle Hazard

Heaven help me, Alana thought disbelievingly. She couldn't deal with this right now. *The Magis* teacher advisor Eileen Messick, perhaps the only remaining conservative teacher in campus, was extremely strict about the paper's publications being in conformity with Church teachings. Alana looked around desperately for another editor to help her explain *The Magis* policy to Cole but there was no one working on a stormy Saturday. "Um, I can't do that, Cole. I can publish your work but the dedication would be against the publication's and the Church's beliefs. It would be like sanctioning homosexual acts."

Cole frowned. "I knew you would say that. Why are you being so discriminating? Isn't Christianity always harping on unity and yet your backward views on issues are so divisive! Gay people only want to be happy."

Alana felt she wasn't equipped for this but she tried to argue anyway, "Well, the Church teaches that homosexuals are not at all evil – only that homosexual acts are sinful. And I don't mean to judge you at all, Cole. I mean look at you – you are such a nice guy. You work for pro-life causes and you play worship songs at the talent show, inspiring more people to worship God and to obey His commandments of thou shall not kill. You are far better than anyone out there, than me! But God knows what will make us happy. After all, He created us and if He says through our Church that its wrong to commit homosexual acts then we have to trust that its for our own good and happiness even though we can't see the point right now. All Christians are doing is standing up for God enacted laws, that's all – just like we stand up for laws against abortion. It's not about judging gay people."

Cole sneered at her lecture. "You would never understand what gay people go through. You are Miss Perfect in your *perfect* size 4 and *perfect* perky attitude with a *perfectly* happy life."

Alana sighed sadly. After two hours of bottled up emotions, all her feelings needed an outlet and unfortunately for Cole, he was the sounding board. "That's not true at all. I have a lot of faults to contend with. My basic instinct tells me to be selfish, to be arrogant and to be angry when people hurt me but I have to act against those same instincts if I am working toward my salvation and sanctification. Believe me, I struggle with my human nature all the time and in fact, today, I so failed. I deliberately hurt the man I am in love with. And if you must know, the man I want is not in love with me so – so much for your *perfect* theory."

Cole turned sarcastic. "So what you're saying is that gay instincts are wrong and we have to counter them and struggle with them all the time, for as long as we live practically. Then we'd all be like priests and consecrated religious in that way: we have to be celibate all our lives!"

His sarcasm was lost in Alana, who was wrapped up in her own little heartbreak. She nodded heartily. "Exactly! Now, you see you're not in such bad company. You're also in the same company as virgins – namely me! – who have to struggle with their passions while they are single. And you're also in the same boat as married couples who have to be self-controlled when they are abstaining from sex while using the Natural Family Planning Method."

Suddenly, Alana was struck with inspiration. She added gently, "God's plan for sex and marriage is to mirror the love of Jesus Christ for His Church. In His own words, Jesus said "I came that you may have life and have it to the full." From this we know that the sexual act belongs in a marital context and has to be done with openness to life. That's why contraception and abortion are so wrong because it takes away the gift of life that God wants to bless us with. Sex and marriage are to be done under God's laws, not randomly and indiscriminately. The thing is Cole, we're all subject to our Creator's laws and we're not all beasts. We've got souls and God gives us the grace to overcome our temptations whatever our state of life is."

Cole sat thoughtfully for a minute or two. Not once had Alana gotten mad at him or judged him the way he feared a priest would. Cole had always held Alana in high regard after meeting her at the Charity Ball. But now he was amazed by her spirituality and her wisdom. His tone was gentle now as some understanding began to creep in. He hung his head. "I guess I can't be a cafeteria Catholic —

pro-life and pro-gay marriage, huh? If I am to be a good Catholic, I'd have to obey the Church Magisterium. I wish I could understand the reasons fully."

"You can try to. It's in theological documents somewhere and they explain it far better than I ever can. But even if you can't always understand, you can obey. St. Ignatius equates obedience with love."

Cole stared at the wooden cross behind Alana. "Oh, I'd give anything to have a different cross."

Alana looked at Cole and felt so much compassion for him. Truly, he had a heavy cross to carry if he was gay. Then Alana remembered that at one time she believed wrongly about the Church teaching on women and how she thought she knew more than the Pope himself. With sympathy, she touched his hand and said, "I know obedience is a difficult word in this day and age, Cole but I believe we have to obey our God-given leaders in our Jesus-given Church."

Cole felt sympathy for her, too. "You're right on that but you're so wrong on Lukas, Lanie. Lukas is in love with you. I don't know what obstacles there are that he's facing but I do know he is a fine man and men like those only come along once in your life. So if I were you, I'd help him get over his issues or stick around until he does."

Alana looked at him disbelievingly. "How did you know?!? Oh of course, the whole world knows I love Lukas. Thanks for your advice Cole. It's actually the best one I've heard. You are a good man, too. If you figure out that you're straight, I'd know a few women who are totally enamored with you."

Cole wagged his finger at her playfully. "Tsk, tsk. Lanie, if I was straight I'd be after you and if I was gay, and Josh broke up with me, I'd be after Lukas."

Alana laughed out loud. "You're a nut! Make up your mind, Cole."

Cole had an impulsive idea. "Oh, you know what? Since you're not going to dedicate my love poetry to Josh, why don't you use it and dedicate it to Lukas on the next issue of *The Magis?*"

Sand and Water

Alana was overwhelmed with gratitude for his generosity. Cole was such a special man. She had no doubt that he would, with God's grace, carry his cross and overcome it, and then she could only imagine the crown he will gain for eternity. "Thanks for the offer. But I'll give credit where credit is due. And thanks again Cole. You have given me so much more than you'll realize."

"So have you, Lanie. See you later."

When Cole left the office, Alana turned on the computer, intending to get some work done. However, she was so distracted that she could barely start.

Alana wanted to talk to Lukas so badly. She had lots of things to say to him now as opposed to her silent morning in his presence. Mainly, she wanted to tell Lukas that she would wait forever for him if she had to. He was worth the wait.

Alana realized now that she had to swallow her pride and let go of her anger. But how in the world could she do that, remain submissive and be willing to wait for his initiative? She was clearly in a bind. With a deep sigh, Alana opened some files on the computer and forced herself to edit some articles.

Midway through her work, Alana was inspired by an idea that Cole had unwittingly given her. Or more accurately, an idea sparked by the Holy Spirit through Its vessel, Cole. She sat up straight, wrote, typed, revised, rewrote, edited and finally by early Saturday evening, she was finished. Alana had big plans for her final months at SILU: she would be published by the final issue and enlist the help of Kerry to make sure it was executed in perfect timing.

Chapter 23

    The final semester whizzed past in a blur for the graduating students of St. Ignatius of Loyola University. They could be found busy almost everywhere – cramming for written exams, forming study groups for oral exams, using their free time to finish their theses, preparing for theses defenses, holding meetings for group presentations, passing out resumes to onsite job fairs, rehearsing for job interviews, and posing for yearbook pictures.

    On top of all the pre-commencement activities, Lukas' hectic itinerary included the twice a month meeting with Fr. Tim to discuss his discernment in vocation. Thankfully, after five months and a half, the official state of life discernment was coming to a close. By now, Lukas was definite on the direction God was leading him to but knowing how Fr. Tim was a stickler for exact schedules, Lukas planned to sit through two more meetings with his spiritual director before he could take the first step to his vocation.

    Lukas checked his watch and picked up his pace. He was systematically putting away the worship books after the noon Mass had finished. He had arranged to meet Fr. Tim for lunch and already, he was running late. Lukas was just holding a stack of worship books in his arms, ready to put them back in their slots when Kerry called him over from the double doors leading outside, to the huge campus.

    Kerry was holding a stack of books herself, and her pile was much higher than his.

    "Hey Luke, can you give me a hand here?" Kerry asked.

    Lukas hesitated, but once he saw Kerry struggling, he put down his stack of books on the pew and decided to help Kerry quickly. "What do you need me to do?"

    "Can you help me bring some boxes in from the dolly outside? I'm helping *The Magis* staff distribute their latest publication so I have to put these on top of the leaflet table in the church lobby." Kerry was under strict instructions from Alana to make sure Lukas grabbed a copy today.

Lukas unloaded four heavy boxes and set them under the table by the entry way. Kerry got busy arranging the books next to the church literature and pamphlets. "Hey," she said conversationally, "why don't you grab a few copies and take them with you?"

"Uh, no thanks. I'm not a big reader these days. I have too much on my plate finalizing my biochem lab project."

"Oh c'mon, I'm sure your live culture will grow better if you read them a story or two," she cajoled, shoving a couple of books in his hands.

"Yes, but I'll put *me* to sleep reading since I'm already sleep deprived as it is."

"You never know if something can catch your interest. I think Lanie said she had a contribution in there somewhere."

At the mention of Lanie, Lukas' muscles tensed. He thought of something fast to cover up his reaction in case Kerry noticed. "Your matchmaking days are over, Kerry," he said tersely.

"What makes you think I'm matchmaking?" she asked, with what she hoped was an offended look on her face. "I just thought you'd want to read something a mutual friend wrote, that's all."

Kerry bent over, taking books out of her boxes, signaling the end of their conversation.

Embarrassed that he read too much into her remarks, Lukas walked back into the church to finish his chore.

The truth was that Lukas had not gotten over Alana's cutting remarks. And if he was honest with himself, he was not over Alana either. The mention of Alana almost sent him into panic attacks. *How was it possible to be so wounded by someone and still be in love with her?* Not that he blamed her entirely for what she had said. He was more at fault for his impulsive actions, anyway.

Lukas was so preoccupied with his thoughts and his pride was still smarting from shame that he never noticed that he had accidentally stuffed the *Magis* books along with the worship books.

Lukas glanced at his watch again. Fr. Tim would no doubt be hungry and waiting for him. He sprinted in the direction of the cafeteria, then changed his mind at seeing the lines. He skipped lunch and joined Fr. Tim inside his quiet office.

Fr. Tim had become more than a spiritual director to Lukas. He had become a good friend to Lukas over the two years that they spent before, during and after the noon Mass.

"Luke!" Fr. Tim greeted him, puffing out tobacco smoke from his pipe. "I was beginning to think you realized you had no use for me anymore now that your discernment is over."

"Sorry I'm late, Fr. Tim. What do you mean its over—I still have a couple of meetings to go, don't I?"

"Well, you're welcome to come see me anytime of course but I thought the last few meetings we were getting somewhere concrete. Have you changed your mind, since?"

Lukas vehemently shook his head. "Not at all. I am positive now that God is leading me into the marital vocation. It's the only certain desire in my heart: to have a wife and raise a family. I just thought it wasn't officially over until the full six months."

"It's over when you hear God speak or until you have other questions you need answered. Frankly Luke, I always sensed you weren't called into the priesthood but it was worth a shot testing it out. St. Paul says we always have to test the spirits as not all seemingly good inspirations are from the Holy Spirit and that's exactly what we're here for."

"I am glad you helped me see that my only duty is to follow where the Holy Spirit leads my heart. I was just confused there for a while with my mom's and grandma's hopes and dreams for their son and grandson, thinking it was mine, too. Obviously, its not."

Fr. Tim nodded and looked at Lukas thoughtfully. He knew almost immediately that Lukas was not called into the priesthood from the moment when he had first spoken to the young man. At that time, Fr. Tim asked Lukas why he wanted to be a priest and Lukas' immediate answer was "I don't." The only reason he was discerning it was in memory of his mother and grandmother. Of course, Fr. Tim couldn't very well point out to him bluntly that he was going into the priesthood for the wrong reason, if that was the case. His task as a spiritual director was to guide Lukas into making the discovery himself. When Lukas realized his marital vocation with certainty, as he did in the last month, Fr. Tim was on hand to reaffirm it.

"Well then, if there is no other issue, I'd say this discernment is over and you won't have to put up with me anymore."

"Fr. Tim, I'd gladly see you everyday but its your smoking pipe that I can live without," Lukas said, referring to the stench of smoke pipe that he had to frequently contend with.

Fr. Tim took the jab in good humor. He held up his pipe. "Luke, this is another reason why you won't make it in the seminary. Your roommates and fellow priests will annoy the heck out you and make you take up the habit of smoking as your only form of release... or vengeance," Fr. Tim joked back.

Lukas laughed. "Oh, I've heard wives can do that, too."

Fr. Tim raised an eyebrow and challenged him, "If you change your mind, the Jesuits are always looking for a few good men. Think of us as God's army – no, the navy seals of God's military."

"No thanks," Lukas said. "The only people who will call me father will be my own kids."

"Hey speaking of army, there's a great essay in *The Magis* about a soldier's life or something like that."

"I'll get to it when I can, Fr. Tim," Lukas said noncommittally. "Right now, I have my final experiment to worry about. As soon as that's done, the first thing I'm going to do is find me a wife."

"Here, better take one of my pipes."

~ ~

As he exited the biochemistry building, Lukas was grinning from ear to ear. All things considered, life was looking good. He had wrapped up his discernment with Fr. Tim five days ago, passed all his final classes with flying colors, was set to graduate in two weeks and just had a promising job interview with a Catholic non-profit company called Biostemworld (www.biostemworld.com) that was making headways in finding the cure for cancer. Lukas was also looking forward to traveling to Portugal with his family right after his graduation. Since Tomas was marrying a Portuguese girl, they had all decided it would be a wonderful opportunity to tour Portugal.

The only thing that was missing in his otherwise perfect life was Alana. If only they had not parted in such terrible circumstances, Lukas would already be at her doorstep, bursting with his news. But he did not know how she would react after she had told him she did not want him in her future at all. And if she slammed the door shut his face, how would his heart react to that?

Thinking about Alana again made Lukas stop in his tracks for a minute. He sat down on the closest concrete bench, trying to figure out what to do now that he had all the time in his hands. He had to know where he stood with her, he had to talk to her. He just had to.

Impulsively, Lukas rounded the corner and headed for the English Department, which was a good walk from the sciences buildings. He didn't know if Alana would be there, but he hoped to catch a glimpse of her today.

Since Lukas was on unfamiliar grounds, he felt ill-at-ease coming up to the entrance. There were students entering and leaving the building in groups of three or four. Everyone seemed to know everyone else and he was sure everyone noticed that he stuck out like a sore thumb—*more like a mad scientist in a library of bookworms*, he thought dryly. Lukas tried to blend in with the crowd by going into the general direction where most students were headed for. To the right of the main hallway was *The Magis* office.

Lukas recalled that Alana had mentioned she volunteered as an editor for the publication on occasion. He thought he might try his luck there. Lukas peeked inside and saw a five foot high stack of boxes of their latest issue. He stepped into the office and grabbed a copy off the shelf beside the door.

"Can I help you?" asked a bespectacled friendly female staff member.

"Oh, I was just grabbing myself a copy."

"There's more if you need them," she said, indicating to the stack of boxes.

"Uh, thanks. One's enough," he said, feeling self-conscious for standing around in the office without any real purpose.

"Hey, where do I know you from?" she asked, a little too loudly.

"Um...um... maybe at the talent show? Psalm 96?" Lukas suggested.

"No, it was from somewhere else. Oh I remember! Didn't you used to come to this building a couple of years ago asking about a Lacy or Stacy—hmm, I forget the name now?"

Great, he thought to himself. *Just what I need—for the entire staff to find out I'm hung up over one of their editors who wants nothing to do with me. The only thing worse would be if they witnessed an awkward conversation between us.* Considering the possibility of a horrible scenario with Alana on top of two already awful ones, Lukas lost his nerve.

"You must be mistaken," he said through gritted teeth. "Have a good day." Lukas quickly left *The Magis* office and hurried out of the building. Lukas decided that he would have a better chance at finding Alana at the 6:30 Mass tomorrow morning. This way he would have enough time to compose himself and think about what to say.

Lukas drove back to his apartment. Patrick was gone for the night on a study group, so he just fixed himself a quick dinner. As he sat down on the bar stool facing the kitchen counter, Lukas noticed that the button on the answering machine was blinking. He pushed the play button while he chewed on his Mac and Cheese. There was one message for Patrick and the next one was from Spain. Tomas' strange, hollow voice played back on the recorder:

"Hey Luke, there's been an emergency. Dad's in the hospital. We don't know what's wrong yet. Call me."

Lukas jumped out of his chair and immediately called home. Stephen's care giver Magda groggily answered the phone. She explained that she didn't know exactly what was going on, only that Tomas was at the Santa Clara Hospital with his dad in room 304. Lukas dialed his father's cell phone. After a few rings, Tomas answered.

"Hey," Tomas greeted him with a weary voice. "Dad just collapsed in his office this afternoon. They took some blood work and something's not right. The worst case is cancer, the best, I don't know. Luke, Luke, can you come? I'm falling apart—with the wedding coming up in a few weeks and Stephen not being able to help me. I'm thinking of postponing the wedding but I haven't asked Catia yet. I don't know if dad will be well enough to travel to the US for your graduation or to Portugal for my wedding. I know this is the worst time to ask you but I—we need you, man."

Lukas felt his blood drain from his face. He had already lost his grandmother to cancer once. He remembered that it seemed like only he and Tomas had been there for each other in their inconsolable grief. He had to be there for Tomas and Stephen in this crisis now. Most of all, he had to make sure his dad received the final sacraments as a baptized Catholic.

There was no doubt about it. Lukas would fly to Spain immediately. Thank God he finished all his schoolwork and was free to leave. He didn't have to go to the graduation ceremony without his family there, anyway. As for his diploma, he could ask Patrick to mail it to him along with some of his stuff that he couldn't pack.

"I'll be there as soon as I can, Tom."

Lukas hung up the phone, his hands shaking. He booked the first flight available and spent the rest of the night packing up most of his belongings. This was not how he wanted to leave America, but he had no other choice.

Chapter 24

Alana could hardly believe it. The moment had arrived. Four years of intense studying, particularly in the final years when she had to shift her major subjects, had paid off. She was going to graduate with a Bachelor's Degree in English, majoring in Creative Writing.

The only thing that marred her happiness today was Lukas' absence. She thought for sure that when he read that essay on *The Magis*, he would know immediately what she intended to say to him. She hoped that he would at least approach her in the last few days of graduation practice but she never saw him. She deliberated asking Patrick or Sean for Lukas' whereabouts during the baccalaureate Mass for the graduates, but she was too embarrassed to ask them, considering that she practically bore her heart and soul on *The Magis* and had gotten no positive response from her intended audience.

Lukas' silence and absence were so mystifying to her. He had to have read it, she thought to herself. Kerry said that she had handed Lukas a copy of *The Magis* herself with the unambiguous statement that Alana had written something in there. Then two weeks ago, when Alana was at the *Magis* office, she could have sworn that she saw Lukas coming in and picking up a copy. That day when she saw him, she was almost positive that he had come to see her, but when she hurried out of the editor's office to speak with him, he had disappeared like a flash of lightning.

The only reasonable explanation she could come up with was that Lukas had finally decided that he did indeed have a priestly vocation and that he had left for the seminary. If that was the case, he clearly had nothing to say to her and Alana had nothing more to say to him. She would move on with her life, beginning today.

Alana prepared to climb up the stage to receive her hard-earned diploma. As she stood up proudly accepting a handshake from the University President, she scanned the audience for her parents' faces. She gave them a small wave, silently thanking God and them for giving this moment to her.

Then Alana grinned wide, mostly to cover up her sorrow. She didn't want her parents to know that what should be one of the happiest days of her life was also one of the most heartbreaking ones. Yet as much as her heart ached, Alana was also consoled with the faith that God was still in charge of her love story and if Lukas wasn't the hero, there was hope that surely there was going to be another candidate.

Back in the safety of her seat, Alana did not have to put on bravado for her parents' sake anymore. A tear escaped as Alana muttered in anguish, "Lord, please, let him come for me soon, whoever he is."

~ ~

The day after the graduation ceremony, the O'Keefe's departed for Portugal.

Portugal is a country is Southwestern Europe, adjacent to the southeast of Spain. In Portugal lies one of the most popular pilgrimage sites for Catholics, Fatima. Fatima is a farming town located one hundred and twenty miles north of the capital, Lisbon.

Between May 13, 1917 and October 13, 1917, Our Blessed Virgin Mary appeared six times to three shepherd children in Fatima: Lucia dos Santos and her two cousins Francisco and Jacinta. Our Blessed Virgin Mary implored the children to convey several messages for the world: requests for prayer, reparation, sacrifice and the necessity of praying the daily rosary to obtain peace for oneself and peace in the world. She was thus known as Our Lady of the Rosary. On Our Lady of the Rosary's final apparition, around 60,000 pilgrims trekked to Fatima and witnessed the miracle of the sun dancing.

The miracle of the sun is only one of the many miracles attributed to the graces of Our Lady of Fatima. There have been numerous medical healings and testimonies of spiritual conversions associated with Fatima.

Jacinta's incorrupt body further reinforces the phenomenon of the Marian apparition site. After a thorough Church investigation, the apparition received Catholic Church approval. In recent years, Pope John Paul II made an unprecedented three pilgrimages to Fatima, expressing a complete faith in Our Lady's messages and apparitions.

About twelve miles from the Fatima pilgrimage site rests a convent and a small house run by the Sisters of the Immaculate Heart of Mary. The order was founded in the early seventies with the intent of housing young pregnant mothers and abandoned children as the counter-offense to the illegal abortion practices and abortion activists propaganda in Portugal. In Portugal, abortions are allowed up to the 12th week of pregnancy to preserve a woman's mental or physical health. Since Portugal has one of the most restrictive abortion laws in all of Europe, many women travel to nearby Spain to terminate pregnancies or resort to illegal abortions.

It was in this convent of the Sisters of the Immaculate Heart of Mary that the O'Keefe's found their precious daughter, Alana. Twenty three years since they first set foot in the convent, the O'Keefe's were now back ringing the convent doorbell, bringing their adult "child" with them. A young novice in a white and black habit opened the door.

"Good afternoon, Sister. My name is Joe O'Keefe. We are here to see Sr. Mary Margaret."

"*Si. si.* Come inside and sit at the parlor. I will go get Sr. Mary Margaret," she said in broken English. The novice nun led them into a tiny room before disappearing inside.

Alana held her mother's hand anxiously. This was it, she thought. She would know *something*.

Sr. Mary Margaret was a small framed, petite, Portuguese-Spanish nun in her late sixties. She was a kindly compassionate woman, and although looked dwarfed in her black dress and black habit, she walked with such authority that Alana could not help but snap up in attention to her commanding presence. Her straight back, unmarred by osteoporosis that damaged the posture of most women's her age, confirmed her no-nonsense attitude in handling the tasks delegated to her. Sr. Mary Margaret had been the headmistress of the young mother's home for fifteen years. The only time she had to give up her position was when she was assigned to Africa to start a similar convent opened by the Sisters of the Immaculate Heart of Mary. In Africa, Sr. Mary Margaret was headmistress for six years.

"Hello, Maria, Joe," she greeted Alana's parents. Her English was thickly accented but the grammar was flawless, indicating her superior educational degree. Then she turned to Alana. "Is it you, Pureza?" she asked her warmly. "I'm sorry... You must be Pureza's daughter for you look like your mother."

Alana smiled. "My parents named me Alana and call me Lanie. It's nice to meet you, Sr. Mary."

"Oh of course. Please sit. I have a box here that has been waiting for you for over twenty years now."

Alana sat down. "Do I, do I really look like my mother? Can you tell me what she was like?"

"Yes, every bit as beautiful. Her name was Pureza, a Spanish name meaning Purity. Pureza came to us in the summer of let's see 1979? She was a nineteen year old Spanish woman who worked as a seamstress in the royal palace of King Juan Carlos. Pureza had always dreamed of working for royalty since she was very young. She thought that was the closest she would come to ever being a princess. In that respect, Pureza was vain. She seemed snobbish, reserved at first but once we got to know her she was very witty and charming. Pureza made friends with all the girls in the house while she stayed with us and they—we were all sorry to see her go. Once she let her guard down, Pureza was incredibly sweet and very positive about everything. One evening when the power went out because of a storm and we had no water for weeks, she called it the perfect romantic setting like those period romance novels. Soon, Pureza and the young girls were imagining the shadows to be their knights in shining armor. You get the impression that Pureza was naïve, innocent with a vulnerability that needed a lot of love and affirmation."

Alana liked the sound of that. "What was her story?"

"Pureza got pregnant by a regular guest in the king's home. She never did say who it was but would only say that he was married. When she found out she was pregnant and told him, he told Pureza to 'take care of it' otherwise he would make sure she lost her job at the palace. He drove Pureza to an illegal abortion clinic, gave her money to have it done and to take the cab home. Pureza told me that she was crying outside the door for a few minutes as she couldn't let herself go in, until an older woman came up to her and gave her a shoulder to cry on. The woman was a devout Catholic who often staked out abortion clinics, praying the rosary or "preying" on the patients. She listened to Pureza and convinced her that it would offend God very much and ruin His plans for the baby's life. She herself took Pureza to us that same day. This older woman has brought us at least fifteen young girls over the years and has saved fifteen lives—no, thirty lives because by stopping the abortion she has saved the pregnant woman's life from regret and anguish."

Seeing Alana's tear-filled eyes, Sr. Mary Margaret asked her gently, "Do you want me to stop?"

Alana was crying softly while her parents held her hands in theirs. She shook her head. "Please go on, Sister."

Sr. Mary Margaret continued. "Pureza stayed with us until you were born. She was baptized a Catholic when she was a baby but her parents never followed through on her Catholic upbringing. When Pureza lived with us, she asked to be confirmed and to receive the sacrament of the Eucharist. Pureza thought about keeping her baby, you, but she had quit her job as she decided she did not want to return to the palace and face your father. Pureza was broke but deep inside her was a dream that she could go somewhere where she could start over. During the last two months of her pregnancy, Pureza prayed many hours with me asking God for guidance. What finally made her decide to give you up was the fear that you would see how her life turned out and follow in her footsteps. Pureza believed she would be a poor example to you. She did not want you to make the same mistakes she did. Two days before you were born, one of the sisters told Pureza that a Catholic American couple had come to Fatima to pray for a baby. Pureza knew she could not possibly give you the life that you would have with them. That is when she made the decision to let you go. We never knew what became of her after that."

Alana sniffled into her tissue. "What's inside the box?" she asked hoarsely.

Sr. Mary Margaret opened the shoebox and explained the five or six contents inside.

"This," she said, holding up a finely embroidered and cross-stitched image of Mary and the baby Jesus, "was your mother's specialty being a needle worker. She wanted you to always remember that you were born Catholic and hoped you would remain so forever. She actually wanted your parents to have it. Pureza wasn't sure she could raise you Catholic herself as she saw her own parents drift away from Catholicism when trial and adversity came."

Alana clutched the fabric close to her heart. There was no denying that she would have been raised a Catholic either way. This was God's plan for her. She was ever so grateful that her parents had raised her Catholic. Thanks to them, her faith meant everything to her. She passed the fabric to her mother.

"This," Sr. Mary Margaret said, holding up a hardbound poetry book written by Pedro Calderon dela Barca, "was given by a rich patron to the girls in the house library. Your mother used to read that to you over and over again until we all decided she may as well keep it since she had folded dog ears on the corners of its pages. Pureza wrote her name on it and then later on changed it to your name. She said she hoped that this would help you out as much as it helped her."

"Oh we even love the same book!" Alana exclaimed, softly touching the dog-eared pages.

"This," Sr. Mary Margaret continued, handing her a Christmas ornament of an angel, "was from her grandmother or mother, I am not sure but she's had it since she was a little girl. Pureza told me to tell you that while we are on earth, we won't always know everything we want to know but someday, when we get to heaven, all will be revealed to us. Her prayers for you were to always strive for heaven where she could meet you and try to explain things more --unless God beats her to it and tells you all that you need to know."

Alana silently took the ornament, noting that the chipped wing and tarnished halo did not lessen the impact of the meaning behind the family heirloom.

"And this," Sr. Mary Margaret said, holding up an old beer bottle, "showed your mother's sense of humor. She liked to drink beer, lots of it. In fact, I think she was drunk when she and those girls thought their shadows were knights. Where they got the alcohol from, I don't know to this day. Pureza said that someday if you came to us seeking her and had the tendency to romanticize her image as perfect, this beer bottle was to let you know that she was far from perfect. You may have very well been the child of an alcoholic."

Alana laughed, at once remembering her drunken state at the Charity Ball. Her laughter lasted longer than she had intended. It felt good to laugh in the middle of all this drama for her laughter had healed a deep-seated wound that she had denied ever existed: the pain of being rejected by her own mother. And beyond that, her laughter meant, too that she realized she had been given a chance at life instead of death and indeed, what a blessed life it was!

As Joe and Maria watched their daughter's tears turned into laughter, they effusively comprehended the healing that had taken place in these grounds.

Sr. Mary Margaret showed her two more things from the box until Alana's curiosity was, at last, spent.

Chapter 25

Lukas was frustrated. No, he was upset.

After twelve hours of flying and airport layovers, he hailed a taxi, called Fr. Juan, dropped off his suitcase at home and headed straight for the hospital. Now his stubborn father was refusing to see the good priest.

"I don't understand, dad. What exactly is it that you have against the Catholic Church? You and mom used to take us to Church all the time, had us baptized, confirmed and made Tomas receive Holy Communion before she died. What was it exactly that changed your mind? Did you think the Church took mom's life away and God stopped being God because he didn't give you what you want?"

Frank Swenson looked at his son, tiredly. "You wouldn't understand, Luke. You have never loved your mother like I did. She was my—life. I never remarried because no other woman could compare to her. I never moved out of our home in her home country because I wanted memories of her wherever I turned. I thought I was going to spend the rest of my life with her and I was cheated by a God I thought was all loving and all powerful. God does not exist, son. If He did, I would have had more than ten years with her. She should be here with me!"

Lukas regretted his harsh words instantly. He looked at his sad father's pale, drawn face, vulnerable on the hospital bed. "But I do understand, dad, more than you think I do. I have loved a girl too and lost her and yet I still trust that our good, loving God has it all worked out even though it doesn't seem like it will."

Something like sympathy flickered behind Frank's eyes. "You are right, Luke. I don't know much about you or Tomas or Stephen. I have worked in my clinic to hide my pain and have never paid attention to yours. I want to be a good father to you but I don't want this God to be part of it. Let's leave it at that."

Anabelle Hazard

Sand and Water

Lukas sighed. He tried one more time. "Dad, I know you still remember what you taught us. You know as well as I do that one can not be a good father without understanding supreme goodness and love, sacrifice and mercy."

Frank held up his left hand weakly. "Please stop. Your grandmother has tried. Other priests and old church friends have tried this conversation. My mind will not accept anything you throw my way. Can we just get on and get me out of here so I can make it to Tomas' wedding in Portugal?"

"You have cancer, dad. I don't know if the doctors will let you travel."

"Of course they will! I've had patients with cancer having babies. It's just colon cancer. I can walk perfectly fine and I will be at Tomas' wedding. I am already aggravated that you have made me miss your own graduation. I will go to Portugal even if I have to give the doctor's orders myself."

Lukas had to smile. He knew where he got his own stubborn determination from.

"Alright, we'll go but we are taking a wheelchair on our trip because the doctor's say that your legs are getting weak and if something happens to you, I will not be able to carry you anywhere."

~ ~

For the first time in fifteen years, Frank took a three week vacation from his successful obstetrics practice. He flew with Lukas, Stephen and Stephen's caregiver Magda to the city of Porto, Portugal. Porto was north of Lisbon, the second largest city in Portugal. From Porto, they had planned to drive leisurely along the Atlantic coastline of Portugal, staying at various resorts until they reached Lisbon, where Tomas and Catia were waiting for them, busy with the wedding preparations. After Lisbon, the four of them had planned to continue down to the South of Portugal, where the most popular tourist beach destinations awaited them.

As soon as their airport taxi dropped them off at the Praia Golfe Hotel Porto, Lukas checked into the suite he shared with Stephen. The rest of the party had preferred to rest after an exhausting trip but the sight of the blue waters summoned Lukas instantaneously. Since Lukas did not want to waste a minute inside the hotel, he changed into his swimsuit, lathered sun block on, grabbed his sunglasses and prepared to leave the room. He was just about to head out the door when he remembered that the travel brochures had advised that some parts of the Portuguese seafront was too rough for swimming. Lukas wasn't sure if that included Baia beach, the one that the hotel sat closest to, so he decided to take some reading material along just in case the waters were off limits.

Lukas zipped open his travel backpack and fished for some books. He found three: the travel guide to Portugal, Confessions of St. Augustine and the latest publication of *The Magis*.

"Hmmm," he wondered, turning *The Magis* around in his hand. "How did that get in here?" It must have been when he stuffed it in the back pocket of his book bag on his last day at school. He must have forgotten to remove it for the trip.

Lukas wrapped *The Magis* and the travel guide with the beach towel and headed down through the hotel lobby to the beach. Lukas found a spot on the fine sandy beach to set up his towel. He took a quick dip in the ocean, but soon became worn out due to his strenuous experience traveling with a handicapped father and brother. Lukas wiped himself off, sat down and picked up the travel guide.

He studied his map intently to plan out the rest of the trip. He noticed that they were nearing a town called Fatima. Lukas distinctly remembered that Mary had an apparition there more than 80 years ago calling herself "Our Lady of the Rosary." He had heard Fr. Juan speaking about a pilgrimage trip to Fatima once when Pope John Paul II was there to consecrate the world to the Immaculate Heart of Mary, as Our Lady had requested. All of a sudden, Lukas was seized with an urge to visit the holy place. It was, he had committed to memory, a site where miraculous healings had taken place: blind could see, deaf could hear, lame could walk, and cancers cured.

Sand and Water

A plan began to formulate in Lukas' head. He searched inside his traveler's guide book. The information on Fatima confirmed everything and told him more. He noted that there were motels very close to the pilgrimage site for the pilgrims from everywhere around the world. Feeling very pleased with himself, Lukas folded the pages of a list of accommodations close to Fatima and planned to call for reservations as soon as he got back to the hotel.

Lukas sat on the towel silently. He buried his toes into the sand and felt strangely tickled by the sensation. The stimulating reaction on his toes made him decide to take a stroll. As Lukas walked along the edge of the water, he suddenly realized why Alana liked strolling on the beach so much. The coolness of the wet sand sinking underneath his feet felt refreshing.

Paying close attention to the waves that came up on the beach, Lukas observed that the clear shallow water seemed gentle and caressing. But when he looked out into the ocean and saw the giant waves tossing about, he was amazed at the power of the wind on water. He knew from science classes that at one time, the powerful waters had crushed stone and seashell into powdery sand.

Right then and there, Lukas was struck by a profound thought. Just like the wind could blow on the great waters, the Holy Spirit could move man into bold, decisive life-changing action. And just as Jesus stilled the waves and calmed the sea, the power of Jesus' love could also stir in a man's soul a patient, faithful, life-giving love – the love that was, is God, the Eternal Father.

Lukas wished more than anything that Alana was walking beside him, holding his hand. He would have wanted to share that insightful reflection with her.

Lukas glanced up and could foresee that the sun was about to set. He jogged back to his towel, intending to watch the sunset. Judging that he had another fifteen minutes before the sun would retreat into the waters, Lukas picked up *The Magis*. He leafed through the pages and found an essay written by Alana O'Keefe. With a start, he realized that he had almost forgotten about Kerry's suggestion.

Lukas read the title "A Soldier's Life" and recognized it as the essay that Fr. Tim had urged him to read.

Lukas lay down flat on his towel and began to read the highly recommended essay:

<u>A soldier's life</u>
by Alana O'Keefe

Poor Ignatius. Day in and day out, his 12 foot bronze statue, genuflecting on his right knee, two arms outstretched, sword laying flat in both hands, eyes looking heavenward, stands guard over the main entrance of his school. Yet, early in the morning, most of us often ignore him as we speed off to catch our favorite parking spot or slip into our 8:00 class barely awake. When the day is over, we hurriedly exit SILU, without so much as a wave at him, preoccupied with trying to beat the rush hour traffic, dreading the paper that's due, or eager to get going to the Friday night party.

The only time Ignatius ever gets attention (other than his annual polishing from the janitorial staff right before his feast day) is during those days when the ski-masked fraternity guys play their pranks on the unsuspecting Ignatius. Does anyone remember waking up to Ignatius in a Jedi cape, holding a bright neon Jedi sword, right after the Star Wars movie opened? Or how about discovering the July 4th dozen red, blue and white balloons that Ignatius held in his right hand which perfectly matched the red, white and blue balloon encrusted hat he had on his head? And who could forget last year's celebrated SILU versus BC game which depicted Ignatius with a tailor-made yellow and blue varsity jacket, pompoms and SILU flag, much to the rival Jesuit school's consternation?

I guess the only thing that keeps our Jesuit run administration from posting guards over our saintly soldier is the belief that Ignatius must have a sense of humor, too. He has to, otherwise; he'd be giving instructions to his buddy St. Peter to send any SILU frat member who arrives at the pearly gates to go "somewhere else."

Sand and Water

Now I don't know about you, but I do wonder about our patron saint. What was he like when he was our age? Was he a playful, happy-go-lucky kind of a guy or was he serious and brooding? Did he and his buddies enjoy a game of soccer or did he like to play poker behind closed doors? Was he a thinker, a writer, a reader, or a football fan? Was he a student council leader or an unknown science fanatic who worked quietly in the labs? Or was he a fun-loving fraternity guy who liked to play pranks on unsuspecting statues?

We are told that Ignatius was born of noble birth to courtier parents who served King Ferdinand and Queen Isabella of Spain in 1491. Prior to his conversion, Inigo, as he was called, was a self-professed vain soldier who liked flirting with the ladies. A cannonball hit him square between his legs after which he voluntarily endured an excruciatingly painful operation to ensure that he would never walk with a limp. During his recovery, he requested for reading material about chivalry, knights and ladies but was instead given books on Christ and the saints. In his boredom, was born a new Inigo. After his conversion, Ignatius is said to have had a vision of the Madonna and pledged to become a soldier for the Catholic faith. He later pursued his studies, wrote the Spiritual Exercises, drew loyal followers and founded the Jesuits or the Society of Jesus. Thanks to Ignatius, there are to date, 50 Jesuit saints, 167 Jesuit blesseds, 4,000 living Jesuits, 125,000 lay, religious and clerical partners and 1,370 Jesuit educational institutions instilling in 2.5 million students the goal of becoming men and women for others.

Ignatius teaches us a technique of imagining ourselves in the gospels, putting ourselves in the heart of where Jesus was—perhaps as an indifferent bystander, a devout apostle, or a skeptical Pharisee—to better appreciate Jesus' teaching. Taking his cue, permit me to imagine Ignatius here, amongst us, not as a statue but a living, breathing college student, in order to appreciate a facet of the Ignatian spirituality.

Being a female English lit major with a penchant for romances, I picture Ignatius as a suave, smooth, good-looking co-ed, majoring in philosophy. He is tall with dark hair, muscular, with a sun-bronzed (pun intended) coloring, demonstrating his love for the beach. He has a slight Spanish accent. Like his favored book heroes, Ignatius is chivalrous, debonair and has an air of mystery about him. When he speaks, he is charismatic, humorous, and extremely kind. Like many of the students in his day, what draws me to him is his irresistible passion for Christ. He never fails to attend daily Mass and sometimes might like to serve as a reader, a sacristan or a musician. Ignatius plays the guitar dreamily, when he can get away from basketball practices. Naturally, Ignatius is the captain of the varsity team as he has earned the respect of his peers and catapulted the team into an NCAA championship.

    I suppose you might correctly conclude that I am in love with Ignatius, along with most of the females in the school. Like silly groupies, 99 % of the female population of SILU flocks to see Ignatius play in the basketball courts. Inside the secret world of sororities and private restroom conversations, there is a fierce competition for his heart. But Ignatius' heart, like most noble men, is called to the priesthood: to serve his one true love, Jesus Christ.

    All the girls are devastated that he will not be taking a girl for a bride, but no one more than I, as did I mention he rescued me from a concussion and possible head trauma in my junior year? I thought for sure Ignatius and I were meant to be together but he broke my heart when he told me that he is off to fight a war—a war for the salvation of souls. I must say Ignatius is the perfect choice for a soldier as he was born a hero. But I cannot help but wish he was destined for me, to become a faithful husband and righteous father of my children.

    He graduates with honors, of course. With a collective sigh, the girls and I cast one last, longing glance at him when he mounts the stage to receive the philosophy degree that would propel him into the seminary and keep us apart forever. There goes our knight in shining armor.

    Ignatius leaves the SILU grounds on his mustang – that is, his purebred white horse. He stops by the main gates, kneels down, draws his sword with his right hand,

and lays the tip of the blade flat across his left palm. He faces his right hand up to support the handle and now his sword stretches across two open palms. In a gesture of complete and total abandonment of his life to God's will, Ignatius raises his eyes heavenward.

Here I am, close at his heels, crying with heartbreaking sobs, wishing, willing him to look back. "Please," I beg silently, "pledge to lay down your life for me for I am a wretched damsel in distress." Oh, how I long to tell Ignatius that if God should change his mind about needing him in the front lines, I will wait here. I will wait forever if I have to because he, like his master Jesus, is worth the wait. Instead, I say nothing because if he truly belongs in God's army, I am not going to be the last line of defense that stands in his way. Besides, by now, Ignatius barely notices I am alive. Next to Jesus, I am but a speck of dust.

Pathetic as I am, I cannot help but love Ignatius. I want to be like him: courageous, selfless, totally surrendered to God's will.

Where do I go now, armed with my English degree? Ahhh, to a school somewhere to educate children who will become men and women for others. Someday, if God wills, I may find love again and raise my own children in my own home – with courage, selfless love and in total surrender to God's perfect will.

As Ignatius rides off to the sunset, I am left with nothing but his memory and the prayer I heard him once utter, which I now repeat:

"Dearest Lord, teach me to be generous, teach me to serve you as I should. To give and not to count the cost, to fight and not to heed the wounds, to toil and not to seek for rest, to labor and ask not for reward, save that of knowing that I do, your most holy will."

I ask my fellow graduating class: who is Ignatius in your life and what memories of him will you take when you finally leave the classrooms, hallways and gates of SILU?

Chapter 26

Thump, thump, thump. Lukas could hear his heart hammering uncontrollably in his chest. He read the essay three times. All three times, it said the same thing over and over. He may not be a rocket scientist, but he knew how to read between the lines of an English essay.

Alana O'Keefe was writing for him and her message was crystal clear: she was waiting for him.

"How can it be possible?" he asked himself, hardly believing his wildest dreams were coming true. Then he realized that this whole love story could only be possible if God himself was writing it.

He should call her right away, he thought. But this was a conversation that could not be done over the phone. Lukas wanted to look her in the eyes and tell her he loved her to her face. Oh he loved Lanie, always had and she loved him back. He would fly to Hawaii right after Tomas' wedding to surprise her, that's all there was to it. He resolved that as soon as it was a decent hour in US time, he would contact Kerry and ask her for Alana's address.

Lukas sat on the sand and watched the sun set quietly. When the sun disappeared and darkness crept on the horizon, Lukas' only thought was: *"The sun must be rising in Hawaii right about now."*

~ ~

Early the following morning, which was a cloudless Thursday in June, Lukas checked out of the hotel for the rest of the group. He loaded up their van and meandered through the tiny streets of the surrounding villages. He had insisted on driving that day as he would take a meticulously planned detour.

The two-hour drive from Porto to Fatima was mellow, serene, almost lazy. Once he passed the street that

Anabelle Hazard

would lead to the entrance of the pilgrimage site, Lukas slowed to a stop.

"Uh-oh," he said, pretending to look worried. "I think we're out of gas. I forgot to fill up. I'm going to see if we can ask for directions or find a nearby gas station."

Frank groaned from his seat. "Well, why didn't you do that yesterday?"

"Sorry dad, I think I see some restaurant or shop there where you can rest. Why don't you get off while I go looking around for a gas station? I need to check the tires and the engine anyway since we have a long drive planned today."

"You should have left us at the hotel," Frank grumbled but agreed to the plan, anyway.

Lukas dropped off his father, brother and Magda while unknown to them, he parked the car. He walked back and mouthed off another set of lies, "I'm not sure if there's something wrong with the engine so I'm just having some mechanic look at it. Why don't we just stroll around the area? I see people going up somewhere. I think this is a tourist spot or something like that."

Lukas pushed Frank's wheelchair up the hill and onto the entrance. The open area plaza, swarming with pilgrims, appeared before them. At the center of the grounds stood a sprawling cathedral with a 65 meter tower. An unmistakable statue of Our Lady of Fatima was imbedded into the carved dome of the tower.

"Wait a minute," Frank said, starting to get angry. "I know where we are! Your mother and I were here many years ago. Why you sneaky son of a…"

"Don't say it dad. You'll be insulting mom," Lukas said, trying to sound jolly, although he was starting to feel edgy about his father causing a scene. Although Lukas knew his father to be dignified and self-controlled, he wasn't sure if this would be the first time he would get into a conniption.

Frank's face was red with anger. He demanded furiously, "Turn around, Luke. I do not want to be here. Do not push me any further. Stop!" Frank put all his effort into stopping the wheelchair from moving, almost falling off the chair.

Sand and Water

"I'm sorry I lied, dad," Lukas apologized. "I thought..."

"Where are we, Luke?" Stephen asked, bewildered. "What's going on?"

"We're at a pilgrimage place called Fatima, Stephen. It's a place that's been graced by Our Lady's apparitions. She has blessed pilgrims with many graces here: conversion, healing, and other miracles."

"You mean she can cure dad?" he asked, innocently.

"That's what I was hoping for."

"No, Stephen. Only doctors have cures. Your mother and I were here when she was pregnant with you. The doctor's told her that she would have to terminate her pregnancy in order for her to live. But she refused to let them harm you. I do not regret that you were born, Stephen, I really don't. But I blame God for not...for not..." Frank's voice broke off. He could not continue what he was about to say. Then the most unexpected thing happened. Frank burst into tears.

Lukas had never seen his father cry. It was heart-wrenching. Lukas touched his father's shoulder's sympathetically. "I am sorry, dad. I didn't mean to upset you. Let's turn around and head back."

"No," Frank said, gulping between sobs. "Let's go in. I am going to give God one more chance. He can strike me with lightning all He wants but I challenge Him to prove that He exists."

Lukas was silent as he pushed his father's wheelchair to the area designated for the sick pilgrims. Stephen followed them, holding on to Magda's arm. It appeared that they arrived in time for the Eucharistic benediction. The solemn ceremony of blessing the sick began with the processional. A priest holding the monstrance containing the Eucharistic Host entered and slowly passed by the rows of the sick pilgrims. It was explained that everyone present received graces from heaven. Although some of the faithful have received physical cures in the past, most sick people also receive perseverance and endurance to carry their crosses.

The moment passed when the monstrance was raised over Frank and Stephen. Lukas did not know exactly what happened, but he knew streams of graces were poured out on his family. Frank and Stephen knew it as well.

The four of them left the area silently, each contemplating the solemnity of the occasion.

"If you don't mind," Lukas said, breaking the silence. "I'd like to go visit the chapel of the apparitions over there." He pointed to a small chapel where a long, moving line was headed. "You don't have to go. I just want to pray to Our Lady of Fatima."

"I'm going," Frank announced.

"Me, too," Stephen and Magda echoed.

They stepped in line along with the rest of the pilgrims and made the journey to Our Lady of the Rosary. Before her image, Lukas knelt down, in prayer for Alana, his father, Tomas and Stephen.

"Dear Mother," Lukas prayed. "I thank you for your unfailing love for me. You have given me so much I cannot ask for anything more for myself. What I do ask is for graces for my father. Hear his prayers, change his heart and lead him to your Son again. Bless Tomas and Catia that they too may be guided by Jesus and the Church as they begin their new lives together. Bless Stephen that he may find God's path for him, into His arms. And finally, bless my Lanie. Keep her safe while she waits and bring me to her side that I may never leave her again and love her forever."

When Lukas slanted Frank a sideways glance, he noticed that his father was struggling to get up from his wheelchair. Lukas made a motion to help him, but Frank held up his hand to stop his son. Lukas watched as Frank came up to the glass enclosed image and touched it. Then Frank bent his head and walked back to his wheelchair. Stephen bowed his head low, knelt like Lukas did and walked on with the moving crowd.

As soon as they stepped outside, Stephen looked Frank in his eyes and said audibly, "I'm going to become a priest."

"What?!?" Lukas and Frank exclaimed in unison.

"You heard me," Stephen said clearly, in a normal voice, "I'm going to become a priest."

Lukas could hardly believe his ears. Stephen was talking without a speech impediment! Lukas was so flabbergasted that he blurted out the first thing that came to his mind. "But Stephen, you're, you're not even a Catholic. He hasn't even received First Communion right, dad? Do you even know what a priest does?"

Stephen calmly looked at Lukas and answered. "Yes, I do know what a priest is. He is like Fr. Juan Mendoza who gives you Holy Communion and that man who held the monstrance in such reverence. I want to serve Jesus, Lukas. This is what I was born to do."

Frank's red-shot eyes were once again brimming with tears. "Oh my son, you're healed! God has heard my prayers. I only wanted a normal happy life for you, for all my sons. You want to become a priest you say. Oh, your mother would be so proud and so am I, so am I! Oh *mijo*, God has not failed me and the Mother of God is surely hand carrying our requests before her son. What a powerful intercessor she is, how blessed we are to have her as our heavenly mother," he cried. Frank hugged Stephen and then he reached out and hugged Lukas, too.

Lukas was still reeling from all that happened. So his father's deepest tragedy was having a son who could not lead a normal life, he realized. Lukas regretted judging his father unfairly because he *did* know something about a suffering father's love.

Out of the blue, a memory returned to Lukas. Lukas recalled that his mother had offered her sons to the priesthood and her dream that one of them would become a priest. Lukas would never have guessed it would be Stephen but after what he witnessed today, it seemed God had other plans and God, as always, knew what He was doing.

"Let's stay for the day, Lukas," Frank suggested. "I want to go to confession and I may need a few hours to enumerate everything that I've done in fifteen years."

"Actually, I need to go to confession, too since I lied to you all about the car," Lukas confessed.

Stephen, Frank and Magda laughed aloud.

Sand and Water

"Thank you for bringing us all here, today," Frank told Lukas sincerely.

Lukas bent over to hug his father. He did not know if Frank was healed of colon cancer but he knew something more miraculous had occurred here: Frank was healed of cancer of the soul.

"Yes," Stephen agreed. "Now all we need is to bring Tomas and Catia here, too."

"Oh, that can be arranged. I have a master plan," said Lukas, winking at his brother and father.

Chapter 27

The rest of the O'Keefe's stay in Fatima was just as healing for Alana's soul as her visit to the convent.

On her first day at the Fatima pilgrimage site, Alana arrived at the entrance gates, filled with a sense of awe at the number of people who had come to honor the Blessed Mother. What touched her most was the sight of the faithful pilgrims shuffling on their knees to the statue of Our Lady of the Rosary, located inside the chapel of apparition. She and her devout mother did the same thing while Joe and Jack walked on their feet. When Alana reached the statue, she wept, in thanksgiving for her life and the gift of her family. There, she prayed:

"Blessed Mother, you are the Mediatrix of all graces, all I have is because of your graciousness. You have given me so many graces but there is one part of my life that needs a lot of your attention. Please intercede for my love story. I want to raise a holy family and I need a husband like St. Joseph. I thought I had found love once before but it seems my choice was wrong. I ask for healing graces for my heart. This day I entrust to you my future husband. Choose one for me, Blessed Mother. Do not forget the Hail Mary's I have offered for him all these years. Enfold him in your mantle and engulf him in your love. Please supply him with graces that he needs: graces of healing, of love, of hope, of joy, of holiness. Please help our paths to cross in God's perfect time. Amen."

Next, Alana performed the Stations of the Cross with her parents. When she reached the thirteenth station, where Mary holds the body of Jesus in her arms, the full understanding of her life's mission began to dawn on her. Alana somehow knew that when she was going to raise a family, being open to life not only meant practicing natural family planning but in her case, it also meant opening her home to adoptive children who would have been victims of the sin of abortion. She realized that she did not have to do

Anabelle Hazard

grand things in service to God. She could serve him quietly, anonymously, in the confines of her home and family. Jesus after all dwelled in the domestic church.

On her second day in Fatima, a gorgeous sunny Thursday in Portugal, Alana and her family did not get to the site until a little after 11:00. As they ascended the hill, they stopped by a souvenir shop before heading to the adoration chapel for another day of prayer. Alana wandered over to a shelf display of old fashioned lace veils that women used to wear to church. She fingered a long delicate white one, wondering when she was going to have the privilege of wearing one for her wedding day.

Maria saw her daughter looking at the veil longingly. She took it from Alana's hands and tenderly draped it across Alana's dark hair.

"Someday," Maria said, reading her daughter's thoughts, "he will sweep you off your feet and you will give us grandchildren as wonderful as you are."

~ ~

Lukas checked his watch. It was 11:15 in the morning. Lukas was heading down from the main entrance to retrieve the packed lunch for Frank, Stephen and Magda from the car. He had just finished confession and was experiencing a euphoric exhilaration inside him. As he always did after his monthly confessions, he felt as if his soul was washed clean.

All in all, Lukas felt great. It seemed as though God was putting order into his life. His father had tasted a conversion experience, his brother Stephen was unexpectedly healed, his brother Tomas was getting married to a nice girl and above all, the entire thing with Alana had resolved itself. She was not angry with him, after all. His heart burst at the thought of her: Alana had been partly responsible for his own conversion just as he was somewhat part of her own reversion into the Catholic faith. Only a God who knew what He was doing would work things out that way.

Sand and Water

Lukas glanced at a souvenir shop on his right side. He had intended to purchase something for Alana before they left but he didn't know exactly what. He peered inside through the window, trying to get ideas of the perfect souvenir for the perfect woman. As his eyes swept across the room, they came to rest on two women: the older, shorter one had draped a long white mantilla veil over a tall dark haired lady. Lukas could only see the younger woman's profile from the side but he could tell she was lovely. He admired the gentle way the veil cascaded from her head down to her shoulders. She would make a beautiful bride, he thought to himself, like Lanie. Hmm, he thought, that woman did resemble Lanie. Then he silently laughed. *I'm so obsessed with marrying Lanie, I'm even imagining her with me in Fatima.*

Lukas proceeded to the car. He planned on returning to the shop before they left Fatima. He would gift Alana with a Fatima statue and a veil. She would look exquisite in it, he thought. Just as she would look exquisite with his grandmother's engagement ring. Thinking about the ring, Lukas opened the zipper of his backpack to check if he had brought the heirloom along. He rummaged through the contents and found it in its original packaging at the bottom of the bag. Just before they left, Tomas had requested that he bring his grandmother and mother's engagement ring to show Catia. Even though Catia did not want to wear it as she wanted to chose her own ring and start her own traditions, she was still curious to see what it looked like.

Being a best man apparently meant he was suddenly in charge of all the rings, Lukas thought wryly. Even rings that aren't officially involved in the wedding.

~ ~

Alana liked the feel of the veil on her head. She had recently noticed that some young women wore veils to church. This was especially true in Fatima, where old and young women alike were veiled at Mass or at Eucharistic Adoration.

"You know mom, I think I'm going to buy this and start wearing it," Alana declared rather impulsively.

"Whatever for, dear? I mean you can wear it of course as I see many young women doing it as if it were the latest church fashion trend but do you know why veils are a custom and tradition?" Maria asked.

"I think Sr. Emma mentioned that veils represent being brides of Christ so I did a bit of research on it. Regarding nuns or consecrated souls, they wear veils all the time because they are brides of Christ but for lay women, head coverings in Church symbolize the goal of union with Christ. When a woman covers her head in communion or adoration, it is a form of reverence for her Lord and Savior in the host and an expression of her desire to be in union with Him, in obedience to Him. It is also a symbol of subservience to her husband who is the Christ appointed head of the domestic church which is the family."

"Hmmm, that's interesting to think about. I've always associated veils with little old women, thinking it an act of piety reserved for old-fashioned traditionalists. During the feminist movement, it was always scorned as something to be dispensed with. No wonder your dad and I had a lot of fights when we were younger."

Alana gave her a puzzled look. "You and dad? I never heard too much yelling going on."

"No but there was a lot of silent mutiny going on—on my part." Maria shot Alana a guilty look. "If I had known I was in serious disobedience then, I could have saved us both a lot of trouble."

"Aha! So I did inherit something from you after all—your rebellious nature."

"That you did. Thanks for sharing your discovery with me, Lanie. What you've just told me has made me appreciate what veils signify because even though the feminists think women have been treated by the Church unfairly, the truth is that the most exalted creature in the Catholic Church is a woman clothed with the sun!"

Alana nodded. "Yes, you only have to look at Fatima and all the other Marian shrines to know that the Holy Trinity chose Mary to be Queen of heaven and earth

Sand and Water

precisely because of her supreme obedience to God's will while she was alive. Imagine how special she was, chosen to carry the son of God in her womb, but in her humility, she obeyed her God and her husband."

Maria looked at the selection of veils on the shelf thoughtfully. "I think I'll get one for me too but I'll get the black one because it goes with my hair and most of my wardrobe."

"Why mom," Alana teased. "Is that a hint of vanity I detect?"

"It's a ton of vanity, I'm afraid and you've inherited that, too."

The two women smiled at each other guiltily. They made their purchases, met up with Jack and Joe and prayed the rosary together with some of the pilgrims at the plaza. Then they proceeded to the Adoration Chapel for an hour alone with Jesus.

Meanwhile, Lukas, Frank, Stephen and Magda ate the sandwiches they had brought along. They sat at a designated picnic area for eating and had a peaceful, uninterrupted lunch.

After clearing up some of the trash, Magda spoke to Stephen with loving fondness, "Your grandmother prayed many, many rosaries for you and she made me promise to pray one for you every day."

Stephen hugged the woman who had taken care of him all his life, the only mom he had known. "Magda, how can I express what I feel for you...thank you for everything...thank you." His voice broke off, but he continued to hug her.

After that touching moment, Frank, Lukas, Stephen and Magda joined in praying the rosary with some tour group at the plaza. Then Stephen and Lukas decided to go to the Adoration Chapel while Frank and Magda performed the Stations of the Cross.

"If *abuela* could see us now, praying the rosary without making faces," Lukas whispered to Stephen as they walked to the Adoration Chapel.

Stephen snorted. "I never made faces. Only you and Tomas did. You two were terrible! I still remember those days: the minute *abuela* closed her eyes to pray, you two would try to make me laugh so I would get into trouble. I've had many nights without dessert thanks to your silly faces and Tomas acting like a monkey. Tomas is lucky I'm not his best man or I'd incorporate a novel full of his best behavior stories in my toast."

Lukas chuckled at the memory. "Well Stephen, tell you what. To make up for my antics, I'll make you my best man."

"Hah! At the rate your going, I'll wind up the priest officiating your wedding!"

Lukas laughed again. "I'll say my vows before you will, buddy. And Stephen, I am so glad you are, uh, well—you know..."

"Fixed?" Stephen joked. "I am, too. Now the fun begins. You and Tomas better watch out."

Lukas and Stephen reached their destination. The Adoration Chapel was packed when they got inside. Stephen motioned that there was a seat beside two veiled women for Lukas to sit in while he would squeeze in front between a priest and another man. Lukas nodded.

Lukas bowed to the Eucharist on the center aisle, then slipped into the pew. He observed that the veiled woman had seen him from the corner of her eye and moved to her left to make room for him to sit. He also vaguely made out the features behind her bent head and recognized her as the woman at the shop he had seen earlier.

Lukas knelt down and was silent for a long time, waiting for Jesus to speak. Jesus was silent, too. Lukas sat down and decided that he would do some spiritual reading to give him a point of reflection. He quietly opened his book bag, and took out the two books he had brought along for the trip.

Definitely, *The Magis* was not appropriate reading in the Chapel. He set it back down on his book bag. It slipped off, causing a dull thud as it landed by the woman's foot.

Alana reached down to pick up whatever hit her right shoe. She was visibly astonished when she saw the familiar publication. Quickly, Alana grabbed it, turned to

Sand and Water

her right side, holding out a copy of *The Magis* ...to a man who looked like Lukas.

She blinked. *"Is it Lukas?"* she thought to herself. As unbelievable as this was, there was no mistaking the dark hair, kind blue eyes and handsome face. Alana couldn't say anything. Dumbly, she just kept holding out the book to him.

Lukas slowly took the book from Alana's shaking hands all the while staring at her, flabbergasted. If he wasn't sitting so close to her, he would never have believed his own two eyes. But here she was, a hair's breath away, more striking than ever, with the same ability to knock the senses out of him.

"Lanie," he finally whispered. "Are you really here? I mean, um, uh, I'm so glad you're here. Do you want to step outside with me? I'd like to talk to you...that is, when you are done praying. Just let me know."

Alana nodded mutely. Her hour was not yet over, but she could hardly sit still and concentrate with Lukas in the same room. "I can go now, if you can."

They both bowed reverently and walked backwards, never taking their eyes of the Eucharist despite their eagerness to be with one another.

Chapter 28

Once they stepped outside of the Chapel, Lukas found an unoccupied picnic bench under a shade. He waited for Alana to sit before he settled himself on the same bench next to her. Then he turned and directly faced her. He could not help but notice that her beautiful sea green eyes were perplexed, to some extent forlorn and also, incredulous.

Alana didn't say anything. She couldn't trust herself to speak considering the last two times they had talked, she said words that she later regretted. She searched Lukas' face for clues to what he was going to say. But when she looked into his blue eyes, an amusing thought struck her: *Those eyelashes belong on a magazine ad for a mascara.* Alana concealed a smile.

Lukas spoke first. He cleared his throat. "Uh, I read your essay in *The Magis* yesterday. I wanted to call you but I figured this conversation is better done face to face so instead I called Kerry and asked her for your address in Hawaii. I'd planned to go right after Tomas' wedding. That's why we're here, you know. My brother's wedding is in a few days. Why are you here?"

Alana answered matter-of-factly, in succinct sentences. "Trying to find my past. My parents and I just came from the convent that took me and my birth mother in."

"Oh wow! That must have been exiting. Or was it? What did you find out?" Lukas' genuine interest in the events of Alana's life diverted him from what he wanted to say.

Alana shrugged. "All that I needed to know."

In his head, Lukas wondered why she was acting so reserved with him. This was so not like the Lanie he knew. Was she upset with him for some reason? Then he belatedly realized that Alana did not know where she stood with him. She had laid open her heart and soul and he, stupidly, had not laid bare his own.

Anabelle Hazard

"Forgive me, Lanie. Let me start over. I read *A Soldier's Story* yesterday afternoon three times and another ten times before I went to bed. I hope I am not being too presumptuous but I believe you wrote it for me and connived with Kerry to make sure I read it before graduation. I'm such an idiot though, I didn't get that hint. If I had read it then, I would have run straight to your dorm, waited all day for you to get home, and told you this: God doesn't need me in the front lines of the battlefield. He wants me here, next to you for all my life, if you will take me."

Alana felt a smile tugging at the corners of her mouth. "And what do *you* want?" she asked, raising an eyebrow.

Resisting the urge to wipe a stray hair off her face, Lukas held her gaze intently. "I have always wanted – loved you, Lanie. Even before I saw you, you had my heart. I wanted to be with you so badly that my motives for finding God was so that I could be with you. Of course that all changed when I realized that God himself is love. And then just when I thought it couldn't get any better, God led me to follow you. I've been following you for a long time, Lanie because at one point, I was convinced that God meant for us to be together since the beginning of creation. There were other times though when I couldn't distinguish anymore if it was my will I was seeking or God's. I mean it was so obvious to me that I was in love with you but I had to discern God's will to be sure it wasn't just my emotions making my decisions for me. I hope you understand what I'm trying to say. It's not as organized as your writing but its -- it's the truth and the truth is that I love you, Lanie and now, I know for certain the source of this love is God."

Alana's heart softened at the words. "I do understand, Luke, and despite what I said, your selfless act in seeking God's will made me love you more. I am sorry for what I said the last time we talked. No one has ever broken my heart so I guess I said the first thing that came to mind, hurtful as it was. When I didn't hear from you since the article was published, my heart broke all over again and I swore I would never let my guard down like that again."

Sand and Water

Lukas shook his head sadly. "The fault was mine, Lanie. I should not have sang that song for you and revealed myself to you and tried to sweep you off your feet without being sure it was in accordance with God's plans first. I'm so impulsive, I used to always get myself into a lot of trouble. Now look, I've gotten you in trouble, too. I'm sorry for breaking your heart, Lanie. I promise I will spend my life making it up to you and try never to break it again."

Alana looked at him earnestly and told him what was honestly in her heart. "I am still a little afraid to trust you now. What other things are you hiding from me?"

"Lanie, I have nothing to hide anymore. I don't know what to say to make you trust me. I just know I don't want to be apart from you anymore. Why don't you come with me to Tomas' wedding? After I play my best man part, I'm all yours. I'll bring you back safely to Hawaii and spend some time there with you, see where you grew up or you can stay in my father's house in Spain and tour Spain like you always wanted to... with me of course."

Alana grinned and posed a challenge, partly to test Lukas' seriousness. "I'm traveling with my family so they go wherever I go. Why don't we see what they think of that?"

Lukas was undaunted. In fact, things were shaping up better than he could ever have planned it. "Your father is here? Perfect, then I can ask for his permission to marry you... that is, if you want to."

Alana gasped. Both her hands flew to her mouth and then moved to cover her flushed cheeks. "Lukas! This is all so sudden. We hardly know each other."

Lukas pried both of Alana's hands away from her cheeks and held them in his. He had a serious look on his face. "Lanie, I've known you since I was 20 and I've loved you since then. We share the same faith, the same goals and dreams. What matters most is we both serve the same boss. Sure, our personalities are not the same, we have major faults to work on, but Lanie that's where our sanctification will come from—you putting up with me and me loving you through the best and worst of times. I know this is part of God's plan for my life, Lanie. Look at us here, now, Our

Blessed Mother surely had a hand in this: she brought us to her son Jesus and Jesus brought us together."

Alana was smiling but she weakly protested, "B-but, where would we live? Hawaii and Spain are on opposite ends of the earth. I mean, the sunrise begins in Hawaii at the exact moment the sun sets in Spain. We can't be chatting online the rest of our married life together."

Lukas tossed his head back and laughed. It was as close to a yes as he could get, considering the short notice. He answered gravely, "We will figure it out or rather, God will figure it out for us just like he figured out for us to meet each other halfway in Boston. Any other objections before you forever hold your peace?"

Alana realized she didn't really care where God would lead them because she would gladly follow this beautiful, wonderful man anywhere, if he was the appointed head of her household.

"I don't but that man with a puckered brow over there might," she said, referring to Frank who was coming toward them purposefully with a look that could only be described as a confused grimace.

Lukas flashed her a grin. "Ahh, that would be my father wondering if I have lost my marbles, hitting on a pretty girl during a sacred pilgrimage. I better go tell him I've not only lost my head but my heart as well. And then let's all have dinner together, my family and yours. You pick the time and place, I don't care. I just never want you out of my sight again. My mind is made up: if you're not coming with me, then I'm going with you." Lukas squeezed her hands, conveying the solemn implication of his intentions. "Please don't make a desperate man out of me, Lanie."

Alana giggled, tingling at the sensation of Lukas holding her hands in his. Then she spotted her own father striding toward them, his face more contorted than Lukas' father.

Alana gulped. "There's my father." Despite the fact that she was an adult, Alana couldn't shake off the guilty feeling of holding a boy's hand in front of her father. She attempted to retrieve her hand from Lukas's grip but his hold on her was unyielding. Nervously, she suggested, "Let's do dinner first and see how that goes before dropping the "M" word on our families, ok?"

"Whatever you say," Lukas said confidently. He gave her an encouraging smile and rose from his seat, pulling Alana along with him. Already, he was mentally rehearsing his speech before her father and his.

~ ~

"Well, how do you think dinner turned out?" Lukas asked Alana, as they strolled hand in hand on the plaza at the pilgrimage site.

The previous night, they had dinner with both of their families. Today, they had managed to spend some time alone together.

Lukas and Alana were now standing with the rest of the crowd, waiting for the traditional procession of Our Lady of Fatima. Every 13th of the month, on the anniversary of her appearance to the three shepherd children, the faithful gathered to watch the statue parade across the grounds and return to the Chapel of the Apparitions. This was always a special time at Fatima. Crowds of men and women would sing "Ave, Maria" and wave white handkerchiefs at the Queen of Heaven as she passed the throng of "children" who came to honor her.

"Pretty well, except that Jack came home to the hotel trying to convince my dad to let me marry Stephen instead of you. He advised my dad to have a play station competition for my hand in marriage." Alana replied, laughing and shaking her head.

Lukas guffawed good naturedly. "Stephen's too young for you and he's engaged to the Church so you're stuck with me, lady."

"I wouldn't want to be stuck with anyone else, Luke. You know, if someone had told me years ago that I would be on a date with you in Fatima, Portugal, I would have called them crazy. But here we are."

"Funny how we can plan our lives to the last detail but then God's plan takes over and the thing is it always winds up so much better, doesn't it?"

"With God, everything possible and nothing is coincidence!"

The procession was just starting. Lukas and Alana sang along with the crowd, anticipating the arrival of the Mother of God. Alana's eyes welled up in tears as she watched the faithful pay homage to Our Blessed Mother, waiting for her patiently to pass them by. The feeling of union with God and the communion of saints was indescribable even to an English literature major like Alana. *This must be what heaven is like*, she thought.

As the statue came closer to them, Alana noticed that the crowd was waving white handkerchiefs in the air. She dug into her purse. She took out a white handkerchief and started waving it, too.

Lukas observed Alana as she waved a white handkerchief in the air, like many of the pilgrims. He looked closer and discovered that the handkerchief had the initials M.E.J.M embroidered in fine blue and gold stitches.

Lukas asked Alana, "Where did you get that handkerchief?"

"Oh, I got it from my birth mother. Remember how I told you that she left some stuff in a box for me? This is one of those things. It belonged to the woman who rescued my mother from the abortion clinic. She gave it to my mother to cry on and told her to keep it. My mother, Pureza, gave it to me so I would always remember the lady who saved my life, at least in my prayers. I brought it today to pray for her wherever she is."

Lukas' eyes grew wide as Alana narrated for him the story behind the handkerchief. When she finished, Lukas squatted on the floor and opened his book bag. Alana watched as he slipped his hand inside, grabbed what he intended and pulled out a tiny old black box. Lukas opened the box and took out a handkerchief with the initials M.E.J.M in fine blue and gold embroidery. It was unmistakably identical to the one Alana was holding.

With tears in his eyes, Lukas got up and told Alana, "This belonged to my grandmother. She embroidered her initials on them, Maria Elena Javier Monteverde. She must have been the woman who spoke with your birth mother. I know she did things like those—staking out abortion clinics and such-- because all her life she was a pro-life activist. She said she would not stop working until the murder of the innocents was over."

Alana excitedly put two and two together. "Then my birthmother must have named me after your grandmother! I saw my original birth certificate. I was born Elena but my parents changed my name and had me baptized Alana for a more Hawaiian flair. Lukas, that means, I owe your grandmother my life."

To her surprise, Lukas got down on his right knee, unwrapped the handkerchief and took out a simple gold ring with a tiny diamond on it. He knew beyond shadow of a doubt that this ring belonged on Alana's finger.

"Lanie," he said, "I've been planning on doing this at some other place and some other time, but now I realize there is nowhere more perfect and no time more right than now to ask you: Will you, Lanie, do me the honor of being my wife?"

Alana put her hand over her gaping mouth, stunned. She had known of course when Lukas had requested to speak privately to her father last night that he had intended on proposing, however she did not think it would be so soon.

In a split-second, the Holy Spirit gave Alana a morsel of wisdom on the concept of time: that God's sense of timing is not always in accordance with her own and that when He leads, there is only the choice to follow Him.

Alana's uptightness subsided and held out her left hand ecstatically. "Yes, Lukas, yes, I would love to be your wife."

Lukas slipped the ring on Alana's finger, got up, embraced her tenderly and cradled her head under the crook of his neck. At that moment, the statue of Our Lady of Fatima passed them by. Alana felt with every fiber of her being that all of heaven was involved in this match and that at this moment, her Heavenly Father and her Blessed Mother were giving them their blessing.

Alana stood up on tiptoes and whispered in Lukas' ear, "You know, since I was a little girl, my mother and I prayed our Hail Mary's to Our Lady of Fatima for the man I was going to marry."

Lukas smiled at her. He remembered his comical first attempt at saying the Hail Mary outside the grotto of St. Monica's. After learning the rosary from Lanie last year and saying it every night since, he would now never be confused on how to say the Hail Mary.

"Hail Mary, full of grace..." he prayed inside his head. Then he stopped at the magnanimity of those words. Our Lady was indeed full of grace. She was pure grace herself.

Lukas tipped Alana's chin up and said solemnly, "Lanie, I know now what it is like to have been loved by grace herself."

"And I know now what it is like to have been graced by love."

Chapter 29

It was winter everywhere else in the West but in the South Pacific Island of Hawaii, the weather was warm and sunny. Inside the tiny parish church of St. Bridgette where Alana and her mother often went to daily Mass, the warmth was caused by the excitement and anticipation of loving family and friends who had gathered to celebrate the Sacrament of Holy Matrimony uniting Lukas Swenson and Alana O'Keefe.

The bride's side was a mixture of her mother's Hawaiian-Filipino relatives, her dad's Irish American cousins and the home schooling families of St. John Bosco's Academy. The groom's side was composed of guests from mostly Spain, some young Americans and one Irish groomsman, who had his eye on the maid of honor.

When the traditional bridal march sounded, all eyes turned to Alana as she gracefully sailed down the aisle in her father's arm. She was an ethereal vision in a soft, wispy white silk dress, with full fluttery sleeves and an intricately embroidered belt cinched around her tiny waist. Her dark wavy hair, intertwined with white flowers, cascaded loosely around her shoulders, providing the perfect compliment to the pristine innocence of the romantic gown. In all respects, Alana resembled what all brides ought to resemble: the immaculate purity of the Blessed Virgin Mary. The translucent floor length veil which covered Alana's face could not hide the radiance of her smile which conveyed to Lukas all the love in her heart. Lukas was sure that his own smile, which was aimed only at Alana, expressed his own profound love for her.

Fr. Juan Mendoza, who had flown in from Spain especially for the occasion, addressed the guests with his homily:

"I want to tell you all that this sacrament you see unfolding before your eyes is not just about Alana and Lukas. It is entirely about God. It is about God who creates us out of love, pursues us, loves us, sacrifices for us, even dies for us so that we can enjoy eternal union with Him. Every love story, especially this one, is a reflection of God's love for you and for me.

"It is no coincidence that marriage is mentioned countless of times in the bible and many of Jesus' parables were concerning weddings and marriage. Let's study for instance today's gospel message where Jesus speaks of a wedding banquet prepared by the host. The parable tells us that the host invites all of us to join in the celebration but to the one guest who didn't come prepared in his fine garments, the gates of the party shut him off permanently. This does not depict a strict God. In the old days, the host always provided his guests with wedding garments. Hence, this story illustrates to us that we are all invited to lasting happiness but we have to put on the proper garments in order to join the feast of heaven. And what are these garments? They are the virtues: faith, hope and love. They are the Sacraments of the Holy Mother Church: Baptism, Confirmation, Reconciliation, the Holy Eucharist, Anointing of the Sick and once in our lives either Matrimony or Holy Orders. But above all things, St. Paul tells us that the greatest of these is love for love covers a multitude of sins. And love is simply illustrated by the cross of Jesus. It is dying to self—seeking always the good of the other no matter what the cost is to ourselves.

"Most of us know the story behind Alana and Lukas. We were all privileged to share in the journey of love that these two talked walked on with the Lord. I wish I could tell you that from this day forward they are going to live happily ever after. But those of us who are married, whether it is to the Church or to a person, know that the solemn vows we undertake on the sacraments of our vocation are only the beginning of suffering—the suffering that comes when we die to ourselves so that Christ can live in us.

"To those of you who aren't married, I don't mean to imply that marriage is worse than a terrorist attack because it's not. Marriage is a sacred covenant between the Triune God and the bride and groom. The sacrament of a marriage bound by God abounds with grace. God supplies us all with grace to remain true to our vows –the grace of joy in time of poverty, the grace of healing in time of sickness, the grace of faith in time of doubt, the grace of love in time of war, and the grace of peace in time of adversity. So I will instead say that from this day forward, I assure you that God will bless Lukas and Alana with the grace necessary to live in love ever after."

The Eucharistic banquet continued. Lukas and Alana said the traditional church vows. Lukas pledged to love, honor, and cherish his bride all the days of her life. Alana vowed to love, honor and obey her husband all the days of his life. After receiving Holy Communion, Lukas and Alana turned to the statue of the Sacred Heart of Jesus and the Immaculate Heart of Mary and consecrated their lives to them. Their consecration meant devoting everything they had from this day forward, body, mind, spirit and entire possessions to the one love shared by the two hearts.

Lukas' long awaited moment came when Fr. Juan pronounced them as husband and wife. In slow motion, savoring every moment, Lukas lifted the veil off Alana's face. He stared at her flawless features and his deep blue eyes bored into her light green ones. What he saw nearly took his breath away: Alana's eyes were overflowing with love... for him, no one else but him. Gazing into that love was almost like glimpsing a flash of brilliance of the Almighty hand that brought them together. Lukas soaring heart flew him to paradise.

Lukas put his arms around Alana's waist, took a deep breath and tenderly kissed her with all the love that he could muster. Alana blushed. A look passed between them, a look that expressed such joy, love and passion. They could not wait to be alone together to celebrate the ecstasy of a union graced by love, knowing full well that the bliss of love making was only a shadow of the joy of union with God in heaven.

After Mass, the happy couple drove off to their reception which was held at an unpretentious hotel in the city. They danced their first dance, nibbled on some lunch, posed for some pictures, listened to several toasts and went around the ballroom greeting their guests.

Lukas and Alana paused by the bar where some of the younger set of guests were gathered.

Laura, the matron of honor, reproached Lanie. "Well, Lanie, this time last year you gave us no indication that you were going to get married. I could have lost ten pounds if I had known then. Who would have thought, huh Jim?"

"Yeah," piped Jimmy, who was sitting next to Laura and holding her hand. "Last year you gave the St. John Bosco's alumni some hope that they still had a fighting chance."

Lukas couldn't help but tighten his arm around Alana's waist possessively. She tapped his hand reassuringly and said, "There was never any chance, Jimmy. My heart was already taken. It was reserved for someone long before I was born, since the beginning of creation."

Laura gave Jimmy a questioning look. "What are you talking about, Jimmy? Half the boys were making fun of Lanie's love for Pedro Calderon dela Barca, including you, while the other half wanted to become priests."

Jimmy looked back at Laura and explained, "Oh, they only pretended not to notice Lanie because she never gave them the time of day. Except for me. I really could not stand poetry of any kind and I was too busy paying attention to someone else...to Caroline Morgan to be exact, who never gave *me* the time of day..."

Laura stuck her tongue out at Jimmy. "Haha. You can take this ring and give it to Caroline then, Mister."

"So tell us, lad," Patrick asked, clapping Lukas on his shoulder. "What is your secret to winning the heart of the most eligible bachelorette of the Catholic home schooling world?"

"There is no secret other than my devotion to the Sacred Heart of Jesus and that I simply received communion everyday. Jesus gave me strength for anything that came my way and *you* know how many obstacles there were... But, let me tell you man, it worked like a charm—as soon as Lanie saw me at Church, she fell for it, took off after me and I couldn't shake her off since then."

Alana jabbed him in the ribs. "Watch it, buddy. I did no such chasing. You were the one who followed me halfway around the world and don't you forget it!"

Lukas gave her an affectionate squeeze. "Too true. I was smitten then and I still am."

"Uh—there is another secret weapon you used on this helpless girl, Luke," Sean interjected. "Have you forgotten fasting on bread and water for a whole year?"

Alana looked up at Lukas in awe. "You did that for me?" she asked, almost shyly.

"Yes he did," Patrick answered. "We couldn't have any fun Wednesdays and Fridays because Luke didn't have enough energy and some days he was just plain grumpy from hunger."

Lukas looked embarrassed but Alana's love and gratitude for her husband rose in tremendous proportions. *So he was largely responsible for my reversion,* she realized.

Kerry, the maid of honor, waved Patrick off saying, "Forget about Lukas' secret. On behalf of the bridesmaids, I want to know Lanie's secret to a happily—I mean, love ever after."

Everyone's eyes turned to Alana. Even Lukas stared at her, his gaze a mixture of curiosity, amusement and anticipation.

Alana almost choked on her drink at all the attention that would be paid to her words of wisdom. After she deliberated on her answer, she replied, "I just have one word for you all..." She paused for some melodrama. "*Mother.* My mother dragged me to the Immaculate Heart of Our Blessed Mother everyday to say our Hail Mary's for a man just like her son. When she knew I'd stopped praying, she quadrupled her Hail Mary's to more than make up for mine. Our Blessed Mother is truly our best advocate to get us to her son, Jesus."

"You know," Sean declared from his seat, "St. John Bosco once said that the only two things that can save us in these days are the two-fold devotion to the Eucharist and to Our Lady. So this must be quite a marriage you guys have, it's almost a union of the Sacred Heart of Jesus and the Immaculate Heart of Mary."

Stephen held up his glass of coke for a toast. "To Our Lord and Our Lady," he announced. He was no longer autistic, but he was still refreshingly honest.

"I'll drink to that," Patrick said approvingly. They all raised their glasses for a toast. Patrick turned to Kerry, batting his eyelashes, "Now, err Kerry my dear, have I told you that I go to daily Mass now?"

Kerry gave him a playful swat on the arm and drawled, "Oh c'mon, I'll dance with you this once, you pitiable groomsman you. Then I'm going to have a talk with the Blessed Mother if you're the best she can come up with for me."

An ecstatic Patrick and a giggling Kerry went off to dance, leaving Jimmy and Laura to continue their argument and Sean and Stephen to discuss possible seminary options.

Lukas gave Alana a spontaneous kiss on her mouth. He was so in love with her, so proud of her and so wanted to be alone with her. "Do you want to stay, Lanie?"

"No," she told Lukas, her eyes dancing mischievously. "But I am bound by a vow of obedience to my husband."

Lukas laughed out loud, grabbed her hand and ordered firmly, "Let's go."

Epilogue

Even a Hawaiian native like Alana had to agree that the Canary Islands of Spain was the perfect place for a honeymoon. Jandia beach at Playa de Jandia was a paradise of golden sand and blue waters in a subtropical climate. During the daytime, Lukas and Alana ventured into the sunlight, walked down the Hotel Riu Calypso's sloping steps that led right onto the beachfront. They spent the days lounging on the sandy beach and dipping into the water. The slightly cooler evening winter temperature did not bother the honeymooners as they enjoyed looking at the view of the ocean from the cozy warmth of their room, wrapped in each others arms.

As the sun broke into the sky, Lukas stood gazing through the window at the picturesque sea. "Today is our last day here, Lanie," Lukas announced to Alana. "Would you like to do anything special today?"

"Stroll down the beach, kiss you, pick seashells, kiss you, build sandcastles, kiss you, go swimming and snorkeling, kiss you..."

Lukas walked over to where she was sitting up on the bed and gave her a loving kiss. He ran his hands on her smooth dark hair and lightly touched face. With an impish grin, he said, "I was hoping to laze in the sand all day like a fat sea lion but since you've planned out a hectic day for us, can we get some energizing breakfast first?"

Alana stuck her tongue out at him. "You couldn't sit still in the sand if I paid you to, Mr. Ants in your pants."

"What would you pay me with?" Lukas asked with a gleam in his eye.

"This." Alana grabbed a pillow and hit him square on the head.

Alana could still hear Lukas laughing as she made her way to the bathroom. Once she got dressed, Alana enjoyed a leisurely breakfast with her husband of one week.

After sipping the last of their orange juice, they walked down to the beach and took their morning stroll.

Lukas noticed that Alana was unusually quiet beside him. He asked her with concern, "Are you feeling melancholic that we're leaving?"

She glanced up at him and nodded. "A little. But I am also excited to see the rest of Spain, where you grew up and to taste the Spanish life that I could only dream about." After a weeklong stay at the hotel perched on a hill, they were going to stay in Lukas' hometown of Zaragoza and leisurely tour the pilgrimage sites that Spain had to offer. Of all the places they were going to see, Alana was most anxious to visit Montserrat to see the altar of Mary's shrine where St. Ignatius had pledged his life to serve the Lord.

Lukas squeezed her hand affectionately. "Ahh my little Spanish *senorita*-at-heart has at last found her way to travel Spain."

"That's Spanish *senora*, *Senor* Swenson," Alana corrected him. "For your information, I'm married to a dreamy Spanish man."

Lukas couldn't resist teasing her. "Good for you. I got duped. I thought I'd married a tropical Hawaiian girl but it turns out she's really got Spanish veins running in her blood."

Alana shoved him playfully with her shoulder. Then she stopped walking, pulled him back and asked him seriously, "Are you sad that we're not going to live in your hometown? I don't have to live in Hawaii, you know. I'd follow you anywhere because far more than I love Hawaii, I love you."

Lukas put his hands on Alana's waist and made sure she was looking into his eyes when he answered. "Lanie, before I met you, I was lost but didn't know it. I was like... like the deep blue waters of the sea, rising and falling, without any direction or purpose. When you found me floating and drifting around in the ocean, you led me to find the heart of God.

"Then, the breath of the Holy Spirit blew my waves into the coast of Massachusetts to search for you. And when

I found you, it was like finding the sandy shore that I belonged in. You are my home.

"So in answer to your question: No, I'm not sad. Lanie, I am happy and willing to go wherever the ebb and flow of God's tide takes us. Yes, I'm giving up a lot but it isn't more than what Christ gave up for me. And this I know for certain: the work God asks of our family is in America— it is a major port in the battleground for the unborn souls."

Breathless, Alana circled her hands around Lukas' neck and buried her face under his chin. She was so moved by what he had told her. She had always thought that submission was the most difficult thing to do but she had never thought that a man's role to lead, protect and love his wife was just as challenging.

Now she realized why the scripture passage on obedience was immediately followed by a command for "husbands to love their wives, as Christ loved the Church and handed himself over for her to sanctify her cleansing her by the bath of water with the word, that he might present to himself the church in splendor, without spot or wrinkle or any such thing, that she might be holy and without blemish. So (also) husbands should love their wives as their own bodies. He who loves his wife loves himself." (Ephesians 5:26-28)

At that moment, Alana fully understood that her Lukas loved her as Christ loves His Church.